A Little Learning Is a Murderous Thing

A Little Learning
Is a Murderous Thing

Lou Allin

Five Star • Waterville, Maine

First Edition, Second Printing

Published in 2005 in conjunction with Tekno Books and Ed Gorman.

Set in 11 pt. Plantin by Christina S. Huff.

Printed in the United States on permanent paper.

Library of Congress Cataloging-in-Publication Data

Allin, Lou, 1945–
    A little learning is a murderous thing / by Lou Allin.—1st ed.
        p. cm.
    ISBN 1-59414-253-X (hc : alk. paper)
    1. Ontario—Fiction.   I. Title.
    PR9199.4.A46L58 2005
    813'.6—dc22   2004029570

Acknowledgements

Many thanks to Professors Richard Martin and the late John Harold Wilson of Ohio State University, and Professors Calvin Thayer and the late John Hollow of Ohio University, inspiring teachers who walked the line between instruction and delight. For her eagle eye, a thumbs-up to Dr. Evelyn Easton of Cambrian College. Tim Jones, my favorite geologist, gave me inspiration for the cheerleaders. And I owe a ton of Greenies to Nikon, the big man with the little guy inside.

Chapter One

Maddie Temple awoke abruptly at three thirty a.m. with a warm, wet tongue searching her nose. "Okay, Beastface. Hold your . . . well, hold everything. I'm coming," she said with a moan as her feet hit the floor and a furry body used her legs as a ramp. Nikon, a black and tan German shepherd, barely ten weeks old, sat his tiny rump on each stair and hopped behind her like a cartoon frog. Then he bucketed through the kitchen, out the patio door, and onto the deck, propelled by flying nun's ears. Once a night was an improvement, and he hadn't flubbed since she'd caught him in midstream by the dishwasher and drop-kicked him outside in a communication infinitely more powerful than words.

Keeping him in bed for house training had been a calculated risk. Her neighbor Ed King claimed that sleeping together made the pet a littermate, disturbing the proper hierarchy. The dog bible assured that it speeded the process: "An animal prefers not to soil the place it lies. A pup is too small to reach the ground from a bed and will wake you with its restlessness."

Hours later at the dawn's light, Maddie padded to the kitchen, swam through waves of programmed coffee aroma, and spooned mashed carrots into a cup of puppy chow. Halfway through Nikon's wolf act, she removed the bowl and dried wet streaks from under his eyes. "Eats until he cries. You're not going to die of bloat like your brother," she said,

7

ignoring his abused look. Bred for deep chests, GSDs needed to be monitored against bolting food or exercising too soon after meals. The stomach could twist like a sausage and lead to a painful death. After her coffee and a croissant with melted cheddar, she tossed Nikon a rawhide strip digestif and took herself to the bathroom.

At a time when many women welcomed makeup, Maddie had long abandoned the charade. Greasy eye shadow, crusty mascara, pore-clogging foundation and powder. Why wake up with a stranger? Life is too short. Dress as you please. Eat what you want. Don't talk with bores. In a hundred years we'll all be dead. She peered into the mirror, blessing the kindness of myopia. Separate reading and distance glasses were awkward, but last time she had tried bifocals, she had nearly fallen down the stairs. As she blinked to shift aggravating floaters, she winced, then grabbed a razor, swiping a dry run across her chin and around her mouth. Secondary sex characteristics. A soft, downy blonde beard. And would that period ever give up the ghost? Hot flashes or power surges?

"I don't care if grandmothers are popping babies right and left," she muttered to the intelligent, wolfish eyes staring up from her feet. "At fifty-two it's a biological joke." Nikon sat primed for instruction in the steady concentration of the breed, only a flicker of his tail signaling separation anxiety.

Getting dressed, she appreciated another perk of the casual nature of university teaching: comfortable jeans, along with a red silk shirt. Few enough opportunities for delicate fashions in the Michigan Upper Peninsula with three hundred inches of snow and four seasons: nearly winter, winter, still winter, and construction. Soon enough she'd switch to wool pants, cords, or lined jeans until March. Desultory brushing arranged her short auburn hair, shading gradually into gray.

As she entered the hall, she spied a tiny molar on the carpet and added it to a miniature incisor she kept in a jewelry box for sentimental reasons. A whine from the dog reminded her that he needed to be confined against chewing instincts. "New regime, Nikon. Mom has to go to work," she said in the kitchen as she ushered him into a metal cage nearly the size of her first car, a '63 VW Beetle. "Look out the patio door to the backyard. Act One: squirrels, followed by chickadees and maybe Ed's cat Peep." He sank onto the thick foam mattress and placed his head on his large paws. Blackmail.

Snatching a canvas tote bag, she walked out the front door of the small Cape Cod white frame house on Prospector Road, only one neighbor in half a mile. The '95 blue Ford Probe squealed like the academic version of Torquemada's rack. Year twenty-two at Copper University. Too young for retirement and too old to bank on a second wind. Would anyone interesting join the department this fall? Not tenured, of course, just sessionals. No one permanent had been hired in years, and even junior faculty were quaking at the cutbacks. Though "lean and mean" seemed odd words for a university, the Ivory Tower had become Babel itself.

Maddie drove into Stoddard, once a proud company town of over forty thousand when trainloads of Finns, Germans, Cornishmen, and other hopeful Europeans swelled its dusty streets. The village had been founded when the Babcock Mining Company had struck its premier lode in 1859. The original boomtown wooden structures had perished in a fire a few decades later. Rebuilt from the bottom up when fortunes were flush and architecture was lavish, the municipal buildings, churches, and banks reflected a systematic Old World charm. The mines had been closed for half a century, but diversification in light industry, tourism, and a reliable quota of students had given Stoddard a second life and a steady population of about thirty thousand.

Surrounding the university were acres of boreal forest protected from the ax. The wrought iron gates and shaded entrance road opened into a plain, where the campus stood like an armory of civilization in a wilderness. When Cece Babcock had endowed the college in 1888, he had insisted on brick buildings. The complex gave a firm sense of place and time: terra cotta window lintels, hammered copper cornices, and the handsome bell tower of the administration building. Once the ornately carved bracket pairs and modillions had been painted as brightly as Roman statues. Copper University, with seven thousand students, maintained an excellent teaching ratio. Until lately, Maddie's classes had been under twenty. Now, cost-cutting measures were filling rooms to capacity, canceling less-efficient seminars, and loading senior English faculty with a basic grammar or introductory lit course.

She pulled into the staff lot, swerving to avoid a minefield of potholes. Couldn't Maintenance afford a load of hot asphalt? Shaking off the increasing evidence of a Third World country, Maddie headed for Denney Hall. After a quiet summer, a fresh start was invigorating, a *tabula rasa* begging for inscription. Today was registration, no classes, but the campus surged with confident seniors, hesitant freshmen finding their paths, and all the gradations. A lilting carillon in the bell tower, operated by a wag from the music program, played "White Christmas." She stepped faster as she waved to former students. The balmy weather seemed more like June than September.

Maddie entered the foyer of Denney Hall, stopped for a drink at the fountain, then looked for cover as vapors of Estée Lauder snaked around the corner like a spoor. Florence ("Do not call me Flo") Andrews. Regarding teaching as an unnecessary anathema, she had been angling for an administrative job for years. In the meantime, biding time at forty-two, Flo settled for the coordinator position: few classes, extra cash, but petty details. Flo loved counting pennies, pushing a Scottish background to the northernmost Hebrides. Once Maddie had seen her in the campus bookstore, furtively grabbing fistfuls of free welcome packs for freshmen. Later, she watched the woman stripping them at her desk like a corn husker, discarding the coupons and advertising inserts to snatch lone sticks of Trident gum.

Dressed in a teal blue double-breasted suit, Flo had chosen a beige blouse with a paisley scarf knotted in variation seventy-four. A regular at staff aerobics, with the double application of shoulder pads onto her slim figure, Flo resembled a tiny quarterback. After an elaborate series of checks on her customary clipboard, she gave a pregnant cough. "At last you've arrived. All the syllabi are ready except for Victorian Poetry. I hope you adhered to the new paradigm."

Maddie sighed. Anyone who used "paradigm" and "syllabi" should be locked inside a closet of thesauri. What an officious little woman. At first glance, her makeup was tasteful, the mascara improving her skimpy lashes. Yet behind the jewel-winged glasses rose thin, plucked eyebrows, perpetually surprised, belying the craft within. And only an ichthyologist praising the ruthless efficiency of the lamprey eel might have admired the razory white teeth framed by a blood-red mouth. "Of course I followed the new . . . format. But I didn't give it to Nancy because of a last-minute book change. The master is in my bag. I'll run it off on the copier."

"It's down. You'll have to go to Morrow Hall." Flo pursed her mouth and flicked a speck from her lapel. "Make sure you have them for your first class. Our clients must be served according to their needs, not yours. That's our mission." And then she trotted off, an exercise bag in tow.

Maddie felt wet under her arms. Flo could spark hot flashes in a refrigerator, inventing problems to justify her job. "Gr-r-r—there go, my heart's abhorrence," she muttered. Sister Florence, not Brother Lawrence. More obnoxious than Browning's hypocritical friar. As if Madame Coordinator cared about quality education, the sophist, playing whatever tune worked. In departmental meetings, she pushed her agenda by verbally outlasting the group. Malcolm Driscoll, the chairman, had a laissez-faire approach, preferring to write limericks and espouse unpopular causes.

Maddie reached her office a minute later, grinning at the sign on the door: "I've gone out to look for myself. If I should return before I get back, please ask me to wait." Students would understand, especially freshmen. She fumbled for her key, wiggling it in the lock, and entered a sauna. The ancient radiators were pumping, oblivious to the Indian Summer weather. Another politically incorrect word? She turned the knob, then forced open the window, sneezing at dust motes rising in the air. The circle she had drawn on the filthy glass in a fit of pique last spring was still there. More support staff cutbacks. She made a mental note to bring Windex, paper towels, and lemon polish, but knew that she'd probably forget. Cleaning at home was bad enough.

Her bag landed beside the creased leather chair with lion's claw feet, rescued from an auction of bank furniture, an immovable object, but so comfortable. The small room contained a battered oak desk and computer with Internet access, a tippy roller chair with arms, three mismatched cabinets, and a wall of bookcases with the wisdom of the ages, or what used to pass for it. Near a reproduction of Rossetti's *The Blessed Damosel* were Turner's *The Fighting Téméraire*, a pen and ink rendition of Gloucester Cathedral, and a plaster copy of Victoria and Albert dressed as Saxons, each wearing an armband with the other's name. Maddie gave her course outline a final proofread, juggling reading glasses onto her nose. Her eyes were smarting again. From the dust, perhaps.

Then she walked next door to Morrow Hall, the Geology Building. Constructed from stones representing each Michigan county, Morrow stood out in muted rainbow eccentricity. With a wave, Maddie saluted the collection of fellow-fossils in the turret room off the foyer, an eight-foot giant sloth clawing a tree her personal emblem of the department. Revving up the ancient copier deep in the basement, she ran off fifteen copies. How long would she be teaching cozy seminars if enrollment kept dropping? Twelve percent fewer students majoring in English this year, and no wonder. Jobs were scarce. Graduates were tired of waiting for the expected retirement of the boomer teachers. Demand went in cycles. Maddie remembered a smarmy letter she had received decades ago. "Barring a visitation of the black plague, there will not be an opening at Balderdash University until after the Millennium arrives."

A coffee would be welcome, she thought, returning to Denney. Just one, though. Some metabolic quirk was giving her the shakes if she exceeded her limit. She made her way to the Common Room, a quiet refuge with curtained windows, scattered armchairs and tables, and bookcases loaded with the musty donations of former colleagues. After filling a cup from the urn, she sat at a long oak table with Marie Tressler, Medieval and Old English professor, gat-toothed as the Wife of Bath herself. Bumping along the halls like a pack mule, ironclad in shapeless wool dresses whose varying thicknesses suited the seasons, her hips saddlebags of toys, she provided comic relief from the academic stuffiness. Only the fact that

13

she kept adopting children from Latin American countries kept her from retiring. At sixty plus, never married, she still had two in high school and two in eastern colleges. Her creased and time-worn face, stern when necessary, hid a warm and generous soul. Marie stabbed a stout finger on a well-thumbed copy of Old English grammar. "Canceled this year. Instead I've got two Lit Surveys. Guess I'll be munching hay in pasture soon like an old plowhorse."

Maddie laughed weakly. "I'll bet I have a hundred for Bonehead Grammar 100. And my Victorian Novel course is on life support. Ten books and they're floored." She spread out her hands in pure bewilderment. "I could read a Dickens a day. Still, you'd think that any English major—"

"Remember the consolation of those wise odes." A wistful smile crossed the craggy old face like an echoing childhood song. "Deor, the wandering minstrel who dreamt of sharing warm firesides with his master. 'Thas ofereode. Thisses swa mae.' That passed and so shall this. Or in our vernacular, that which does not destroy me, makes me fatter." She pressed a shiny-wrapped toffee into Maddie's hand and bounced off.

Getting up from his armchair in the corner underneath a tarnished brass-standing lamp, George Zulandt joined her, a feisty bantam of a man, in charge of Restoration and Eighteenth Century. "Pass me Yorick's skull, so that I may better brood upon my life," he said. "My Swift seminar has been canceled. I've been shoved into Bardstown, and I don't mean Kentucky. Guess whose idea?" His neat black moustache bristled at the insult while his small hands kneaded a rolled newspaper.

Maddie passed the toffee to George. She'd pulled out enough fillings. "Not Malcolm. He knows how dedicated we are to our specialties. Why do you have to teach Shakespeare?"

"Flo is our Renaissance man, but with her duties as coordinator, no classes this semester. And Willy is more popular than ever, all those Hollywood pretty boys playing Hamlet." He gave a low growl, then slapped the table. "What's next? I suppose she'll ask me to teach all thirty-five plays in one week, or get holograms made and run without us. Virtual university."

"Come on, George. You'll get the course back next year," she said, trying to summon an absent conviction. A far cry from the halcyon days when they'd had three more full-time faculty. Cliff Cardinal, the Modern British professor, was on sabbatical, his courses postponed with hardly a ripple. She'd been hired strictly for the Victorian period, yet her domain had been extended to include the Romantics.

One more stop. Reserving a selection of reference books for the seminar. Otherwise, some overzealous student might check out key texts for weeks. Minutes later she was crossing the Oval, a grassy expanse which centered the university. Ahead was Collier Library, circa 1890, six stories of sandstone and brick, capped with a leaded roof and twined with Virginia creeper ivy ripening into a brilliant carmine. Round-arched windows on the bottom floor surrounded reading and reference rooms; above, the windows of the stacks. Flanking the wide steps, two recumbent stone lions stood guard below the university crest of a crossed pick and shovel: *Semper Utilis*. Since it was Frosh Week, the big cats' toenails wore a coat of purple poster paint. From somewhere came the rich strains of a cello. The sky brightened and Maddie blinked at the sudden light, wishing that she had brought sunglasses. She was reviewing whether to have chili or stew for dinner when she heard a scream.

Chapter Two

Bouncing back and forth among the buildings that ringed the Oval, the cries echoed in the sultry afternoon air. Maddie stood in confusion. Her middle distance vision wasn't sharp, and in the periphery, people ran from all directions on the footpaths which crossed the green. Leaning against the War Memorial obelisk, a cello at her feet, a plump student in a Copper t-shirt pointed with the bow, weakening sobs spurting from her guppy mouth. Behind a hedge close to the library lay a small figure, a pile of discarded clothes at first glance.

"God. That sound. Hitting the ground." The girl began to retch and dropped to her knees.

Hardly hearing what she said, Maddie headed forward in reflex action. She slowed in the last steps, fearful at the prospects, finding instead a quiet tableau. A girl lying on her back, fine blonde hair streaming like a crumpled halo, her neck at a twisted angle. She'd landed on the spongy turf, missing a concrete utility pad by inches. No blood stained her delicate skin. Still, what internal injuries she might have, Maddie did not like to speculate. With gentle fingers, she touched one wrist, warm and supple. No pulse, and the eyes were wide open. Images of literary deaths flashed across her mind. Not Ophelia, floating in billowing garments down a weedy stream, hands gesturing in stylized beseechment. Here was a broken figure. Porphyria, strangled by the unnamed groundskeeper by the cheerless grate she had made blaze up ("No pain felt she; I am quite sure she felt no pain"). As if following Browning's poetic clues, Maddie considered the neck, obscured by a bright blue scarf. Something about the girl's face called forth a vague memory.

Ben Jones, one of Copper's superannuated security guards, limped up, hot and flushed from the effort. He took great gulps of air as he looked at Maddie, who shook her head. Still, he stooped with an arthritic grunt and tried for a pulse. "Couple of fellows came after me in the office. Ambulance on the way. Doesn't look like it'll do much good. Poor kid. How'd she . . ." With a groan, he set back his cap and gazed up to an open window.

Maddie rose slowly and called out, "Where is the girl who screamed?"

The student stepped forward, wiping her mouth with a tissue. "I didn't see her fall. Just heard the, the . . ." Her voice trailed off and a woman in a tracksuit hugged her, offering supportive words.

A lean, muscular boy in Spandex shorts spoke out as he parked his bicycle. "They're all sitting at the windows today. It's hell inside. Turn the goddamn heat on in this weather."

Maddie stared at the body. Who was she? What were her dreams? Her clothes were the standard jeans and t-shirt, in casual contrast to the shapely almond-polished fingernails. Above one breast, a silvery angel pin winked. The shoes were the same Nike model as Maddie's. How perverse to think about such banality. Something drew her back to the eyes, liquid and almost alive, as if asking one final question. Guided by early photography theorists who believed that final images remained on the retina like a negative, British police had photographed the eyes of Jack the Ripper's victims.

As the ambulance drove onto the green, horn blaring, followed by a police cruiser, the crowd fanned out politely, whispering and gesturing. Then while the gurney was wheeled in efficient silence, Maddie averted her gaze from the activity and looked up. Fourth floor, the literature stacks. Copper had over two hundred English majors, in addition to those taking a course as an Arts requirement.

"Professor Temple?" Ben was shaking her arm gently. "You'll have to give your report now." Behind him, two officers rushed up the library steps.

Maddie turned to face a redheaded woman in a Stoddard Police uniform, smiling, neat, and starched to perfection. The officer opened a small notebook and asked her name.

With a dissociative calm which surprised her, Maddie reviewed what she had seen, giving her address and phone number. Covering those pitiful and decisive seconds didn't take long. Then somehow she found herself standing in a trance inside the library foyer, hardly realizing how she had arrived. Only the sharp click of passing heels on the cold, streaked marble snapped her back to reality. Too much strong coffee? In a mist again.

Decorative Corinthian pillars reaching to a ceiling painted with gauzy murals of the Nine Muses recalled times when money had been generous at Copper. Caroline Majuscule, the Head Librarian, called from the entrance to her office near the circulation desk, where no book left the library without passing through a metal detector trellis. "What's happening? I heard a siren. Then two officers ran in without a by-your-leave and disappeared. Those freshmen must be up to more mischief. Yesterday we had a dog running through the stacks. Wearing a little cape with the school colors. Can you imagine?"

Maddie said quietly, "It's serious. A girl fell from the fourth floor."

"Fell! My God! Those windows should never be open. We don't have the staff anymore to check regularly. She wasn't—"

"Yes, I'm afraid she's dead. A grim start to the semester." As they spoke, a slender figure approached a loaded cart behind the desk. One arm hung pendulum loose at the man's side, but the other busied itself organizing books with a mind of its own. Ian Macdonald, sporting his trademark tartan tie, was a senior professor of American history who had suffered a debilitating stroke over a year ago. A rather prickly character, he had few close friends. Maddie knew him only by reputation. What was he doing here? Had the administration in its miserly stance refused his disability? Forced him to take a job on the support staff? Unions had difficulty at universities mobilizing efforts for what was perceived as a blue-collar concept; as the faculty's only protection, the Senate was a grumbling bunch of impotent fools.

Embarrassed at approaching, Maddie made a pretense of consulting a sheet announcing the library's new reduced hours. Ian had lost the ability to speak, except for the word "yes." Imagine being limited to the affirmative after all those assertiveness books about learning to say Carlyle's "Everlasting No." What a prison.

The gray head peered up like a centennial tortoise, stretching folds of skin. "Hello, Ian," Maddie said, her voice cracking as she confronted personal fears about the ravages of age, the pitfalls around each corner.

Wise old eyes glimmered with quiet intensity and a thin-lipped mouth contorted slowly as if struggling to remember primal patterns. "Yes." Then the tall body regrouped as the cart was shuffled off, pushed by one unerring arm and a persistent foot.

Caroline followed Ian's progress. "He is a brave one. As part of his therapy, he comes in every week to shelve books,"

she said with a womanly cluck. "I wouldn't have the gump-
tion. Probably hole up in my bed with talk shows and choco-
lates, and wait to die."

Maddie nodded. "His research on William Jennings Bryan
nearly won a Pulitzer Prize. Now I hear that he can't even
write."

The woman sharpened a pencil until the point pleased
her, poking it in her bun along with three others in a Cio-Cio-
San effect. "He's keen enough inside, God love him. Come a
long way the last few months. Don't underestimate the man.
If there's something important to communicate, Ian will find
a way."

Maddie dropped off the list of books at the Reserve Desk
around the corner, then picked up a fresh selection of magazines in the Periodicals Room. *National Geographic*, *Ms.*, even
People, anything to take her mind off what she had seen on the
Oval. As she was passing the elevator, something made her
punch the fourth-floor button. It might have been that she
wanted to check a reference to Tennyson's connection of
"Morte d'Arthur" to Prince Albert.

The door opened and a smiling maintenance man greeted
her, a smear of grease on his pug nose. He had the inside
panel removed. "Going up?" he asked. "Guess it's okay to
take passengers. Police have left. Had to check the floor
where that girl fell. Looking for witnesses."

"Did they find anyone?"

"No, ma'am. See, this is the only way out, fire exit alarms
on the stairs and all. And I've been here for the last hour
fooling with these confounded Braille signs. Almost got her
done." His battery-powered screwdriver buzzed, and he
reached for a small square of pressed metal.

When she stepped onto the floor, Maddie forgot her pretext, gauging her location until she found the window, now

tightly closed. The air was stale, the temperature stifling. On such a hot day, who would choose to study here unless he needed to consult the books? The carrel, merely a desk with an eye-level locked metal container for valuables, bore no sign of activity. Maddie surveyed the nearby shelves. PR, the American literature section. On an empty row sat a copy of Jay Martin's *Harvests of Change, American Literature 1865–1914*, open and face down. She picked it up. The chapter concerned Frank Norris. Perhaps the girl had been an English major. One of their own.

On the way down, the elevator stopped suddenly. Aware of the problems, she waited patiently. No sense in pushing the red emergency button like a hysterical woman. On the wall were scrawled several rude messages about professors, none in her department. Another sign of their inconsequence. She finished correcting the spelling when the elevator jerked back to life.

Home at last to a caged dervish, Maddie busied herself with Nikon's training regimen: ten sits and downs, a couple of fetches in the yard rewarded by a pocket of liver snack treats, and a walk down the road. Ed King waved his John Deere cap at her. For a moment she felt like telling him what had happened at the library, but decided against it. She wanted to relax and forget. And he'd probably read about it soon enough.

"Fall's a nip away. Mid-September already and no frost," he called, digging up dahlia tubers, knocking them free of dirt, and enfolding them in newspaper with a loving hand. "See them leaves redding on the maples? First to go. Others line up like soldiers."

Maddie wouldn't dream of correcting him, though she sometimes felt like playing Midnight Grammarian with other neighbors. Their expensive routed signs could be traced to an illiterate vendor at the local mall. "The Jackson's." "The Smith's." Those misbegotten apostrophes begged her to wield a paintbrush some dark, concealing night. Yet she shrugged off the stereotype of a crabby, self-righteous school-marm. Inside her flagging, middle-aged body was a ten-year-old eager to jump the fence. "I'll need more tulip bulbs to fill my bed. The few that showed their faces died of loneliness. Hope those moles enjoyed a free lunch."

"Got some jim-dandy stuff at Miller's Greenhouse. Critter Ridder. All natural, mostly black pepper oil and capsaicin. Harmless to dogs." He tickled Nikon's hairy chin. "Don't worry about those ears. They'll take their time. My brother's Sam was six months before they perked up."

"Looks are fine in a man, but I prefer obedience," she said, giving the dog a tug for attention when he jumped at a squirrel chattering in the cedars.

"Don't I know it." Shoving the wrapped tubers into a gar-bage bag, he winked lively green eyes at her like the rogue he pretended to be. A trim sixty with a lion's mane of silver hair, he had recently retired from contracting. There wasn't a leaking faucet he couldn't seal, a sheet of drywall he couldn't patch, or an electrical short he couldn't locate. In the yard, Ed was an artist with a chainsaw. After a messy divorce five years ago, he had moved next door, and his reassuring pres-ence provided security without compromising privacy. "Got a different BP med last week. Nothing left to buy but the champagne." He added a thumbs-up gesture.

New Year's Eve. Even if the prescription didn't work its magic, there was comfort in custom, a bond surpassing the dewy fresh skin and flexed sinews in her classes, lovely though they were. "I'm looking forward to it."

She turned and headed for the end of the road. For some

reason Nikon had been reluctant to leave the property. The dog whimpered against the tyranny of the small leash, running sideways until he fell on his nose. A sense of territoriality was fine, but this was embarrassing. Her last dog, Honey, had passed on just as the bright May sun coaxed the lilacs into lacy bloom. The thirteen-year-old had lurched with arthritis, hind end outstripping the front, like a city bus with an accordion middle. The pup was the same, struggling for authority over ungainly legs. Soon he would grow strong and fine as he showed Maddie the world through new eyes. Around the turn, he became distracted and ceased mewling, snatching unsteadily at a blue bead lily, which she extracted from his inquiring mouth. To him the cobalt fruit resembled his favorite blueberries, but lilies were toxic, at least to humans.

They took a path through the bracken and second-growth maples and poplar, emerging at the crest of a hill overlooking the azure platter of Lake Superior, a glorious and humbling vista which defied all concept of distance. "Tell me the landscape in which you live, and I will tell you who you are," said Ortega y Gassett. Today was deceptively calm, but locals, aka Youpers, awarded it a respect born of experience. Every year unwary ships sank into the icy graveyard, from the legendary *Edmund Fitzgerald* to an errant tourist canoe setting out north of the Sault, fooled by the lapping waves behind sheltering islands and finding out too late that death lay beyond. Life jackets were useless toys in that frigid water. Hypothermic within minutes and dead in half an hour, victims floated along shoreline currents for miles instead of washing up on the beaches.

By the time they returned, Nikon was trotting demurely at the heel, one black-tipped ear flopping like a Victorian lady's morning cap. Lately he had skewed in front, and she had taken fancy steps to avoid him, afraid to injure a small paw, but the bible warned that this behavior signaled domination, so she plowed into him a few times, deaf to the yips.

Chapter Three

Maddie parked next to a familiar green Buick LeSabre, the "old lady" car she coveted for a comfortable cruise to retirement. Might as well go downhill in plush leather-heated seats. Enough of these sports models put on like a glove. Handling the Probe raised the heart rate, but the UP roads and climate weren't Grand Prix style. Many of the staff owned four-by-fours to deal with the brutal winter. Even Flo drove a Jeep Cherokee, but to Maddie, paying more for a vehicle than for your first house seemed preposterous, aside from the atrocious gas mileage.

A tall African woman closed the Buick's door, a lizardskin attaché case in her hand. Under an open Burberry raincoat, she wore a bright caftan, blues and red shimmering with gold threads. Grace Lwasa, Twentieth-Century American Literature professor. Maddie had vetted her résumé during the hiring process. Educated in New York universities, she had taken American citizenship. As the first non-white female on Copper's staff ten years ago, she had experienced nasty harassment: flat tires, hate mail, anonymous phone calls. Grace's hair was meticulously braided, a *Vogue* photo shoot. But no model would have cultivated the blank expression in her dark eyes, the deadness in the smile she attempted.

"Anything the matter? Can't be first-day jitters," Maddie said, matching the long steps of the younger woman with a tug at her hamstrings.

The broad cocoa face, expressive even in repose, seemed strained. Instead of the regal bearing that carried her like a queen, her posture was tired. "The student at the library. I was her thesis advisor."

Maddie reached for her arm, then stopped, afraid of intruding upon cultural norms. The woman held herself in reserve, never confiding anything personal to her colleagues. "Grace, I'm so sorry."

Grace walked on, then paused at the bronze sundial in front of Denney Hall, tracing the grooves with her finger as if turning back time. "Cheryl Crawford would have graduated in December." The musical vocal cadences, a rare tropical bird singing alone in the cornfields of flat Midwest dialect, usually tickled Maddie's ears, but today the lilt was gone.

"Cheryl Crawford? Now I remember where I saw her face." British Lit Survey class three years ago, along with seventy-five others. Always at the back in a corner taking notes, quiet as paint on the wall. "I was nearby when it happened." Not wishing to compound the distress, she added no graphic details. "Those open windows. Was Cheryl careless? A daredevil? That doesn't sound like the girl I recall."

"Never. Very sober, an honor student with a full scholarship. If anything, too hard a worker. Never satisfied."

"Straight A's on all my assignments." Maddie knew the type. Unable to meet their own impossible standards, frequently they collapsed like an imploding star as the term ended. "Trouble with her thesis?"

"Not to my knowledge." Grace spoke slowly, as if casting her thoughts back in time. "Last spring there was some distraction, but recently her thesis was proceeding well. I saw her work in progress before the summer interlude. This semester she was finishing the final draft, waiting for the arrival of two Masters' theses she had ordered. With her characteristic thoroughness, she had searched the Internet to discover sources outside the published bibliographies." She waved a delicate brown hand, silvery bangles on her wrist. "Of course, she probably found nothing new at that amateurish level of research, but I admired her persistence."

As they parted company, Maddie wondered how she would have felt if she'd been Cheryl's advisor. Last semester she had five seniors to supervise. When you mentored them one-on-one, they became the closest thing to children.

After setting up lesson plans, she went to the Refectory for lunch, a faux-medieval grotto in the basement of Campbell Hall, the Engineering Building. Usually she brought a frugal sandwich, along with a thermos of juice, but on the first official day of class, a splurge was allowed. Despite typical student carps, the cafeteria food was decent and affordable, with three entrees and even a salad bar, galaxies apart from the mystery meat meals and wilted lettuce with vinegar in her college memory bank. Upon making her selection, she found a booth and forked into a heaping portion of hamburger macaroni casserole, a winner for simplicity and bonus of leftovers. This version could stand a smidge more chili powder.

As she sipped an iced tea, a teddy bear of a man plunged his tweeded rump into the opposite side of the booth. Malcolm Driscoll, her chairman. Before getting into administration, he had prided himself on brightening his dry eighteenth-century period by assigning risqué poetry and arming himself with ribald jokes. The Duke of Rochester was his idol, a dissolute satirist. Rumors hinted that Malcolm had been promoted from the classroom to avoid embarrassing complaints from the ever-vigilant religious right who blundered into his courses. Yet he was too conservative to fit the role of roué, pottering about on his large property, an old bachelor who raised game birds.

He unbuttoned his coat to reveal a matching vest with gold watch chain, then arranged his plate and silverware with precision, placing an Aran hat on the seat, flicking its colorful feather from his flock for approval. Born and raised in Michigan, he affected an English accent to match his appearance, dropping it only when furious, as if taking off kid gloves. "Maddie, dear. Try this one: 'The management of tyros of eighteen/ Is difficult, their punishment obscene.' "

"Ugh. Did you write that?"

His cough wafted a hint of brandy into the air. "I'm not good enough to be so bad." From one pocket, where a silver flask winked, he presented *The Stuffed Owl*, an anthology of wretched poetry.

"How very perverse to find delight in the dreadful. Like people who watch Grade Z movies."

Making an archer's gesture, he said, "I like to prick the balloon of pride. That quote was from Cowley, but every great poet has penned his share of groaners, even your precious Victorians."

"Never." She set down her fork and came to wary attention.

"How about Mrs. Browning: 'Will you oftly/ Murmur softly'?"

Maddie assumed a hurt expression. "So she's saccharine. Point conceded. 'How do I love thee' can't hold a brief candle to the feeblest Shakespeare sonnets, though I'd never admit it to Flo."

"Tennyson?"

"You're in dangerous territory with a poet laureate."

" 'He suddenly dropt dead of heart-disease.' " Malcolm watched her wince. "And there's more. Robert Browning himself."

"Please, not my hero."

" 'Irks care the crop-full bird? Frets doubt the maw-crammed beast?' " With a chuckle, he fluttered a liver-spotted hand over his tie. "Always ask the quail that at feeding time. Put in a new pen over the summer. They should be quite toothsome."

"What's next? Emus?"

"Too strenuous for this country gentleman." He bit into a club sandwich, a dab of mayonnaise dribbling down his Van Dyke beard, making him look like a graying schnauzer rising from its bowl. "Classes going well, then?"

"Except for the mob of your tyros I expect in English 100. Marie's upset about losing her Anglo-Saxon section. And George is furious at being assigned Shakespeare instead of his beloved Pope."

"Pope! That bitter old hunchback. Can't abide the man and his vitriol. Swift's the primal focus of the period." Putting down his sandwich, he leveled his bloodshot eyes at her, framed with wrinkles but charged with purpose. "It's the damned cutbacks, Maddie. Getting harder and harder to offer a full English program." He leaned forward as she nodded in frustration. "I remember, and so do you, when we had faculty for Milton, for Spenser, not to mention Marie's inspiring seminars. Woof and warp of our language. But times have changed. Students are abandoning English for computer studies, environmental issues. Even public relations."

He turned up a patrician nose at the idea, but Maddie knew the expediency of economic realities. "Who would blame them, Malcolm? They want jobs. Sometimes I think that we're only propagating ourselves in an incestuous sham."

"God forbid, we might end up as a mere service department. And what money trickles down is furthering useless causes." He yanked a sheet of foolscap from his battered leather briefcase. "Let me read you the draft of my latest letter to the editor of *The Peninsula Register*."

Maddie swallowed a final mouthful of casserole with difficulty. Malcolm attracted trouble. "Whatever it is, I'm against it" was his credo. Expanding the local landfill, returning the drinking age to eighteen, refurbishing the detention facility, opening another native-run casino. This time his wrath fell upon Copper's new initiative for the handicapped, or in more politic terms, SWINC, Students With Individual Needs Center. Bolstered by government grants and private donations, the five-million-dollar complex had no rivals in North America. Thanks to the energetic lobbying of Anisha Mukherjee, the director, and Reggie Conrad, a wizard seconded from the Marketing Department, the project had succeeded in a time when general downsizing was not only nibbling but gnawing at the college core. Reggie's friends called him enterprising; his enemies called him unscrupulous. More than once, he had nearly burned his talented fingers in questionable juggling of funds and other creative accounting techniques.

"It's a scandal. Always picking our pockets," Malcolm muttered, cocking a thumb toward a poster announcing a Trash or Treasures sale in the gym, proceeds headed for SWINC. Maddie had contributed her Pentium 2 computer. "Classroom windows cracked, cleaning haphazard at best, secretarial staff halved, sessionals instead of permanent contracts, and now this misbegotten idea. Another swimming pool, a specialized reference library, even vats of hot wax, I hear. What the hell's that for?"

She flexed her hands, stiff from grubbing carrots. "Nothing sinister. I heard it was connected with the new sign language program. Or maybe the occupational therapy people who deal with carpel tunnel or arthritis."

30

Malcolm's face darkened, and his voice drowned out the piped-in beats of the campus radio station as the mellow British vowels vanished in the heat of rhetoric. "And that artificial abortion. Mukherjee Manor, I call it. Simply destroys the integrity of our campus." Apparently, with modern costs of labor and materials, recreating the Victorian architecture had been impossible. Some said that the Center resembled coupling pink elephants.

Maddie drew a deep breath, resisting the urge to duck and cover. At the next table, a muscular girl in a wheelchair, pulling on leather driving gloves, whispered to her male companion in a letter jacket. He glared over at the old man.

"You can't oppose a project like this, Malcolm. It's such an apple pie issue," she said.

He pounded a gnarly fist on the table. "Someone must sound the clarion call. There are facilities in the immediate area that are underused. The School for the Blind, the AmVets' prosthesis program, those private learning centers the paper advertises. In plain and simple language, this expense is scandalous."

She spoke quietly, pressing his arm as if human contact might urge the argument upon him. "Be realistic. The university saw the opportunity for matching funds and jumped at the chance. And if I may play Devil's advocate, the classrooms, the pool, and the library might be accessed by the rest of the student body once things get organized. Remember when Anisha ran that workshop last year about diagnosing learning disabilities? She's a reasonable woman."

No use. He was going to make powerful enemies this time, Maddie thought, as she dropped off her tray. Anisha would guard her new realm like a cobra. The man was harmless, but he persisted in swimming against the current.

English 100, Bonehead Grammar, started at two p.m. Pathetic to have to teach high school graduates the elements of a sentence, but the college dealt with realities. Revamped, it seemed, the very minute she had matriculated, the public school system labored at making students feel worthwhile by rewarding them for dubious creativity that ignored spelling and syntax. Coddled by this well-meant but misguided principle, some could barely read a hundred words a minute, and few could write their way out of a ripped paper bag. So it was back to the basics of a foreign language.

She approached the corridors of Lord Hall with a shudder, knowing the sinister reason that she had been assigned the large lecture room. Copper was saving money by increasing class size. Whether she had enough desks was Flo's only care. Maybe the next step to fiscal meltdown would be classes without furniture. Outside. In the stadium. A bullhorn. Whip and chair. Stun gun. Students running through irregular verbs like trained tigers jumping hoops.

As she opened the double doors, she reeled at the noise. Giggles and whoops filled the air. From every direction, bodies squirmed like puppies. Odors of chewing gum, cloying perfumes, and locker room sweat from the athletes swept forward like a noxious tide. A paper plane drifted from the back row and nearly parted her hair. With a gulp, she climbed to the stage and braced for action behind the podium. Thank God for the microphone. She flicked it with a fingernail, and an acoustic shriek turned heads. "Your cooperation is requested, ladies and gentlemen. We have a challenge here to maintain order and still manage to communicate." Thumps and bumps, and rumps pushed into the narrow seats, snapping up the hinged writing arms. As one fellow turned quickly and tumbled into the aisle, she narrowed her eyes. The crowd quieted, listened attentively to her orientation, accepted the handouts, and shuffled off with their backpacks.

"Pro-fessor. Uh, ma'am?" A shape barely her five-foot-four peeked from the edge of the stage. Dressed in sharply creased dress pants, a freshly ironed white shirt, and bow tie, he was speaking loudly and clearly but very slowly, as if she were a child. Frizzy red hair the color of a fire engine seemed electrically charged. A freshman hello sticker on his chest read: "Barney Smallwood." Did he have a hearing problem?

"I am sad that we did not have a whole class today. I do not know if I can get the book this week, because I need to set up my bank account." A stuffed animal nestled under his thin arm, perhaps a prize in the welcoming activities.

Maddie felt guilty about dismissing class early, though she did so on the first day when many students came without texts. "We'll march the full period next time. Sit next to someone with the book and take lots of notes. Subjects and verbs to start. Easy stuff. You'll be fine." In a strangely middle-aged gesture, Mr. Lonely Boy used a finger to adjust the bridge of his horn-rimmed glasses, nodded, and walked away.

Maddie enjoyed teaching freshmen, heads open and ready for delivery, like Gradgrind's pitchers in Dickens' *Hard Times*. Unlike some other instructors, she rarely encountered rudeness. Her patented dead-serious expression and firm but friendly tone worked like a Distant Early Warning system. Decades ago as a rookie teaching assistant, she had been asked out on dates by older students. Then she had become a mother figure, and now nearly the right age for an ambitious grandmother.

Down the hall, she slipped into the ladies' bathroom and considered the three shabby stalls, more evidence of budget slices. Women had been complaining about defective locks and large gaps around the metal doors. She chose the most secure and took a seat, noticing too late that the cubicle was out of paper. Luckily, one lone tissue remained in her pocket. Then she heard voices.

"Can you believe? She took a dive right out that window."

"Yuck. Did you see it?"

"No, and I'm glad I didn't. Crissie did, and she threw up in the bushes. Of course, she might be preggers."

"The girl who died?"

"No, stupid. Crissie." Through the gap, Maddie glimpsed an arm shove out in jovial guy-fashion. "Anyways, remember that dumb angel pin she wore? What a loser. Tried to get her psych notes last year. Just blew me off. Never came to any of the mixers either. Said she had to study." There was a snicker. "Adios, Miss Perfect."

Purple Doc Marten boots scuffed in front of the wash basins. A rainbow shock of hair moved across the space, and the hiss of hair spray muffled the words. Snapping gum exploded, over the girl's face, Maddie hoped. Then the outside door swung shut.

Poor Cheryl, she thought. College was meant to socialize as well as educate. For all of her scholarship success, it sounded like a narrow, unhappy life.

Chapter Four

Maddie paused for breath on the final landing before reaching the top floor of Denney Hall. "Thank God I'm going down," said a gravelly voice above. "Dear Dietrich was right. You can lie about your age, but you can't beat a good flight of stairs."

"And when I can't cut the mustard anymore, I am going to retire," Maddie called as she passed Marie.

Under the sloping eaves was a tiny piece of nineteenth-century Oxford defying the roughshod American Midwest. Despite the occasional mouse, she always requested the remote nook for seminars. At one end stood a long-unused fireplace with an oak mantelpiece carved with gargoyle faces and equipped with nickel firedogs, which she had been tempted to appropriate. Threadbare Turkish carpets organized a motley collection of sofas, love seats, and armchairs, an occasional tuft of stuffing poking through the worn upholstery. Originally the room had been used as a faculty lounge. She imagined Oscar Wilde pontificating to his backwoods brethren, an orange tiger lily in his hand. Perhaps he had done so. A marathon lecture tour had dragged him across the Midwest to California, as far south as Georgia, and back through Ontario. How the miners had loved him in Leadville.

She walked in, her sneakers whisper-quiet. A dozen students were chattering, looking up in surprise as she cleared her throat pointedly. "Good afternoon," she said. "This is

Victorian Poetry 400, a senior seminar. I'm Dr. Temple, but Maddie will do." Mere titles didn't confer respect, and she was comfortable on a first-name basis.

Settling into a brocaded armchair with one leg supported by a yellowing Monkey Ward catalog, she pulled out the course outlines, handing them to a familiar face from last year's Romantics class. "This will list the textbooks and assignments. A midterm, final, two short critiques, and one research paper of twenty-five pages." A universal groan circulated.

"It's English literature, folks. Write we must. If you want to make films or design video games, check out another major. Last chance." A few laughs broke the silence as she assigned the homework. Most of them hoped to become high school teachers, only a select few going on to graduate school elsewhere.

A full professor, she had written two books on the Pre-Raphaelites and fifteen articles. As years went by, she wondered about the usefulness of chewing dry cuds, saying something obscure about someone notable, or something notable about someone obscure. Barring an attic of Keats' love letters, a collection of fat-free recipes by Shakespeare's dog's vet would fetch a thousand times the rewards of academic publishing. One enterprising and well-compensated writer convinced *Playboy* to publish "Goblin Market," an innocent children's poem by Christina Rossetti. Furry men lurking in the forest with their forbidden fruits. Phallic symbols abounding, mildly pornographic cartoons for truckers to thumb at rest stops. "Twilight is not good for maidens." Still wasn't, for that matter.

After class, Maddie plunged into the departmental storage closet for a pack of fine-line red pens. "Nancy, how did your summer go?" she asked the secretary.

A devout vegetarian, Nancy Grady munched a sandwich of curious brown bread spread with what looked like chocolate flakes. "My kid is at the awkward age. Too old to send to summer camp and too young to get a job. I need a vacation from my vacation."

"What unusual bread. Did you make it yourself?"

"Of course. Good for what moves you, if you know what I mean, at our age," she replied. "It's spelt."

An archaic past participle, but students often wrote "learnt," even if they hadn't. Maddie waited for her to continue, but the woman kept chewing in a Trojan effort. "It's spelt how?"

Nancy swallowed and then sucked from the nipple of a bottle of spring water. "Got you there, Prof. Spelt is an ancient grain of the Aztecs or Mayas. Maybe it killed them off."

In Maddie's mailbox were piled the usual advertisements from book companies, memos about departmental and college routines, hours of library and gym services, and a yearly account of the anemic accumulation in her pension.

Back at her desk, she set up the lesson plans. English grammar resisted change, "irregardless" of the constant barrage of new words. For her literature classes she tracked the latest scholarship, if you could call it that. Trends came and went. Byron was a hero, a blackguard, gay, a woman in disguise.

Hours later, Maddie pulled out of the parking lot and tuned in 550, a station dedicated to boomers. "Twist and Shout." Gray Power. People glued together by memories of the Beatles gyrating in front of dour Ed Sullivan or the taste of a pepperoni pizza when they learned Jack or Bobby Kennedy had been shot. A generation older, her father recalled watching Gary Cooper in *Sergeant York* the day Pearl Harbor had been bombed.

George Temple lived in a small bungalow with aluminum siding in a subdivision of Stoddard old enough to grow shade trees. It had been a struggle to get him to sell the massive colonial with three apartments, where their family had lived for thirty years. Rental property was the only kind, her mother Francy had cautioned. Dressed in her rompers, a succession of skimpy, spaghetti-strap sunsuits designed to counteract hot flashes, she wore hanging from her bright red lips an ever-present cigarette with a drooping ash. How she avoided renting to women was a triumph of guile over law. Though she claimed that she didn't like their hosiery hanging up (even in their own bathrooms), the truth was that Francy hated competition. She was queen of the house until her death in an auto accident on I-75 during a blizzard.

"Hi, guys," she called as she opened the door to greet an ancient, smelly dachshund sniffing at her shoes. "Lucky, on Halloween you can masquerade as a pot-bellied pig."

Her father ambled around the corner, blue eyes brightening as he hitched up pants with neon red suspenders. "Hello, my Madeline," he said, the name borrowed from the series of children's books. His hug brought a scent of Old Spice from his baby face.

Steeling herself, Maddie pointed to the dog's underhang. "You can't keep stuffing him, Father. That stomach is touching the floor. Dachshunds are prone to serious back problems."

He ran a hand over thick white hair trimmed to a butch cut. "Word of honor I don't give him an ounce more than what the vet says. One cup of that dry, diet stuff. Crime, though. You want to eat that?"

They moved into the living room where her mother's portrait dominated the decor, her eyes following every move. Maddie knew that the effect was a painter's trick, but couldn't ignore the eerie feeling. They settled into matching recliners and turned on the shake-and-bake feature, a heated massage. For several minutes, only the drone of the mechanics filled the room.

"You heard about it on the news, I guess. A student was killed on campus. Fell from a window in the library," she said, turning off her switch.

His lower lip tightened. "Damn shame. Those kids. Fooling around, would you say?"

"I'm not sure. Nobody saw the fall." Hoisting Lucky onto her lap with difficulty, she stroked the animal, its breathing relaxing, the tiny heart strong beneath smooth brown skin. One cup chow plus steak trimmings, butter pecan ice cream, and the errant oatmeal cookie at snack time. The old man could have dropped twenty pounds, too, even if at seventy-five he walked three miles a day.

"How's the exercise?" she asked, searching for a positive note. Children turned into parents, "chadults" was the word on the talk shows, middle-aged women trapped by the disparate needs of two generations, except that she had an unruly teenaged dog instead.

Her father tapped his watch. "I get up at ten minutes to six, never fifteen minutes to six, never five minutes to six. Water the mutt at his favorite pine tree, around the block, down to Wal-Mart, come back, and watch the news. Billy's not out of the sack until eight."

Something delicious drifted into the living room. If Billy was anything, he was a good cook. She cocked a thumb toward the doorway. "Stew?"

"Wednesday. Must be. Had some gas last night from the lasagna."

Maddie eased into the kitchen, the louvered door swinging shut behind her. Billy Cleghorn had lived in the basement suite of the old place, sharing an alcoholic bond with her hard-drinking mother. How close Maddie didn't want to know. Returning one night from a high school game, she thought that they had moved apart too quickly, leaving the porch swing shuddering. Then a holiday binge had lost Billy his position as a groundskeeper at Copper. Francy let him stay to handle the yard work and cleaning, or so she said. Now her father had a good pension from his job as a sergeant at the police department, and Billy retained enough brain cells to manage the house. George Temple was an affable soul, confident that her mother had been a saint. Maddie would never have disabused that notion. She nurtured the old man's pride like Billy trimmed his prize caragana hedges. Billy raised no eyebrow at his encyclopedic war stories, merely opened another pack of Winstons and dumped a burgeoning ashtray into the trash.

A gallon of cheap vodka hid under the sink behind a bleach bottle, but as long as he was functional, he escaped life in a shelter. She maintained an uneasy peace with this complex man. Without him, her father probably would have moved in with her, an alarming prospect for anyone wedded to the single life. To lay down the law to Billy unless absolutely necessary would upset a precarious symbiosis. What would cause that reckoning? When he cracked up the car because he was dead drunk? Billy turned at her approach, bone thin, a pair of razor-creased washpants and an ironed shirt covered by one of her mother's aprons.

"Smells good," she said, noting on the counter a file card from Francy's legendary recipe collection.

"Stay for dinner if you want. Bull Moose pays the shot," he said with a shrug, his voice raspy. Despite a throat cancer operation and brutal radiation two years ago, he hadn't stopped smoking. Never would, until the pack was wrenched from his cold, dead hand. None of his excellent meals would add to the hundred twenty pounds on his six-foot frame.

"I'd love to, but Nikon needs a walk. I've been gone all day." They'd had nasty times all of her years at home. Fueled by booze, he'd made snarky comments to her in private. Once she had been holding a neighbor's baby as he passed by. "I pity any child of yours," he snarled with a coward's confidence because they were alone. In tears later, she'd told her father. After that, Billy minded his manners. "What did you say?" she had asked.

"Told him that if he ever made you cry again, I'd kill him." The threat was at odds with his peace-at-any-price personality, born out of life with her mother. On the job, he gained a reputation as a common sense guy who could talk the most violent offender into surrendering quietly.

Billy coughed into a handkerchief and headed upstairs. Watching him go, Maddie surreptitiously inspected the fridge, tossing out a mayo jar outdated by two months. Her father's bouts of stomach trouble might be traced to this oversight. With his chronic colitis, Billy wouldn't have thought twice. No other Tupperware containers turning to furry Petri dishes, she noticed with relief. God bless them for soldiering on. They had their independence. And Father's rusty Dynasty. And Lucky.

Chapter Five

"Behave yourself, Nicodemus," Maddie said, flipping a pig ear into his crate as she left, a treat that would keep him busy. Unfortunately the crispy brown snack had grotesque links to the little porker in *Babe*, especially with the blurry tattooed number. "Your personal trainer reminds you that there's only one letter difference between 'friend' and 'fiend.'"

Later that day she was browsing in a conference room with textbook displays, lured by free coffee and doughnuts. She leafed through the index of a grammar book, appalled to find no entry for the question mark. As she turned toward the door, through the small rectangular window like an arrow hole in a castle battlement she glimpsed a familiar red mophead in front of a hall locker. Barney Smallwood twirled the combination lock and pulled to check that it was secure. Then he disappeared, only to reappear seconds later and repeat the process like a film rerun until Maddie felt guilty about spying on the poor creature. Obsessive-compulsiveness ran in her family, too. Her grandfather's suicide.

Back outside, she strolled past the Student Union as signs were going up for the first guest speaker of the year, a noted sex therapist with a weekly television show. The perfect subject to get their attention, and with the rise in STDs, a classic blend of instruction and delight. One poster touted the G-spot for men. Another asked whether people with disabilities could have orgasms. Anisha Mukherjee would be proud that her students were included. Thinking of Ed, she searched a table of pamphlets for information on Viagra, but the display was student-oriented.

As she returned to her office, Jack Birchem was leaning against the door, reading a copy of *The Crucible*, Copper's weekly paper. "Hello, Professor. Sharpening that red pencil?"

A blink ago he had been a callow freshman with a cheek so smooth that she wondered if he needed to shave. Now he'd stretched another four inches. The sweatpants, ripped t-shirts, and ponytail were history. His chestnut hair was gelled to attention and his chinos pressed beneath a light sportcoat. Turning over a new leaf or a new girlfriend? "I use a pen, Jack, as you should remember," she said. "So, did you get on again at the Refectory?"

"Dish jockey. Pays the rent, even if it's only min wage." Last year when he hadn't been able to afford the textbook, she'd passed him an extra complimentary copy. "Wonder what my chances will be in June, though? Jobs look grim for graduates."

"Too many of us old bags hanging around. But we need to pay the rent, too, and invest for retirement," she said. "How's the writing going?"

"I've started a couple of short stories. Science fiction. Not your kind of stuff, I guess."

"Go for a best seller. Too late for the millennium thriller, but another fad's always around the corner. Men are even writing romances now." She flashed him a smile, then saw a sadly familiar face on the front page of the paper he held. "Wasn't it terrible about Cheryl Crawford?"

"I couldn't believe it. Jesus. Must have seen her studying in the stacks a hundred times." Together they scanned the lead story, a brief review of her scholarships and a few words from a roommate, Alice Blake, in Rocky Quad.

"Were you close friends?"

"Not really. There was something, well, solitary, circumspect . . ." He looked to her for help.

"Jack, never use a polysyllabic word when a plain one will do."

He rubbed the back of his strong, young neck in boyish fashion, uncomfortable at the sudden seriousness. "Now, don't get me wrong. She wasn't a snob. Just never seemed to play the usual dating games. I asked her out, and she turned me down, politely but firmly. Guess all her time went to her studies. Hard to keep a four-pointer going."

Finally Maddie headed home, her route skirting Creswell Park, site of an abandoned copper mine. The pet project of a surprisingly environmentalist mayor at the turn of the century, Creswell proved that sensible reclamation and a hundred years could work magic. The park spread over seventy acres edging Lake Superior, and had been adopted by each mayor in succession. In an unofficial contest to outdo the last incumbent, they added small ponds, groves of maple, birch, and oak, long vistas of fast-growing red and white pines, shaded walks with sturdy wooden benches, and last year an asphalted bicycle path. In-line skaters were multiplying like June blackflies, and Maddie preferred the dirt paths, kinder to aging knees. What had it been like under excavation: bare hills, piles of rock dredged from the bowels of the earth for its red-gold metal? Superior had been many levels higher after the last Ice Age, the beaches lapping at a series of islands where the peninsula now stood. It was no coincidence that the line of mines leading to Copper Harbor followed this path, nor that the natives, known poetically as Ancient Miners, had nosed canoes toward the richest sources centuries before the white man had arrived with trinkets, organized religion, and smallpox. One mass had weighed over six tons.

Samples of identical copper had been found in Egyptian jewelry, confounding the anthropologists who doubted the possibility of Pre-Columbian oceanic travel.

Maddie hadn't visited the park since Honey's death. The old dog had loved Creswell, amused by opportunities of meeting new friends. Tennyson was right: "The old order changeth, and giveth place to the new." She shook off the temptation to dwell on grief. If she collected Nikon now, there would be time for an hour's exercise.

Twenty minutes later, hearing her enter the house, the dog began wailing, keening the pain of abandonment. When he wasn't loosed immediately, he launched into an invective only canines understood. Maddie resisted the urge to hurry. The bible cautioned against making a big fuss: free the pet when he quieted. "I must be cruel only to be kind. But you get a bonus today. A new place to explore," she said, opening the pen and noticing that he had dislodged the sheet on his foam mattress to tooth out a few shreds. "And stop that nonsense with your bed. It's willful." Stupid to talk to him in sentences, she thought, recalling a cartoon where the dog heard only "Blah, blah, blah, blah, Tippy."

The sky was clear and the air crisp, hinting at a hard frost. She cast an eye over the feathery tops of carrots in the remains of her garden. Ed had collected the last green tomatoes a few days ago, and he was wasting no time. The breeze brought the piquant aroma of chow-chow. She folded down the Probe's back seat, spread out a sheet, and boosted Nikon into the car.

Later, as he hopped out at the park, Maddie noticed that he had vomited quietly into the coin holder. What a sensitive stomach. Why had she pressed those turns so sharply, she wondered, as she grabbed a roll of paper towels. On a long, retractable lead, the pup took immediately to the idea, running after pine cones, nipping at scattering leaves, and accepting admiring pets from joggers. "Isn't he the cutest thing?" said a young woman pushing a stroller as he planted a kiss on her ear. He loved people: kids, adults, anything breathing. What kind of a watchdog would he be? No house on her road with a dog had ever suffered a burglary. The mere idea of a German shepherd would dissuade robbers, not to mention the fearsome bark. So far, "roo-roo" had been his best effort.

Reaching a remote area, Maddie paused to appreciate the subtle music of a small pond, the reeds singing a dry brown song while the frogs handled bass clef. Freed from the leash, Nikon snatched a cattail, an exploding cigar which covered him with fluff. Then they took a footpath to the dunes, a choice overlook. When the area was logged, great trees were sent crashing down the hundred-foot sandhills to be collected on the beach and floated onto the lake. As kids, she and her pals liked to slide to the bottom and climb back. The trip up the steep slope in sand was brutal for thighs that weren't young and strong. She'd probably have a heart attack trying it now.

Maddie relaxed on a bench behind a low stone wall and gazed across Lake Superior. Choppy today, cat's-paw waves Swinburnian-full of sand and foam. In the shadowy distance, blazing with lights like a sea-going circus, an iron ore boat churned east to where the massive locks of the Sault would usher it through to Huron and the steel mills.

The steamer blew a horn, so mesmerizing in its massive power that Maddie lost track of the dog. Irritated by her carelessness, she called, "Nikon, come here, Mannie." Then with their customary whistle, she expected padding feet to sound, but all was quiet. She jumped up and flailed about the undergrowth of alders, flinching as a sparrow fluttered away. Letting him off leash had been a big mistake. Obviously he was drunk on freedom.

"Nikon!" she yelled, clapping her hands like a fool. "Never sound angry," the bible cautioned. "A dog seeks a merry voice where fun is in order." Fun be damned. She felt like administering a lesson with a two-by-four. So much for the Infant Phenomenon.

After an annoying wait, Maddie's wrath turned to fear. She began imagining dire encounters. Pray God not a porcupine. What about a bitch in heat? Had hormones surged before his tiny balls had dropped? Perhaps a dognapper. Those five-hundred dollar genes were evident to even the unpracticed eye. Her frantic gaze finally focused on the dirt path, where telltale pawprints headed off. She set out on a run. That little bastard.

Creswell Park bordered on the town golf course, and as she stopped for breath, Maddie could see through the thinning birches up a hill to the ninth hole. Two people were getting out of a cart. She narrowed her eyes, waiting for those bothersome floaters to settle. It looked like Flo and . . . Dean Nordman. He was bending over her, whispering in her ear as she prepared to putt. When the ball fell into the cup, he looked around furtively and gave her firm little fanny a pat. Butter wouldn't melt in Flo's mouth, yet here she was tooling around on the golf course. With the gossip about his health problems, her husband Bruce was hardly a companion for sports.

Nikon's tracks doubled back on another path to the lookout, where she found him waiting at patient attention, as if she had been the truant. From his smiling mouth hung a partridge feather. "Couldn't wait for dinner?" she asked with a snarl as she took him back to the car, hurrying against the oncoming darkness. A cloud bank blotted what sun remained. Like many of her older friends, Maddie had begun avoiding driving at night. The glare of headlights blurred her vision so much that she nearly stopped several times. Maybe she should try those bilberry capsules from the health food store. No, better go to the optometrist, despite the new prescription in April.

A bottle of chow still warm from the canner was waiting at her door when she got home. Ed's secret recipe. Nikon gobbled his kibble in minutes, but all she could manage for herself after that harrowing drive was a bowl of cream of mushroom soup spiked with a dab of Harvey's Shooting sherry, crackers on the side. She drank one glass as an appetizer and another as dessert. Simplified things.

Then she picked up the Victorian lit anthology and tried to lose herself. Her hand stopped at Porphyria again, mute, helpless, a flower plucked in perfection, her pathological killer imagining that she smiled in death to confirm their union. Even OJ, a free man forever in limbo, had said in an unguarded moment, "If I had killed her, wouldn't that prove that I loved her?" She closed the book with a self-critical sigh. Why was she getting so dramatic over a simple accident?

Putting away the bottle, Maddie discovered a mere half-inch and finished it out of good housekeeping practice. She had counted on the anesthetic effect to calm her nerves, but instead she grew more analytical, examining far-fetched theories. Was liquor involved in the fall? The drinking age in Michigan was a puritanical twenty-one. That didn't eliminate booze runs to the Canadian Sault, though, a popular student pastime. She shook her head. Stick to the facts. From what she'd learned, Cheryl had been a lonely creature consumed by the need to achieve high marks. Accident, suicide, whatever the case, everyone needed to move on. So unfortunate that the thesis was unfinished. Closure was important.

Before soaking in a hot bath, she caught herself blearily in the full-length mirror, turned overnight into her mother.

That extra twenty pounds. No waist, not that she ever had one; snake hips, her grandmother had said. Nikon's head was barely tall enough to rest on the tub edge. With his brown eyes surveying her, she soothed away knots behind her shoulders, muttering to herself. Answering back. That wasn't healthy, even if you did win all the arguments.

Chapter Six

Maddie made an eye appointment before she left the house. Later, in the corridors of Denney, she met Malcolm chugging towards the office. Wearing his usual tweeds, brandishing an umbrella with a wicked tip, he might have been Mr. Toad of Toad Hall except for the aquiline nose. As a young man he must have been an attractive figure, but Maddie found it hard to pare away the avuncular poundage of age.

"How's this for a smashing limerick?" he asked. "A wily old harlot from Akron/ commissioned a hymen of Dacron./ 'It can't be too limp'/ She said to her . . .'"

She winced, but conceded a certain rhythmic flair. "Dacron. Out of fashion since Lyndon Johnson left office. What about Gore-Tex? That waterproof stuff?"

"Rhymes with Wessex, Essex," he said with a grin. "But I need an American context. I'm sending it to *Playboy*. Sometimes I miss the Damoclean sword of publish or perish. After I don my golden parachute, you should apply for the chairman's job, Maddie. It's time for a woman." Then he ambled off, whistling "Roll Me Over in the Clover."

Strange that he hadn't mentioned SWINC, his *bête noire*, but perhaps he was selecting lures for the final cast. Whatever his odd preoccupations, the staff enjoyed his easy-going managerial style. With shrinking funds, he'd wangled them office computers and Internet connections, she thought later as she pounded out sheets of grammar tips. The departmental copier was functional again, so she loaded the paper tray with plastic transparencies. Push a button and presto, a pile of visual aids. A quantum pedagogical leap from her college days. Except for passing around a box of rocks and fossils in geology, her teachers had preferred the talking-head method.

Once in the lecture hall, however, Murphy's law was operating. The overhead machine beamed a bright square, but the screen wouldn't lock. Up and down it flew like a recalcitrant Venetian blind as she groaned, then summoned an arch expression. "Enough entertainment from me. I want a man with slow hands." Laughter broke the tension, and a blond giant in baggy blue jeans ripped at the knees and a Blackhawks jersey strode onto the stage and tried to wrestle the screen into submission. Still, it resisted. Maddie shrugged. "Good lesson to us all, especially future teachers. No matter how many times you double-check, technology hides a custard pie up its sleeve."

With a "Yee haw," the student whipped off his belt to a series of gasps from the class, looped the leather around the handle, and roped the screen to a nearby chair.

"Bravo, Sir Galahad," said Maddie, acknowledging his bow as the class applauded. "Necessity and invention and all that stuff."

"Punctuation is important," she said, her face totally deadpan as she flashed the first foil. "Don't. Stop." and "Don't stop." "Life can get complicated if you miss a period." The sharper pencils caught her drift and exchanged amused glances. Armed with a medical epithet, she switched to the colon rule.

Barney waited as she left the platform at the end of class. In his hand was a creased worksheet, under his arm a stuffed rabbit with a pink hair (hare?) ribbon. Was a girl animal a safer choice than a boy? His face was serious, scruffy eyebrows sparring with each other. "Doc-tor," he exclaimed in that loud voice. "Can you tell me the difference between 'genius' and 'ingenious'? Is 'ingenious' the opposite, or does it mean the same thing?"

She took off her glasses to peer at his paper. "The first is a noun and the second an adjective, similar definitions." With sudden inspiration, she fingered the tiny lock on his backpack. "You might say that this lock is ingenious. Invented by a genius. Get it?"

"An ingenious genius. OK," he said agreeably, though he stared at a nearby wall. "But I still think I am going to fail this test."

She smiled and shook her head. What an ingenious/ingenuous question. Another Mr. Dick from *David Copperfield*. The thin line between common sense and absurdity. Did he merely need reassurance? Maybe he was a candidate for SWINC. Until the first test, she couldn't be absolutely certain. It might be an idea to contact Anisha Mukherjee.

In her office, Maddie punched in the complicated code on the new voice-mail system, more frustrating than useful if the caller didn't pronounce his name clearly or indicate his class. A message said to call Lieutenant Jeff Phillips at the police station. What more could they want?

Phillips picked up on the first ring. "Professor Temple. Sorry to bother you. I know we took your statement, but we're rechecking details."

"Why? It was an accident, wasn't it?" Cheryl's image flashed across her mind like a stubborn, uninvited ghost.

He paused, his tones ordinary and official. "That's our guess. The library may want to install security devices on the upper floor windows. Investigations can be boring, nothing like television. Just tell me your observations, please. I won't keep you long."

She answered his questions patiently, stressing that she hadn't seen the girl fall, nor apparently had anyone else at the site. Then he thanked her and hung up. Maddie felt a small worm of discontent. The police weren't revealing much, but they knew their jobs, she supposed, even though the Upper Peninsula was a quiet law-and-order zone. Not enough population to generate the endemic problems of serious drug trafficking, smuggling, or illegal aliens. No logistical interest to the Mafia, and too cold and snowy half the year for street gangs milling around in search of trouble. Neighborhoods too friendly/nosey for urban crime. And she hardly recalled the last murder, a woman abused for thirty-five years finally stabbing her drunken husband with a pair of sewing scissors.

Her father said that plain shoeleather served an officer best. Perhaps he might able to tell her why questions were still being asked. Often he took doughnuts to the station for a good jaw with his old buddies.

Later, Maddie saw Grace headed for the parking lot. "Come for dinner tonight?" she asked, doubting a positive answer. Insulating the woman was a certain mystique, unlike Maddie, who wore her heart on her sleeve. Though she had been in the U.S. long enough to acclimate, the African woman remained a stranger in a strange land. She never attended department parties, nor mentioned any activities with friends.

Grace mustered a small smile and nodded, hoisting a fat bundle of papers. "A break would be very welcome."

As she made a quick trip to the supermarket, selecting the last choice cut of beef, Maddie wondered what, after all these years, had caused her to ask Grace for dinner, and what miracle had made her colleague accept. Somehow Cheryl had brought them together, a certain deadly kinship, an unspoken responsibility of the living for the dead. And detecting was in her genes. She had wanted to pursue police work like her father, had thrived on Conan Doyle, sported a deerstalker hat and puffed frosty breaths from a corncob pipe on Halloween. At the time, no forces recruited women, and as for the locale, Holmes would have needed more than a seven percent solution to wallow through sixteen feet of snow.

Shortly after dusk, Nikon's puppy woofs announced the arrival of the Buick. The succulent roast beast had not died in vain. "You might turn into a decent watchdog despite yourself," she said, yanking him into a sit as she opened the door. Grace stiffened, stepped back, then relaxed as she realized that the shepherd was a miniature model. She extended a box of truffles from the local chocolaterie, then bent to scratch the dog's ears, which rolled him upside down in shameless submission, pink belly presented for a rub.

"An Alsatian. Very popular at home," she said. "Sadly, the choice of Amin's secret police. But also cherished companions." She lowered her gaze as if recalling a painful experience. "I had to leave my Goldi behind with a cousin. To this day I have never heard what happened to her."

"The dog or the cousin?" Maddie asked, disarmed to catch a personal reference.

"Both."

Rattled from her faux pas, Maddie settled her guest in the living room. Onto the CD went five discs of resonant violin music by Itzhak Perlman, while a South African Cabernet the color of blazing garnets filled the glasses. She couldn't help noticing deep circles ringing Grace's eyes, despite her efforts at makeup. Though always lean and sculpted, she seemed nearly gaunt, breastbone stark above a scoop-necked fawn wool dress decorated by an elegant beaded shawl. Her thin wrists looked vulnerable, ringed by the silver bangles. Perhaps Cheryl's face still haunted her dreams.

"Paarl makes excellent wine. I missed it during the years of the boycott," Grace said. She sat back in the deep sofa cushions, looking expectantly toward Maddie. When she heard about the investigation, her shoulders tightened. "And yet the police told you nothing?"

"That's how they work, but the additional questions are curious for an accident. I'm wondering if they found a witness. Many buildings face the Oval." Maddie took a hasty gulp, spilled a drop of wine on her hand.

Drawing the shawl around her in a protective gesture, Grace shuddered. "Yes."

Maddie rose to turn on the gas fire. The flames leaped and darted behind the glass doors, warming the room as Nikon snored in the corner in a post-prandial daze, having enjoyed an early supper. "I hesitate to bring this up, Grace, for fear of upsetting you. But what do you think about the possibility of suicide?"

It was clear from Grace's unhappy expression that the suggestion had presented itself. "My knowledge issues from a privileged position as her advisor. Whatever might have tormented her, now she is free. I am not sure I should—"

A timer rang in the kitchen, postponing the agony. Maddie excused herself with a smile. Minutes later they sat at the dining room table, enveloped by a reassuring aroma of pot roast simmered in tomatoes and basil. The Yorkshire pudding, puffy and golden with butter, bubbled at the edges as she lit the two long candles.

Maddie picked up a filigreed knife and traced the monogram, MIT. "Rambler Rose pattern," she added, trying to lighten the mood. "My enterprising mother got everyone to give me sterling silver for birthdays, Christmas. All those predictable little velveteen boxes taking the place of real presents. When the set was complete, she started using it herself."

Cheryl's shadow might have been seated in the opposite chair, for Grace resumed the earlier conversation. "At first I thought her troubles stemmed from a young man. Passions run high at that age."

"I spoke to a student who knew her. Apparently she was quite solitary."

"She never did mention any man in her life, other than her father. His approval meant everything." The lithe cinnamon legs crossed one way, then another, as if seeking an exit from pain. Her broad lips barely formed the words with a sad hush. "I wonder if the family knew about her therapy."

"Therapy?" Winkling facts out of Grace was more onerous than cutting Nikon's claws. "She was disturbed enough for that?"

Grace folded her hands, considered the licking flames of the candles as she added each word with deliberate care, wetness moistening her eyes. "I know that she was getting professional help. Once or twice she rescheduled our conferences for an appointment."

"On campus?"

"I would suppose so. Students do not have much money, and the Health Clinic is a useful service."

The conversation drifted to classes, the cutbacks, the cold weather. Perhaps the soft, ripe wine reminded Grace of her sunny homeland, for she drank heartily and accepted more of the Yorkshire dish, intrigued by the concept of a savory in pudding disguise. On prompting, she offered a few hints at Ugandan cuisine, despairing of finding hairy, baseball-bat yams or the nefarious palm oil outside New York City.

They returned to the living room after dinner, the bright strains of Paganini prevailing. "Cheryl's death was tragic," Maddie said, serving the coffee and truffles. "We may never know the truth. But a positive step might temper the sting. I've had an idea. How far along was her work?"

"She was completing the final draft, but knowing Cheryl, it would have been near perfect. After defending her thesis, she would have matriculated in December. She had hopes of going on to graduate school. The University of Michigan and then Johns Hopkins. Excellent programs."

"If that's true, what about arranging a posthumous degree? Of course, we'd need to find the thesis first. See what shape it's in." Grace's face came suddenly to life, so Maddie continued in Sherlockian fashion, waving her hand casually. "We'll call her roommate. Look through her desk. Maybe talk to the family."

Darkness returned to Grace's brows, which suggested that Maddie had exceeded the boundaries of good taste. "I am a private person. I respect the privacy of others. Do we have the right to do this?"

Maddie drew back, measuring the conviction in the woman's voice. Cooperation was critical. Best to couch the inquiries in an ethical frame. "Not only the right, but the duty. She was one of ours. We both know she worked hard. Let's find a way to reward her efforts."

She clinked her coffee cup against Grace's, who after considered seconds, took a hesitant sip. Wakened by the noise, Nikon began attacking his tail as if it were a separate and treacherous monster.

Chapter Seven

The kitchen was dark and quiet, except for the tubercular wheeze of the coffeemaker. Maddie liked to rise before six and regain her senses at the breakfast nook with a dose of *The Peninsula Register*. "Come on, lichen breath," she said as she collected the paper at the door and let Nikon out, watching him skate on the frost that covered the deck like a coat of icing sugar. His first winter was approaching. Everything old is new again. With flailing paws, he shambled down the stairs and bounced off into the far reaches of the yard.

Minutes later he returned, traces of grubbing on his mouth. "Dig up any moss? Rocks? Gravel? You're a cheap feed, but digestion may catch up with you," she observed, prying open his jaws to extract a blackened mushroom. He yawned and fell back to sleep on the linoleum, gangly legs outstretched in puppy impossibility. He was growing so fast that he didn't know what fresh Frankenstein monster might greet him each morning. His dreamy scrabblings in her bed might soon relocate him onto the sheepskin rug where Honey had slept. A leg with a thirty-pound thrust, however unintended, could be a jarring experience.

She scrambled two eggs, then enjoyed them with Dick's spicy chow and a toasted English muffin as she read the news. A certain presentiment dampened her appetite as she turned to the letters to the editor. The outrage at Malcolm's diatribe covered half a page. Parents of a handicapped high school se-

58

nior asked if Hitler's final solution would be her chairman's next plan. A clergyman called for his resignation.

The Refectory was bustling at nine as she collected a coffee. Sitting alone at a table was one of the part-time lecturers employed as slave labor. Married women, eager young graduates, they were an undulating amoeba, faceless numbers on a roster. This transient labor pool shared a pen in the nether regions of Denney Hall, surrounded by steam pipes and janitorial closets. "Rita, anything this semester?" Maddie asked, joining her.

The woman clasped a cardboard box filled with her life at Copper. "I waited until the last minute to clean out my desk. Thought that maybe . . ." Her voice quivered, sea green eyes brimming at the corners. In a bright calico dress, her hair a mass of reddish curls, she looked like a depressed Raggedy Ann doll. "I don't want to move to a larger town, but it's hard to keep going with uncertainty when bills need to be paid."

Maddie's warm cup lost its savor. Rita was a single mother, divorced from a wandering husband who had left her with a ten-year-old Civic and a crushing mortgage. Her two boys were in junior high school, master consumers of food and clothes.

"It's not fair. You've been doing a great job for us for so long." Once Flo sucked a teacher dry for a year or two, she advertised for fresh blood at the lowest hourly rate, then restarted the cycle for those laid off. Administrative vampirism. And yet, meagerly paid sessionals were often the most earnest and diligent teachers.

For a moment, Maddie wished that she could run the department. Hand on Rita's shoulder, she affected a reassurance slenderly felt. "Call in next week. Sometimes we open another section of remedial grammar to keep the athletes eligible."

Minutes later, Rita struggled out with her burden, leaving Maddie mulling over the Darwinian law of the jungle: Adam hunts the mastodon while Eve tends the fires. One poor choice and out of the gene pool. Despite recent maternity leave laws, it was still a juggle for a woman to balance child-raising and an academic career. After Dan and Maddie had shaken hands over two decades ago, foresworn all their vows, she had forged on without another thought at partnerships and their biological complications, surrendered brain and body to her career and expected the rewards.

Back in Denney, she dropped into Gary Carter's office. Last hired, he needed a few more years for tenure, and she had a feeling Flo would use her power on the committee to black-ball the appointment and fill his place with a sessional. Despite what the average citizen thought, tenure was not a foregone conclusion. The occasional failures crept away quietly, well aware that their inability to publish had doomed them. Gary taught nineteenth-century American literature, but his passions warmed at comic book heroes like the Green Hornet and Captain Marvel. He'd had some success placing articles in nostalgia magazines and *The Journal of Popular Culture*.

His usual enthusiasm had been replaced by a frown, his mouth firmly set. "Guess this might be my last year," he said, drawling out the syllables with a heavy Oklahoma accent. "No way I'm getting tenure from Flo. None of that matters to her." He gazed up with silent pride at three framed testimonials to excellence in teaching, an annual award from the Student Council.

"Don't sell Malcolm short. He'll go the distance for you if he can. Have you sent any material to academic journals?"

"It's all so chewed over. I love teaching the stuff, but dissecting literature with a microscope? Maybe you know that feeling."

"No denial here. But publish or perish is the accepted standard, right or wrong. Find a concept that interests you and give it a modern spin." She ran a finger along his bookshelf and stopped at *The Fall of the House of Usher*. "Poe's the best bet. His plots are still churning out movies. The Stephen King of his era."

A faint light appeared in Gary's eyes, and she returned to her office. "Chewed over," he had said, and he was right. The old house needed a good cleaning. She pulled out a text kept for sentimental reasons: *Dictionary of English Literature 1883*. The Victorian Internet. What was still relevant? Ten percent of the Gradgrindish facts? Five? The Fudge Family in Paris was as dead as *The Lousiad*. But a mention of "The Raven" made her smile, an odd durable, along with the pillars of Shakespeare and Austen. She revised her estimate to one tenth of one percent, a fellow-feeling of her personal irrelevance even more disheartening.

On the way out at last, she passed Rick Houghton's office. He crooked a finger at her in his maddeningly understated way. Such a poseur. Teaching twentieth-century American poetry and drama, he locked into the Ginsberg stage, though he'd barely been born when the bearded wonder held court in Greenwich Village. His shirts always looked deliberately unpressed, perhaps to add verisimilitude to his lectures. On the desk, next to an overflowing ashtray, sat a shallow wooden box of sand. Smoke rings wreathing his balding head, one nicotine-stained hand plied a miniature rake, teasing patterns around several small rocks. She fanned the air.

"Cat die?"

He snorted. "A Zen garden in the style of Ryoan-ji."

"A litterbox to calm the nerves."

"Hey, it's better than the jagged little pills George gobbles or Malcolm's booze." He dribbled an ash onto the floor. "I'm into natural stuff."

Intrigued, Maddie considered the circling trails in the sand. On a large scale, the concept minimized garden care in a climate just south of the Arctic. Maybe Ed would lend a hand in the spring. With chunks of pink granite . . .

"Christ. What a year it's going to be. Those idiots in English 100. Maybe I should get back to my novel."

"So what else is new?" His perennial masterpiece, a Generation X answer to *On the Road,* was a departmental joke, but she knew he wouldn't take the bait.

He flapped a blue speedy memo reply in her face. "No more PD dough. Got turned down for my annual trip to the Big Apple." One perk at a university was the professional development budget. Maddie traveled every other year to England for research. Recipients were expected to churn an article or two out of the disbursements, yet all Rick seemed to bring from New York was an unconvincing Brooklyn accent and a bag of exotic dope. More than once, she had nosed sweet suggestions in the corridor after five o'clock.

"Flo claims the frigging budget is frozen until further notice. What a burr on my ass."

"So write our own *Grammar for Dummies.* Admitting ignorance is a new badge of honor. There's one for sex, decks, sound effects. Ten simple-minded units, copious exercises with self-check answers. Presto, thirty dollars times millions of grateful students." What worried her was that he seemed to be mulling over the idea as she left.

That afternoon she called Cheryl's roommate, Alice Blake, and arranged for a visit. The girl sounded pleasant and helpful, if a bit weepy.

A four o'clock appointment with the optometrist didn't go as smoothly. From his perch on what resembled a dunce stool, Dr. Maki peered owlishly at her and scribbled notes. How Maddie hated squinting into that medieval torture machine to choose which side was less blurry, rolling her eyes to shift the floaters, alarmed by the brightness, worrying about the wrong answer. "Your prescription hasn't really changed since April," he said.

Was she imagining a hesitation on "really"? "Not the right eye? I can't read traffic signs as well. And bright lights are a bother." On the way to the appointment, she had closed one eye and then the other, trying to decide which was worse. Move over, Barney.

"So minor as to be negligible." He selected a monocle from a case and placed it over the offending eye with a patronizing sigh. "Better?"

She wavered, reluctant to fail the test. "I think so."

"If you insist on a new pair, I suggest non-glare. Less distraction." He gave her a stern glance. "You are using those bifocals, aren't you?"

"I can't get used to them." She snatched a hand mirror from the tray and lifted her eyelid, peering intently. "And while I'm here, what about these yellow patches on the whites? It looks like pigeon poop."

"*Pingueculas.* Harmless yellowish spots on the *conjunctiva*. Another aging process. Get too bothersome or cover the iris, they can be scraped off." She shrank against the chair, and with a dry laugh, he glanced at his watch in ill-disguised irritation. "But you are picky about your vision. And with the problems of keeping track of two pairs of glasses, you'll soon come around. They all do."

Her ears burned as she left insurance information with the clerk. How old was Maki? Thirty-five? Optometrists should be at least fifty. Post-presbyopic. Then they'd know.

She went to bed that night obsessed about her vision.

Normal, or something more sinister? The man wasn't an ophthalmologist. Photosensitivity could mean potential cataracts or even a detached retina. She hadn't had any light flashes, though. Perhaps she'd taken her health for granted. Aside from an appendix attack, she'd never been inside a hospital.

Chapter Eight

Maddie didn't need to make an appointment with Anisha Mukherjee to discuss Barney. A memo routed to his instructors arrived in her mailbox the next day: "You have in your class Barney Smallwood. According to his mother, he has certain disabilities which may require a minimum of accommodations. If you wish to know more, please call me."

Predictably, the line was busy, so Maddie walked over to SWINC. A vast, pale pink series of winged, breastlike caverns, it hadn't opened officially. Yellow tape and sawhorses with ropes sectioned off bare areas as workers prepared to landscape. Mounds of sod were piled at intervals, water hoses snaking along the ground. As she passed through the automatic sliding doors, a robotic Disney World voice greeted her: "Welcome. You are entering the Students With Individual Needs Center. Straight ahead is . . ." Behind an information desk in the large foyer, a young girl in a wheelchair circulated nimbly among phones and computer screens. A hand on the woman's shoulder, quietly giving instructions; Anisha looked up and beamed.

"I appreciated your memo about Barney Smallwood. Do you have a free moment to talk about him?" Maddie asked.

"Delighted, but how about a grand tour first? I'm expecting the VIPs at the opening, so practice is welcome." Anisha's accent was upper-caste Bombay with British icing from her Oxford schooling. Lustrous, curly black hair was swept into a bun at her nape. Kohl-lined eyes looked out from her café-au-lait face, and her full lips were a dark peach. Under five feet tall, she wore two-inch-heeled golden sandals to compensate. Maddie never stopped marveling at the assortment of exquisite saris, one for each day of the month. This design was pale blue with a seam of silver.

Leading the way, Anisha stopped and ran the toe of her sandal across a pebbly line on the floor. "Notice the row of rough tiles down the middle of each hall. Easy to follow for a low-vision person using a cane."

In each of four spacious classrooms, a bank of Pentium 4 computers with twenty-inch monitors could be adjusted for all postures, even lying down. Side rooms contained machines to transcribe Braille or even read a book aloud through optical character recognition. Anisha spoke into a computer, and a printer rolled out the script. "Milton, we call it. After the poet became blind, he dictated his works to an amanuensis."

"How is this possible?" Maddie asked in astonishment. "What about accents?"

"Initially the program took forever to sort out individual pronunciation. In quality control trials, this Dragon system got Mae West's 'Glad to see me?' perfectly, but couldn't handle Kennedy's inaugural address or Brando's godfather," she explained with a light laugh.

In a workshop, technicians fine-tuned tape recorders, microphones, wands, and other assistive devices. Offices for individual study contained warning lights to signal fire alarms to the deaf. A hall of well-appointed tutoring rooms bore plaques with the names of corporate sponsors Reggie had rounded up. Dedicated to disabilities, a library contained the latest reference material. One room with hospital beds allowed wheelchair students to rest between classes, and the bathrooms were equipped with special hoists and space-age spray toilets. "Accidents happen," Anisha said cheerfully. "No need to leave campus now. The Athletics Department donated a box of sweatsuits the students can wear while we wash and dry their clothes in the laundry."

In the compact kitchen which served as a lunchroom, Maddie spotted a plastic container with the famous wax dip. On invitation, she plopped her hand several times into the warm liquid, fragrant with spearmint. Emerging, despite a ghostly gray pallor, it felt magical. "Leave the coating on for five minutes," Anisha advised.

Outside, they inspected the "Poo Poo Park" for guide dogs. "The students must clean up any mess. Plastic bags and receptacles are provided. All the plants and grasses will be selected to resist urine and fecal damage." Anisha pointed toward a roped-off area where workmen were laying bricks in a walkway. "Next spring that will be a scent and touch garden. The Botany seniors are making it their special project. Nicotiana, lilac, honeysuckle. Comfortable benches and shade trees." She smiled warmly at Maddie. "A place for everyone."

Passing a trash can, Maddie peeled off the new skin with reluctance, feeling disturbingly serpentine, her hand twenty years younger. What she had seen impressed her. And certainly Anisha's no-nonsense attitude was balanced by humanity. But when she entered the director's office, a palace of plush navy carpets, oak furnishings, and floor-to-ceiling smoked windows, she bit her lip. Was it mere jealousy, or Malcolm's proportional argument, an inordinate amount of money for a tiny fraction of students? What were the estimates? Two hundred out of seven thousand?

Anisha grinned in proprietary pleasure, flashing the winning expression that had garnered her success in fundraising drives. A picture on the wall showed her applauding with Reggie as President Bowdler wielded a shovel at the ground-breaking ceremony. Why fault them? The squeaky wheel gets the grease, Mother always said. Maybe Reggie could work miracles for the flagging numbers in the English Department? Directing Maddie to a pillowy charcoal leather sofa, Anisha reached for a file. Then she plopped into an ergonomic chair in matching suede. "Barney has a very high functioning level of a rare type of autism. Asberger's Syndrome. *Newsweek* mentioned it recently."

Maddie's grammatical side marveled at the precision of categorizing a grab-bag of quirks. "And what is the signal feature?"

"An absolute inability to assess behavior in social situations."

The words snapped her to attention. "Exactly. And that loud voice? Suppose he were asked to speak more quietly."

Anisha waved a delicate hand in dismissal, jingling tiny bells on her bracelet. "He'd forget the request a minute later."

"What else?"

The pages turned rapidly. "Let's see. Impairments in the use of multiple nonverbal behaviors, such as eye-to-eye gaze."

"True enough."

"Failure to develop peer relationships. In other words, he can't work with others. Wouldn't have the slightest idea how. But he's bright enough and willing. And his high school marks are above average." She gave a brief sigh, followed by a confident smile. "With a bit of luck and some guidance from the Placement staff, he'll find his niche in the back office of some company, sorting files or checking inventory. Yet, who knows? Many Asperger's people are accepted as mere eccentrics, well-tolerated for their talents despite their idiosyncrasies. One of them probably trotted off by himself in the Stone Age and invented the wheel."

"You could be right. His questions about grammar show promise. Anyway, I'll pair him off in the exercises. And I'll let you know his score on test one." She paused. "Barney the Autistic dinosaur. The poor kid. Researchers say names affect success. Forget your Elmers and Ednas."

"A tribute to Grandfather, as I recall," Anisha observed. "One more thing. Routines are very important."

Maddie nodded, still hearing his voice, confused and a bit accusative. "That's why he was so upset when I didn't hold a full class the first day."

"Imagine life like a drive down a highway. Following that white line. Any deviation causes extreme distress. Yet he will be faithful to his course, cleave to it like a bloodhound. Anyway, thanks for caring." She paused, her gaze narrowing as it moved to a folded copy of *The Peninsula Register* on the desk. "I wish all the faculty could be as cooperative."

"What do you mean?" Maddie said, maintaining a studied innocence. This innuendo had to involve Malcolm.

Anisha waved the paper like a flag of distress as her voice turned bitter. "You've seen Driscoll's insane letters. Everyone has. And a senior member of the university. Totally irresponsible." Was she angry or hurt? Perhaps both. Umbrage took many forms.

Anisha looked for a moment out the tinted glass toward a metal sculpture with the SWINC logo, a stylized wheelchair with wings. "Reggie and I, and countless other responsible citizens, have invested our hearts and souls into this dream. And can you believe that old fool has support in the community? Such small-minded people." Her face turned deep plum, and her little fists clenched. "This evil campaign of his won't succeed."

★ ★ ★ ★ ★

Maddie was grateful that Friday night returned life to normal. The first home game. Her father drove them to the stadium, stopping to collect roast beef submarines, a jumbo bag of tortilla chips, and a "farmer pack" container of cherry ice cream, which he stuck under the bleacher. They had fortified themselves with long underwear, snug woollen pants, and down coats the size of a small garage. As the sun surrendered to the artificial day of the stadium lights, they sat expectantly on the forty-yard line to watch the Copper University Anodes jog onto the field in white jerseys, a huge red "C" with a small "u" underneath, surrounded by flames. The original team had been called the Redmen, in honor of the metal, but complaints from the local Ojibwa nation had prompted the change. A flock of cheerleaders, the "women in red" or the "copper bottoms" as jokes went, brandished their pom-poms with commendable spirit, or perhaps to keep warm. As the band played the alma mater, a version of "I Want to Go Back to Michigan (Down on the Farm)," against the wind's steely teeth, they tucked red-striped Hudson Bay blankets around their legs. The hot chocolate laced with brandy had been Billy's idea.

"Listen, Father, I need a favor," she said, breaking open a chemical handwarmer pack and pushing it into his pocket, where it brushed against a spoon.

"Yes, my darling daughter. So hang your hat on a hickory bough—"

"I never go near the water. Even in mid-July, Superior's too cold. Here's the point. Are you still dropping by the department, chatting with the old guard?"

"Every Wednesday, sharp as clockwork."

"I guess I'm what you'd call an amateur sleuth."

He looked puzzled, and she explained. "That student who died last week. When Jeff Phillips called me to double-check the facts, a little light went on. Maybe they aren't sure that it was an accident."

He inspected the sandwich to make sure that no mustard had been added, then dug in with a will, blotting his mouth carefully with a napkin between bites. "Phillips. He's on the ball. And you want me to dig around at the station?"

"Of course. At my advanced age I don't have a boyfriend on the force." He punched her arm gently in an awkward show of support, as she knew he would. "So what about it? Ask a few questions. Find out what the coroner said."

"Will do. I'll wait until Wednesday, of course. Less suspicious." He furrowed his brow, adjusted plaid earmuffs against the wind. "Say, what about Dan Leary? Heard from the boy lately?"

The "boy" was now bald and had a bum knee. In her first year of doctoral work, Maddie had married the raven-haired six-footer with compelling green eyes and Irish charm. Twenty-five and should have known better, but what wonderful omelets. Mushrooms, artichoke hearts, hollandaise sauce, a cheap romancer for students on a budget. Then Dan had turned out to be gay. She understood why in those dangerous days, which made "Don't ask; don't tell" sound permissive, he'd given his best efforts and nearly convinced them both. They had parted good friends. Now he worked as a civil engineer in Cleveland, the Mistake on the Lake. They exchanged Christmas cards with minimal but friendly notes.

"He's doing well. Probably retiring in five years," she said wistfully, her pension a fading glimmer over too many distant hills.

"Wonderful fellow. Never understood why you . . ." He stood up abruptly, letting the blanket fall to the floor. "Got to hit the can."

"It's almost half-time."

"When you gotta go, you gotta go."

" 'Cause if you don't go when you gotta go, when you go to go, you're gone,' " they said in unison, hooking little fingers for a wish. Parents passed on not only genes, but truths, myths, fables, and foibles. Her wish for him was to smile and laugh and find another bowl of ice cream around every corner until his last day on earth.

When he returned, she put her arm around his shoulder, the heavy coat hiding the old bones and thinning muscle as age asserted its dominion. He pointed down the field and yelled, "Go, man, go!" The quarterback's hail-Mary pass in the last five seconds brought them to their feet, cheering wildly as Copper tacked up a lead of 17-10. Together they were kids again.

Chapter Nine

Malcolm tottered toward her in the corridor, chuckling like a raccoon prying open a brimming trash can. His wattles were jangling merrily. "Sell that limerick to *Playboy*?" she asked.

"The moving finger writes," he said, drawing numbers in the air. "Common Sense 1, SWINC 0."

"I beg your pardon?"

"Round two. We may stop them in their misbegotten tracks. I had an enlightening chat with the Vice President of Finance. Funding is getting thinner than Flo's eyebrows. That redundant swimming pool is heading down the drain. Capital! Don't throw good money after bad, I say. Several influential people have joined my campaign. Stephen Glogore, for one. And Cynthia Dartmore."

That explained his delight. In a university, as in a business, territoriality was hard fought and harder won. The more allies the better. Glogore, Head of the Theatre Department, had been lobbying for a new venue for years. The antediluvian lighting system in the ancient Maxwell Auditorium had turned last year's *Macbeth* into a July Fourth extravaganza. Only with convincing bluster had he been able to persuade critics that the explosions during the banquet scene had been deliberate, that the sleepwalking demanded tri-color fireworks to mirror Lady Macbeth's inner turmoil. Meanwhile, a group of intrepid stagehands had scurried behind the set with fire extinguishers, foaming everything that didn't move.

Cynthia Dartmore brought an uncomfortable reactionary element to Malcolm's team. Great-great-granddaughter of Copper's founder, wife of a department store owner, and queen of her own little world, she viewed the campus as an elitist haven. She flirted with ill-disguised anti-Semitism and was a fervent isolationist, her latest hobbyhorse a plan to triple fees for foreign students under the patriotic philosophy that only "real" Americans deserved subsidies. Maddie wouldn't have been surprised if she had suggested forming a Eugenics Department to weed out home-grown undesirables, though from some toothsome nuggets regarding her son at Copper and his former babysitter, she should have been tending her own garden, Voltaire-style.

"There's going to be a rally. Glogore is getting the theatre students to picket SWINC at the opening tomorrow."

"Malcolm, that is such a bad idea. Glogore enjoys the dramatics, and a bigot like Cynthia will give your campaign the worst kind of publicity."

"Nonsense. She's the perfect town-gown balance. Root and branch, old Cece Babcock. And Stephen will keep her in check. People will listen to reason. Don't get those knickers in a knot." He chucked her under the chin with a gesture both patronizing and tender. "Come out and join the fun. Wouldn't be surprised to see a veritable covey of reporters."

Late that afternoon, Maddie heard from her number one scout. "Come on over. Got some news for you," her father said with undisguised excitement. Cradling the receiver behind her ear, she weighed the attractions of a quiet dinner: a frozen pizza jazzed with black olives, sun-dried tomatoes, and fresh-grated Parmesan. She had a cubic ton of tests to mark.

"Tell me now," she asked, knowing full well that he wouldn't.

"Damn it, girl. Billy's making Chinese stuff from your mother's recipe. Get rolling. That's an order." He paused. "Bring that grandson of mine. The furry one."

Recalling that she hadn't cleaned the oven since a potato scallop had boiled over, she shoved the pizza into the freezer. "Okay."

"Prep school," she said a half an hour later to Nikon as she dropped him off in the yard with Lucky. For young pups shy of manners, the old dog had a fuse shorter than his stumpy legs, providing a good test of peer limits. Nikon gamboled around, rear end up and wiggling, paws extended in the play gesture. Lucky gnawed on a soup bone and observed him out of the corner of one wary Teutonic eye. An interloper bent on stealing food? From the back porch, Maddie admired a thriving bush of gigantic white puffball blooms turned coppery with the frost. The flower beds had been put to rest and the roses covered with burlap. Billy had a faithful relationship with his plants.

An expansive smile on his ruddy face, her father passed her a tall brown bottle as she came into the kitchen. Beer wasn't her choice, but Billy's vodka supply was a dubious alternative. When she grabbed a tin mug from the dish drainer, her father's hand brushed her wrist. He whispered, "Not that one."

Maddie jumped back as if a snake had bitten her. "Why not?"

"It's his spit cup," he said. And she shuddered, replacing it quickly. Billy had trouble swallowing and frequently needed to clear the mucus. Rarely did the men enjoy a meal out unless they could count on a secluded corner booth.

"Where is the old prune, anyway?" Joining him at the kitchen table, she tipped back the bottle and savored the hearty flavor. An excellent local German variety, Hunzpfeffer. Ed might like it.

"Upstairs taking a bubble bath. Say, don't you want to know what I found out?" She knew he would milk his discoveries shamelessly, and why not? He was back on the job again. "Thought it was murder for sure. Then . . ."

With an unintended gulp, she choked on the foamy liquid, counting to five as she mastered her gag reflexes. "Then what? Don't keep me in suspenders."

Another family phrase brought a grin to his face. "Jerry Horowitz's still at the station. Remember him? Gimpy leg from taking a bullet during that bank holdup in 'ninety? Likes to gab. Told me the coroner found a slight bruise on the front of the neck."

Maddie replayed the mental tape of that quiet, horrible moment. A scarf had hidden the throat, but still . . . "That's odd. She landed on her back."

He pulled a tattered notebook from his shirt pocket. "Fatal fractures. A rib pierced her heart."

An impulsive shiver made her wish that the beer weren't so cold. "You took notes? How did you explain that to Jerry?"

"Got a great little recorder gizmo at Wal-Mart. Starts perking when anyone talks. Had it in my pocket. Then I wrote everything up later."

An amused smile tickled the corner of her mouth. "Go on, detective." How she wished he could have made the grade, but with only a tenth-grade education, he'd done well.

"Some fellow in Philmer Lab across the Oval said he thought he saw an extra arm. And the girl turned oddly just before she fell."

She downed the last of the beer, felt a belch rise, and excused herself. "An extra arm? No one else was around when the police arrived. And the elevator was out of service."

"Right you are. I remember donkey's years back before Copper had its own security staff. Did some weekend work when the old Plymouth Fury needed a valve job. Those stacks are a closed system. Fire doors to stairways set off alarms." He stopped abruptly and pounded the table, his bushy eyebrows puzzled. "I don't like it. Something's fishy."

"Philmer's a long way," she said, recalling her own vision problems. "What else could it be but an accident or . . . suicide?"

"Girls don't fool around like that." He considered her skeptical face. "Well, maybe you would. But suicide? A young kid?"

"She had some personal problems, Father. At that age, what we take in stride assumes giant proportions. Suicide is up there with auto accidents as the leading cause of death. Depression, stress over grades, troubled relationships. Lives of quiet desperation."

A shriek came from outside. Nikon galloped kiyiping toward the back door, his nose bearing a definite scratch, or maybe a bite from tiny dachshund teeth. A cheap lesson. She resisted the motherly urge to run and comfort him. The bible again: "Speak confidently. Don't coddle a fearful pup."

Billy shuffled downstairs, slicking back his thinning brown hair. He gave them a sidelong glance, and one gaunt finger hit the microwave control. Then he grabbed a bottle of peanut oil, plugging in the wok and removing a paper towel from a plate of neatly cut broccoli, cauliflower, pea pods, and green onions. While Maddie would have chopped them indiscriminately, he had tailored each with an ornamental shape.

"What's that big white flowering shrub out back?" she asked. Other than late chrysanthemums, her yard was bare of color.

"*Hydrangea arborescens*. Best varieties are Annabelle and Grandiflora. Hardy up to Zone 3B. That's up in Canada, Thunder Bay."

Although she noticed that he sipped a clear liquid which might have been water but likely wasn't, his speech was sharp, his tongue navigating around botanical terms like Mario Andretti at the Grand Prix. Minutes later the nutty smell of basmati rice filled the air.

The food balanced heat and flavor. Hunched over his plate, Billy nodded gruffly at the compliments, saying little, turning away from time to time to address his spit cup. To him she was a necessary bane, and the feeling was mutual. Her father punctuated the conversation with an arsenal of war stories. Tonight was the anniversary of the Invasion of the Philippines. That MacArthur now. Always said he'd be back, the big phony. Staged that beach scene like Hollywood. Shoe salesman Truman put him in his place. Great speech to Congress, though. Old soldiers never die. They just . . . Billy's lips formed the words. Then Maddie left to do dishes while they watched "Jeopardy." Their arguments drowned out the television.

"It was the New Deal, that Roosevelt thing. Not the Square Deal, you nitwit."

A throat clearing was followed by a guttural hawk. "Some expert. You thought Dale Carnegie was a steel tycoon."

Tossing and turning that night as shards of moonbeams splintered her pillow, Maddie was unable to dive into dreams. Maybe it was a fiery chili eaten by mistake, maybe staggering hormones, but most likely the fresh suspicions about Cheryl. How could that frontal bruise have been caused in the fall? She felt herself suffocating and threw back the cover, only to pull it back seconds later. Had Cheryl acquired the injury earlier? Was there violence in that solitary life? A secret boyfriend, or God forbid, a father? Searching with Grace for the thesis might reveal some answers. Question was, did they want to know? Her colleague and reluctant

78

partner was meeting her for breakfast tomorrow before going to the dorm.

Flicking on the light, she got up and went downstairs, stopping first to brew a cup of rose hip tea, then entered the study. Nothing like a pile of grammar tests to induce instant sleep. Checking for modal auxiliaries and independent clauses was as numbing as a dose of Valium, or whatever people took these days. She settled down under a bright lamp and plowed along, noting that as usual, they knew it or they didn't. "The ladie's room is' next to the mens'." Her abdomen churned from a punch no hot pepper could deliver. Then out of curiosity, she turned to Barney's paper. Sweat marks and erasures testified that he had worked methodically. Best of all, the sentences showed syntactical sophistication, crabbed penmanship aside. She drew an eloquent B with her red pen, adding a smiley face. What an odd duck he was, but a smart duck.

Half an hour later, she climbed under the covers and breathed deeply. So silent, her little house, the only sound the gentle snores of a dog on Honey's old sheepskin next to her bed. Nikon had adapted to the new plan. Not too much too soon, though. During her absences, he would stay in his pen in the kitchen until she could trust him to keep his teeth to himself.

Chapter Ten

Maddie tossed on a velour turtleneck over her jeans, doubly glad as she stepped into the morning chill. On her drive to Stoddard, she noticed that the flashing yellow of the leaves had been joined by splashes of orange and blood red. That frost would speed the brief glory. Soon poplars would add rich golden tones, and last to change, the durable oak, settling its burgundies rich as wine. Hosts of conifers kept green vigil among the changing tapestry. Payment for such beauty lay in the baneful chore of raking, which she left until the last minute on the pretext of saving her back. Well-timed laziness would bring a snowy reprieve until spring.

Grace was meeting her at Huhtala's, the city's oldest restaurant. Staking a claim in the center of town nearly a century ago, it had attracted immigrant workmen with nourishing meals and a friendly atmosphere. Since ethnic cuisine had become a magnet for the middle class, the clientele had diversified. Sober, earnest chess games were still played, and descendants of Nils Huhtala in spotless white aprons waited on tables. Miniature blue and white cross flags sat by the cash register, posters of quaint Helsinki and deep, beckoning fiords lined the wall, while the sounds of Sibelius vied with clattering plates and arpeggios of Finnish from the kitchen. Scarcely had she located the only open booth when a waitress materialized to pour coffee into a giant European-style cup.

Then Ben Jones sidled up, rubbing his hip. "Mind if I join you, Prof?"

Giving him a welcoming smile, she drizzled Huhtala's eighteen percent cream into the steaming brew, recalling too late that Finns had a high rate of heart disease. "I was hoping to run into you. The police called me about the accident. Seems they might have had a witness. What's the inside story, Ben?"

Shifting his bones for comfort, the old security guard puffed out his saggy cheeks and narrowed his wrinkled eyes, relishing the temporary spotlight, something more serious than a panty raid. "Pete Beddoes, a lab assistant over in Philmer Lab. He was hot on some experiment, had his eye on a test tube, but he could look out the window, if you get my drift. Right over to the library." He leaned forward, drawing out the pause. Then he pounded the table, his voice gravelly. "And that's when he saw her, back to the window. Arms moved around. Then she jumped."

"Nobody jumps backward. It must have been a fall. 'Arms moved around.' She must have tried to counterbalance herself."

"Got me there. See, that Pete guy, he didn't have his glasses on. Didn't fit under the safety goggles. But he sees close up okay." He shook his head, deflated at the complications. "Guess he was mistaken. The cops have wrapped it up. Beats me as to why they flapped their gums about it at all."

Maddie noticed Grace, frozen like a spotlighted deer at the front of the restaurant. She waved, and her friend took Ben's place as he centered his cap and sauntered off to greet an old timer with a demure Sheltie at his side. Not the first time she had noticed a dog inside. Why not? Commonplace in Europe. Maddie passed over a menu. "Try the pancakes with lingonberry syrup. The food's wonderful."

Grace showed more nervousness than interest as they ordered. A whole wheat carrot muffin with her coffee was the limit. Sugar spilled from the spoon, a tremble in her delicate brown hand. "I know I agreed to help you find the thesis, but my heart overcame my reasoning. This is sounding like breaking the law. And we do not have departmental approval."

Why did Grace have to make a federal case out of everything? Hiding her impatience, Maddie smoothed out her tones. "There's nothing illegal here, Grace. Why bother Malcolm unless we find the thesis?"

Grace shook her head. "We have different backgrounds. Remember that I come from a police state."

"What was it like in Uganda?" Her seventh-grade geography class had memorized every country, thirty-seven of them in Africa. Most of them had changed names.

"For generations, my family owned a large tea plantation. When a change in government brought fresh winds of reform, my father entered politics. Later he was posted to New York City in the diplomatic corps. My mother was ill, I had only a year of school to complete, so I remained behind to matriculate."

Maddie paused as the muffin arrived. "And then you came to the U.S.?"

"Out of necessity. A sudden palace coup threw my father's faction out of power. My mother had died, I had no siblings, and many relatives and friends were in jail. Through secret and very dangerous arrangements, I left the country. I can never go back." She jumped at the crash of a broken plate a few tables away. "Sometimes I still imagine . . ."

Maddie said nothing, absorbing the waves of tragedy. What currents lay under still forms, the chaos and bloodshed this woman had witnessed? Quiet years in a remote corner had not lightened those burdens. What did she fear now?

Grace's haunted doe eyes darted around; then her hand returned to the coffee like a sweet tranquillizer. "After the violence I witnessed, even New York with its shabby streets and homeless seemed like paradise. I walk freely. My last ten years here have been happy and uncomplicated. I do not want my life upset, selfish though it may sound."

Maddie gave a brief check to the time. They were due at the Quad in twenty minutes. What did this have to do with their mission? "Come on. I can't carry out a search on my own. It would look intrusive, if not nosey. After all, you were Cheryl's adviser."

Grace shifted in her chair, watching the butter on her muffin congeal, but Maddie continued. "You worked with her; you sensed her pain. At that last spark of life, I was the only witness. A kind of a triangle, a bond, connects us: a triangle of women." A gruesome white lie about the spark, but why not? And a feminist appeal might seal the bargain.

Clearly, Grace shrank from the inquisitiveness that thrilled Maddie's pulse. All that came from across the table was a barely perceptible swallow and a reluctant nod. Maddie leaned forward and began walking her friend through the plan like she coaxed freshmen through an essay outline. "It's simple. We'll find her thesis, then talk to Malcolm. Then, if the degree is approved, we'll have to contact the family. Does her father live in town?"

"I do not know." She looked into Maddie's eyes, still pleading her case. "This personal trespass is anathema to me. I can promise little."

Maddie looked approvingly at the steaming plate of pancakes arriving at the table. She gave the waitress a thumbs-up. "Follow my lead, Dr. Watson. You won't have to say a thing."

★ ★ ★ ★ ★

Rocky Quad, outliving the joke about being the fourth in a series of boxing films, had been built in an expansion period for Copper which coincided with a five-million-dollar bequest from a graduate who ran one of Michigan's largest aggregate companies: Cement and Gravel R-US. The main entrance to the quadrangle contained a recreation center with video games, television nooks, billiard and ping-pong tables, and a shiny row of junk food machines. As they passed through, a dozen students were watching a popular soap opera, half of them mooning over the buffed leads, the rest mocking. As they passed into a hall, a hulking young man tried to wrestle a pop machine like a recalcitrant buffalo. "People have been killed that way," Maddie observed in a loud voice. "One more out of the gene pool."

They knocked at apartment B on the second floor. Alice Blake met them at the door, wearing a terrycloth robe and fingering gel through her hair. Behind her was a small living room with the basics of sofa, chair, and television. "It's been pure hell," she explained after the introductions. "I had three tests in my engineering courses this week. Then the police asking questions, dorm rats sniffing around. One guy even asked if he could have her laptop. Little shit. Now her sister's driving in from Lansing for the clothes and the rest of the stuff."

Maddie spoke up. "As I told you on the phone, we're hoping to award her a degree. But we need to find the thesis."

"That would be nice. She deserved it. Poor kid." She sniffed at her bubbling nose and pulled a tissue from her pocket, dabbing at her eyes. "There goes the mascara. Better get my butt in gear," she said, pointing down the hall. "That's . . . Cheryl's room."

Maddie smiled at her with a mixture of compassion and

opportunity. If only Grace had the proper spirit, she could quiz the girl while Maddie busied herself in the bedroom. Nodding, she gestured to her colleague, lifeless as cold tea.

It was a typical student retreat, monastic and practical. A prim single bed, dresser, sturdy desk and chair, CD/radio, brick and board bookcases. Occupants came and went, adding a dent or a ding to the borrowed carapace. Books were neatly arranged by subject. Only a poster showing dog breeds added a personal touch.

"What should we do?" Grace asked in a nervous tone.

"Check her desk. You know what she was working on."

Maddie sifted through the closet, feeling ghoulish. Jeans, sweaters and t-shirts, a few plain dresses suitable for church. With only her scholarship, Cheryl had little money for name brands. A shoe box contained high school medals and pictures of an older man with what looked like a Great Dane.

Grace turned awkwardly and gave a small gasp as a toilet flushed down the hall. "Nothing. A few term papers from last year. I am feeling quite uncomfortable."

While her partner stood motionless, hands folded in front of her like a penitent, Maddie searched the desk. Pencils, pens, erasers, fat notebooks filled with writing, paper, an unopened box of disks. A checkbook held normal deductions like groceries and utilities. Pinned to a corkboard was a to-do list: laundry, groceries, deadlines. A small desk planner showed a pencilled appointment at ten on consecutive Thursdays for March through May. "Did Cheryl meet with you every Thursday?" Maddie asked, eyeing a calfskin backpack by the bed.

"Nothing routine. Whenever she completed a few chapters."

"What was in the backpack?" Maddie asked. Deciphering Grace's raised eyes as an indication that she hadn't looked, she rummaged for a moment. Blank notebook. A lipstick and powder, pack of tissues, pens, a wallet with twenty dollars and change, no credit cards or helpful phone numbers. Not even a driver's license.

As they left the bedroom, Alice saw their empty hands. "No luck, then. You know, it's funny. I didn't tell the police. Didn't even remember until now. Her laptop computer never showed up. They brought back her pack from the library where she . . ." More tears flowed down her face, smearing the fresh mascara.

"Don't blame yourself. The library is a popular place for theft." Maddie put an arm around the girl. "Or could a friend have borrowed it?"

"I've been her roommate for two years, but that was the draw. We sort of passed each other like ships in the night. Ate at different times. Weekends I work at an electronics store." She paused, a sad look crossing her face. "Cheryl didn't have any close friends. That's what I told the police."

"What else did they want to know?" Maddie ignored a pained look from Grace.

"They were asking funny questions about her health, but she wasn't depressed or anything. Pretty normal the last week or so. Happy, even. Like she had figured out something. Said she stopped seeing that shrink months ago. Guess she worked out her problems. See, doesn't that prove that she was okay? Maybe she got dizzy and fell. From the pills." Her simple, pleasant expression begged for reassurance, blacks and whites, no grays.

Maddie tossed a glance at Grace, who seemed determined to stare out the window, her thin fists clenched. Figured out something. So typical of suicides to cheer up when the decision is made. "Do you know what medication she took?"

Alice bit her lip, trying to recall. "Prozac, maybe. Wasn't

my business. She didn't like the side effects, but they did help her through a pretty rough spell. One week in the spring she barely got out of bed."

"And this wasn't an illness like the flu. You're sure?"

"Nope. No fever or chills. All she'd take from me was chicken gumbo soup. Said she liked it as a kid." She paused and hugged herself, leaning her head against the wall. "Know what freaked me out? She never cried. Not once."

Grace refused to speak to Maddie as they left the dorm, her giant strides marching ahead as if alone. Reaching the Oval, she turned abruptly. "That was very, very distressing. Looking even into the wallet. A personal invasion. How did I ever let you talk me into this? What could have possessed you to ask such dreadful questions?"

"Sorry, Grace. I got carried away." She spoke quietly, as if thinking aloud. "Don't you find it odd that none of her thesis work was there?" A suicide tidying up? Erasing her life? Why not toss out all of her belongings?

Suddenly, the sounds of a strange band filtered around the corner: percussion, whistles and horns. The Theatre Department students, wearing pig masks and hoisting placards, were protesting the opening of SWINC. "We Pay Tuition, Too"; "SWINC Stincs. Share the Wealth." A pink limo eased into the Center's guest parking lot, unloading Copper's President Bowdler, State Senator Lepke, Mayor Bloom, and business leaders from the community. With Reggie Conrad ushering them along, they stopped uncertainly as a picketer blocked the path, clanging a cowbell. Reggie blustered forward, his face a boiled beet. "Who's in charge of this mob? Where's your parade permit?" He grabbed at the picketer's coat and shoved him out of the way, drawing boos. Maddie hoped the scene wouldn't get ugly. One campus security guard looked nervous, and the other was talking on a cell phone.

In the simple black suit of an Amish farmer, hands grasping a papier-mâché fork wrapped in shiny foil, Stephen Glogore stepped forward. His elongated face and spidery legs and arms recalled Lincoln more than Grant Wood's portrait. Maddie had often wondered if he suffered from Marfan's Syndrome. Like many egotistical directors, he enjoyed playing the occasional part. She'd never forget his portrayal of George, the bog in the History Department in *Who's Afraid of Virginia Woolf?* His voice boomed like a cannon shot across the green. "Touch another of my students, Conrad, and you'll be charged with assault. We have a legal and a moral right to protest this pork barrel project. Stop hiding behind handicapped people to line your own pockets." He gestured with the pitchfork, aiming it provocatively toward Reggie's groin. "Explain those hotel bills in Detroit. Champagne suppers at the Hilton. If it's too late to stop this fiasco, all we're asking is equal access to the new facilities."

Reggie squared his shoulders, shaking his head as if his accuser were demented. Then a regal woman in a lustrous mink coat elbowed a guard aside. Her blue-rinsed hair was permed into a crown, and pellucid skin stretched over her cheekbones like onionskin paper. "My great-great-grandfather was the founder of this university. It was intended to provide a sound education in arts and sciences for worthy students. I deplore squandering resources on those who will never pay it back. The welfare state is certainly not the American way. That's why our unemployment rate is half that of our socialized Canadian neighbor." When mocking groans greeted her illogical bigotry, she looked around, shielding icy eyes against the snapping flashbulbs of a pack of fledgling journalists from *The Crucible*. "Where's that Paki woman? An opportunistic terrorist. Send her back where she came from."

An earnest young female in a suede jacket was thrusting a

microphone toward anyone with an open mouth. Never known for his backbone, President Bowdler shrank into a prickly caragana hedge, his blubbery lips pulsing like a leaky heart valve. Reggie shepherded the visitors, spoke to them guardedly, then gestured to the roof of the new complex. A huge pink balloon with the SWINC logo rose into the sky, distracting the crowd. As the automatic door opened slowly, Anisha emerged like a vision from *The Mahabharata*, long silver dress sparkling with metallic threads. With a proud turn of her head and a swoop of her arm, she led the guests along the pink-carpeted entrance, smoothing a wrinkle with her toe. A mechanical voice boomed. "WELCOME! YOU ARE ENTERING . . ." as Reggie motioned to Campus Security to lock the doors behind them.

Removing their pig masks, the theatre students seemed dejected at the sudden deflation of the afternoon's entertainment. "Damn that Malcolm," Glogore grumbled as they drifted away. "Where the hell is the old fart?"

Marie had been observing the entertainment from a stone bench. Her gray locks tossed as laughter shook her roly-poly body. "More fun than *Gammer Gurton's Needle*. We need more popular theater. SWINC. What an unfortunate acronym. 'Swink' and 'swive,' onomatopoeic Old English words for the world's most popular pastime." Crunching the last of an ice cream cone, she made a universal gesture with her pelvis and toddled off.

Only then did Maddie notice Grace sitting in a sheltered doorway, covering her ears, eyes wide with fear. "The mob. The noise. I was afraid someone was going to be hurt."

Maddie helped her to her feet. "Relax, Grace. Kent State was a long time ago. This is nothing more than good old Yankee Doodle freedom of expression."

As they headed back to the office, Maddie caught a

glimpse of a familiar figure in a tweed suit. He was leaning against a side entrance to Morrow Hall, nearly hidden behind a lamp post. His shoulders were heaving. If she hadn't known the man better, she would have sworn that he was crying. Had he received some devastating news? Why else, after all of his hoopla, had Malcolm missed the rally?

Chapter Eleven

Maddie drove to work early as a typical autumn fog rolled across the land from Superior, a metaphor of the mysteries of Cheryl's fall, that elusive thesis, not to forget the missing laptop. Yet a methodical scholarship student must have had a backup disk. As she approached the campus in its shallow plain among the trees, only the tops of the tallest buildings were visible, like toys under a damp blanket. The top floors of Collier Library winked through the haze. How had she forgotten? The stacks. One last place to look.

Around ten o'clock, she found Grace at the copier. "We're not lost yet. Cheryl was in the library every day, and I'm sure she didn't lug all her materials back and forth. She probably had a carrel with a locked compartment. I doubt that the police even thought about it."

"Perhaps so, but if we find nothing, that must be the end of this inquiry. Let the girl rest in peace. I mean it, Maddie." Her surprisingly stern face emphasized the words.

Caroline took them up to the stacks. "Our records show that Cheryl occupied carrel 4990. It slipped my mind. December and June are the tickers for that paperwork," she said as they got off the elevator. With a master key, she opened the metal compartment over the desk.

Inside was a pocket dictionary, a well-thumbed thesaurus, and a large, zippered plastic sleeve. Maddie sorted through the pencils and pens, retrieving a disk with a label marked FINAL DRAFT.

A faint glimmer lit the depths of Grace's dark brown eyes. She received the slim object like the Holy Grail, her voice hopeful as she left with Caroline. "I will look at it in my office after class."

On the pretense of needing a book, Maddie lingered, smug at the discovery but still discomforted by the memories of that fall. At the window, closed against the autumn chill, she looked down. So far, so fast. How quickly did a body drop? With a mischievous impulse, she opened the latch, levered out the glass, and sat on the ledge, bracing herself on the frame. Grace would have found the experiment morbid. With the cornice of the building jutting out several inches, one would have to lean far over the sill to fall. She pulled back, noticing as she locked the window, some curious almond streaks on the white frame. Paint? The walls were pale green. A still frame flashed into her mind: a small, perfect hand. Cheryl's nail polish. An effort to save herself from an accident, or a suicide with second thoughts?

She blinked against the sun's glare. Her eyes were hurting again, so dry, as if the tear ducts had shut down. Was this alarming condition damaging her corneas?

Gauging her time, Maddie drove to the drug store to besiege the pharmacist. Listening patiently, one hand smoothing a thick black pompadour, Carlo advised against conventional drops and recommended a tear gel. Then as she watched an assistant knife pills into a prescription bottle, she remembered her questions about Cheryl's medication. "Oh, yes," he said, thumbing through the physicians' guide. "Prozac, like many antidepressants, can cause dizziness. Anyone taking it should be very careful about driving until the side effects are assessed."

Sitting on a bench outside, Maddie opened the gel and applied a liberal portion, blinking away the excess. The non-greasy preparation soothed her eyes and her vision returned to normal. No wonder pharmacists topped the list of professionals for ethical credibility.

At three fifty-five, the elevator doors opened and Maddie stood dwarfed by a dual-level cart carrying a VCR and twenty-eight-inch television anchored by a heavy strap. She gritted her teeth. Eight apparently healthy bodies stood gazing out like guileless puppies. She'd had no lunch, her shoulder hurt from hauling the cart over floor seams, and now this. A hot flush turned her face crimson. As the door began to close, she jammed her foot forward to trigger the safety mechanism, then pointed at a prominent sign. "This elevator is for the handicapped and people with equipment. All able-bodied please exit." There was a brief chorus of sighs and only a slight movement forward. Meanwhile, the hum of a wheelchair brought a student from around the corner, navigating by a joystick in one clawlike hand, her head slack, only the hazel eyes alive. The men lumbered off with embarrassed grunts, but the elevator was still half full. Had they no shame?

"That's it!" Maddie yelled. She reached inside, slammed the stop button, then hit the alarm. "If you think manners can't be legislated, watch this." Muttering "bitch" and "get a life," the girls shuffled out. The woman maneuvered herself backward onto the elevator with the precision of a brain surgeon. Was it imagination or was there a wisp of a smile on the impassive face?

Heart pounding from the efforts, the double wheels of the cart as recalcitrant as a cheap stroller ferrying an elephant, Maddie pushed into her poetry classroom. A chorus of sneezes and blowing noses greeted her, the first onslaught of coughs, colds, and flu. Maybe she should buy an autoclave to sterilize assignments. She made the sign of the cross at a red-nosed girl with a box of tissues on her lap, a tube of lozenges spilled open, and a menthol smell lingering like a medicinal swamp. "Give that virus to me, and you're a dead woman!" she said. The student trundled her pharmacopoeia to a chair ten feet back.

"Pop videos, turn-of-the-century style." Maddie explained how Thomas Edison had taken his phonograph machine to England, and unable to collect any royals, had hunted up writers instead. On the scratchy tape, Tennyson intoned "The Charge of the Light Brigade," Conan Doyle discussed in trenchant seriousness his abandonment of Holmes to explore the fairy world, and while Maddie mourned to herself, her hero Browning tried to read "How They Brought the News from Ghent to Aix," so senile that he stumbled over the lines.

Just after five o'clock, Grace came into Maddie's office with a frown on her face. She sank wearily into the armchair and tossed a manuscript onto the desk.

"The thesis?" Maddie asked. "Nancy ran it off already? Anything wrong? You don't look happy."

Grace fingered the beads of a stunning coral necklace as if it were a rosary. " 'Wrong' is not the word I would choose. It is basically finished."

"Basically? I hate that word. So a bit of polishing and Cheryl gets her degree."

Grace shrugged and weighed the bundle as if it sat on a medieval scale of morality. "The research is documented. For the most part, the editing is careful. But something integral is missing."

"Missing?"

"Let me explain." She leafed through the introductory

chapter. "Cheryl was examining illness and disabilities in the twentieth-century American novel."

"That sounds morbid. I never could stand Tiny Tim."

"*Ethan Frome, The Heart is a Lonely Hunter, Winesburg, Ohio.* But the part on Frank Norris is sketchy. Roughed out, as it were, and certainly incomplete. His bold, atavistic depiction of venereal disease in an artist. *Vandover and the Brute.*"

"The brute? Less than subtle. What kind of a writer was this Norris?" American lit was not a strong point, the choicest cuts of Hemingway, Faulkner, and Cather her limits.

"Many call him a . . . I think the word is 'hack,' suffering an attack of Richard Harding Davis and his cardboard characters. His finest book is *The Octopus* from 1901, a modern romance for its time, as well as an exposé of the wheat industry."

"Romance and muckraking about wheat? Only in America."

Grace's voice picked up strength. "California, actually. Some passages are astonishingly lyrical. You might enjoy them. Despite that, his focus was naturalism, quite out of fashion now. The Boy Zola, he called himself. Some of his female characters have been rediscovered by feminists. Travis in *Blix* or *Moran of the Lady Letty* in the eponymous novel, for example, a boat captain."

"A lady boat captain? Sounds promising."

"I fear that she dies for her convictions."

"Some dark and stormy night when I run out of Dickens and Thackeray, I'll give him a try. Getting back to our problem, how do you explain the gap?"

"I have a theory. It must involve those theses copies I told you about."

"Maybe she couldn't afford the order after all." Students were proverbially poor, and in more generous times, discretionary funds from the department covered such fees. "Or maybe they didn't arrive."

"I signed the form and sent it to the library. The department was charged." She swallowed in deep distaste at the memory. "Florence was furious at the expense."

"Whether Cheryl saw them or not, she didn't use the material. Our question is . . . can the thesis pass as is?"

"We both understand that a senior thesis is merely an exercise in research, a trivial flexing of muscle, a jumping of precious little academic hedges. Who else is going to read it, Maddie? Still, you and I know the truth. Will it be ethical to omit the Norris chapter?"

"Why not? Cheryl could have used a friend."

Checking her mail later that week, Maddie saw Malcolm's backside perched on Nancy's desk as the secretary entered figures into a database. When the phone rang, he picked it up. "You don't say," he exclaimed, eyebrows wriggling like tangoing caterpillars. "You don't say?" he added, and waited another minute, nodding as he tapped a pencil. "You don't say," he concluded, hanging up.

Nancy looked up in puzzlement. "What was that about?"

"He didn't say." Malcolm exploded into laughter. "Got you there, girl. Infernal phone system has dyspepsia again. Some conversation about uniforms for the basketball team. They couldn't hear me at all."

He drew Maddie into his office where busts of Dr. Johnson and Dean Swift glowered at each other, icons of lexicography, rhetoric, and satire. From a cherrywood holder on the desk, he retrieved a curved meerschaum pipe. In former days, he wandered about ringed with smoke like a merry Santa. Now he was content to fondle the bowl in nostalgia.

Malcolm didn't mention the rally, though he seemed in

regular humor. Despite his energy, it occurred to her that he might not be well, that florid complexion signaling hypertension, heart problems, nameless lurking horrors. "Damned tragic affair, that girl. Grace told me about the thesis. Good show all around." He stroked his beard in a serious pose, a slight tremble in his hand. "Least we can do, eh? There's protocol for it, too. As I recall, we awarded posthumous degrees once or twice during the Vietnam War. So many young lads left before commencement and never returned. Nancy can tidy up the manuscript if need be. I'll contact the Registrar about the formalities. Put her on the graduate roster." Then he clamped the pipe in his jaw. "A few words of tribute. Have the parents receive the diploma, what?"

Maddie frowned, fearful of pushing Grace once more into overdrive. "We'll need to contact the family as soon as possible."

"You handle it, Maddie. I trust you. Diplomacy incarnate. Grace might feel awkward with the locals, and we can't leave such a sensitive business to our Flo." He picked up a shiny nickel letter opener and thrust it into a piece of mail like a rapier as he winked at her. "Needs a woman's touch."

Nancy located Cheryl's files, but the girl hadn't listed a permanent address, only her dormitory. "If there's a roommate, perhaps you can ask her," she said.

Maddie drove home with a certain glum anticipation, cheered only by the purchase of a well-marbled chunk of filet mignon for the barbecue. Answering the phone around dinnertime, Alice reported that the sister had come and gone; an unfriendly type, she left no contact number for herself or the father. Alice suspected that he lived somewhere in the country. Once Cheryl had shown her a picture. Big dogs, fields in the background. Great Danes?

That night she and Nikon watched *Never Cry Wolf,* an embroidered tale of a biologist sent to the Arctic to study *canis lupus*. Never let facts stand in the way of a good story, Canadian author Farley Mowat had said. Fact, fiction, truth, myth, as puzzling as the elements of Cheryl's life. Why had the girl been so disturbed? A simple case of overachieving? Meanwhile, the quintessential naturalist though he had read neither Norris nor Zola, Nikon sat, ears pricked to every blood-curdling howl echoing across the shimmering northern lights. Maddie turned her thoughts to the drama on the screen. Despite the ravages of accidents, hunting casualties, or starvation, no pups ever went parentless. For the welfare of the group, they were always adopted by the pack. Where had civilization gone wrong?

Chapter Twelve

A piece of cake for a researcher, Maddie said to herself in a neural starburst the next morning. Why didn't I think of the damn obituary? In her basement she leafed through newspapers saved for recycling until she came to the week Cheryl had died. A brief paragraph said that she had been survived by her father, Mitchell Crawford, and sister Dulce. A sweet old-fashioned name, more imaginative than Tiffany and Ashley. No mention of charitable donations, a frequent tip-off of ordinary mortality: Heart and Stroke Foundations, the Breast Cancer Clinic. Maddie ran a quick and unprobing hand across her chest. That biannual scan was due in March.

The phone book showed a Mitch Crawford near the small town of Massway about thirty miles from Stoddard. A hobby farm? A listing below added a "kennel line." The link with animals prejudiced Maddie in his favor. Yet owning pets was no guarantee of character. Watching people perform at obedience school with Honey had taught her the dark side. A prim grade school teacher had dragged her cowering boxer by the ears when it wouldn't come on recall. Domination, not love.

Since the start of school, Maddie hadn't been outside the city limits. The drive refreshed her, and she rolled down the car window to enjoy the fresh country air. The recent overcast days had depressed her, but now the UP rustled its fall frocks, the reason "trolls" south of the Mackinac Bridge charged up I-75 to snap photos. Poplars shot fountains of golden coins across the scenery, dazzling against sky matching the cobalt blue crayon in her grade school Crayola sixty-four pack. Nestled in distant hills of evergreen fir and pine, occasional maples in gradations of red and yellow peeked out like shy girls at a dance. Her eyes tearing, she clipped on a pair of sunglasses against the glare.

Homemade signs offering tours, camping, and RV hookups advertised the Old Bonanza Mine, one of countless abandoned digs scratching the backbone of the peninsula to Copper Harbor. An enterprising retiree, equal parts historian, anthropologist, and geologist, had bought the long-defunct mine. What had been a bleak rape of the land since the Civil War had become a pleasant wood full of ghost stories and crumbling foundations.

"Take Me Home, Country Roads" on the radio, Maddie drove sedately down pathways far from West Virginia, but equally as picturesque. Farmers with tractors pulling burgeoning hay wagons sent a friendly wave. At some crossings, a timeline of history presented itself for a ready camera. The original settler's log house falling into ruins behind huge lilac bushes, the two-story clapboard Victorian with delicate gingerbread scrollwork nearby, now boarded up and graying, and the vinyl-sided bungalow of the present owners. Even the barns told a story, huge elephantine structures raised with the help of neighbors, massive lofts for the winter's bales. Those which had not collapsed teetered into extinction, tin roofs rusting and boards gapped like broken teeth.

Crawford's property looked prosperous, a stand of showy sugar maple mingling with golden aspen bordering the fields in a peach Melba effect. A mare and her spring foal frolicked in a lush alfalfa pasture, along with a herd of butterscotch creamy-coated Jerseys chewing cuds in placid content. Tidy, fresh-cropped fields stretched behind, round hay bales under tarps forming ziggurats. Behind an unassuming frame house were two steel Quonset huts serving as barns. At the entrance, a painted sign bore a noble Dane head: Sweetcakes Kennels, probably the name of his first stud or bitch.

As she drove into the yard, a pair of dogs larger than the foal loped forward, giving tongue. Leaving the car with caution, she stood her ground. Kennels always carried insurance, and no one insured biting dogs. They stopped at an invisible demarcation line several feet away, quivering in friendly anticipation. Handsome beasts, but with the heartbreaking short life span of giant breeds. She groped in her jacket pocket for a training snack, then decided against it. No one but a trusted friend should offer a dog food. "Hi, guys, or is it girls?" she said, extending a hand. The multi-colored Dane sniffed her fingers, then wheeled with the grace of a ballerina.

A short, sturdy man emerged from one building, a mucking fork in his hand. "Don't be afraid," he called. "They're pussies, as you can see. Looking for a pup? Cleo's three now. Don't like to rush things. We'll have a litter by June if Caesar cooperates." He gave the male a signal to sit, lie down, roll over, putting him through his paces. A proud parent's eyes twinkled at her.

Maddie watched his delight, delaying the sad objective of her visit. The animals were so handsome, it was easier to make small talk. "I'm a GSD owner myself, but I've always admired these gentle giants."

"And so they are. German, you know, not what the name implies. Show quality if you want, or just a super pet for the family." Was she imagining it, or did his voice stumble at the last word? Perhaps he wondered if she were married. She still wore her engagement ring, a splendid art nouveau design of a dragon swallowing its own tail that Dan had insisted she keep.

She stroked the female's smooth coat and dreamed of reducing her vacuuming. Now that the male had turned to follow a vee of honking geese, his sex was more than evident. If looks told all, he was a fine stud. "What do you call their colors?"

"Cleo's brindle. Caesar's fawn. They also come in blue, black, harlequin, or Boston." He eyed her car, ill-suited to rough country roads. "Danes adapt well to city life, though you need a big yard. Their short hair doesn't allow them to be stay outside in the winter. Pardon the suggestions, but I like to know where my dogs are heading."

She felt not only uncomfortable but downright dishonest. It was time to explain her mission, not let the man imagine he had a customer. "Mr. Crawford, I'm Maddie Temple from the university. I teach in the English Department."

His voice dropped, the syllables hesitant. "I didn't expect a visit. It's kind of you." A flash of pain crossed the tanned face, graven with the winds and sun of outdoor life.

"Condolences," "sorrow for your loss," all those canned and sterile greeting card phrases. Speak up. Say what you mean. She took a deep breath, but found her voice lacked force, as if a sudden asthma attack swelled her bronchial cavities. "We'll miss Cheryl. She was one of our best students. And that's why I'm here. We want to award her a degree."

"A degree?" The sun emerged suddenly from behind a puffy cloud, and he blinked at the light. "How can . . ."

Maddie's suspicions about family pressure were rapidly disappearing at the sincerity of the man, the hope in his face. "It is unusual, but there are precedents. The thesis was . . . finished, and Cheryl deserves the recognition."

His gaze drifted across the pasture to where the foal nuzzled the mare's udder. Then he retrieved a mammoth red print handkerchief, wiping his eyes and mopping sweat from his dusty brow. "I'd be pleased if you'd come into the house. I always like to talk about my little girl. My angel, I called her."

They passed through the kitchen into the living room, where he pointed to the mantel. Two toddlers in identical blue smocked dresses held hands with their mother, all three grinning into the camera. The woman looked painfully thin, long hair artfully waved to hide the feverish, hollow eyes and the prominent cheekbones, desperate in an effort not to spoil the mood. Other photos showed the girls teaching a gangly puppy to sit, fishing at a creek, gathering around a Christmas tree heaped with presents. Two high school diplomas were framed on the wall, along with graduation shots, serious and sober and fresh. Yet an understated museum. The chintz curtains were faded, though clean and ironed. The books on the shelves appeared untouched. No magazines, drink stains on the glass coffee table, or telltale clutter. "Light of their mother's heart," he said. "When she passed on, they were just starting school. She told me I'd have to take her place."

"They must have been a great help."

"Sure were," he said. "The dogs, too. Always keep you going. Sense when you need bucking up. Come in the den."

In a small room with two easy chairs and a television was a shrine to his other family, the Danes. The walls were plastered with winner's circle pictures and ribbons, reaching back in muted blue variations nearly thirty years. "That's Sweetcakes," he said, pointing to a brindle Dane getting best of show. "Beginning of the line."

Mitch served coffee at the kitchen table. Farm equipment catalogues and a *Peninsula Register* sat on the counter, along with the breakfast dishes, in the air a lingering fry smell of savory sausage. Sweeping the table free of crumbs with a wet dishcloth, he offered cream and sugar, then took a thoughtful sip. "What was the university planning to do, then?"

She welcomed the steaming brew, strong and honest, like him. No doubt Cheryl had sought to please him, but out of love, not fear. "We found her thesis on a computer disk. It'll be typed and bound into a final copy, then given to you." She swallowed at the word "final," avoiding his eyes. So far Cheryl's gruesome death had been absent from the conversation. "She'll be awarded a Bachelor of Arts degree in the winter graduation. That's the week before Christmas. We'll let you know the date and time. Can you come to accept the diploma?"

"I'll be there," he promised. "Her sister, too, I expect."

A car crunched into the gravel of the driveway. "There's Dulce now," Mitch said. "Drove here yesterday to . . ." He hesitated, then cleared his throat. "To collect Cheryl's clothes for the Sally Ann. Couldn't face it myself. Lives down to Lansing, she does. Married a big city lawyer."

Through the door came a tall, thin woman, the earth tones of her coat and baggy dress adding little to her sallow complexion. Her hair was the same color as Cheryl's, but lifeless, the similar facial features drawn without energy. A set line to her mouth, the woman put down two sacks of groceries, opened the fridge, and began transferring the food. "You had nothing in the house, Dad. Can't live on bacon and eggs. I got stew meat, chicken, hamburger, and I'll cook up enough meals for a month." Then she turned and stared at Maddie, as if resentful at the intrusion.

"This is Professor Temple. She's going to see the university gives Cheryl her diploma. What do you think of that?"

"But she . . ." The girl's jaw muscles tensed before she answered in a monotone. "Sounds great, Dad. I know she worked hard." She hung her coat on a wall rack and folded the paper bags with precision before placing them in a drawer.

A bawling issued from the yard. Mitch excused himself to tend to an unmilked cow which had lingered behind that morning coming in from the fields. Maddie considered the dregs of coffee. Time for a less-than-graceful exit. Shaking out a cigarette and lighting it, Dulce sat in the opposite chair. Thin drifts of smoke leaked from her nostrils in a chilly appraisement.

"How well did you know my sister?" she asked, her small, green eyes hard and penetrating.

Maddie shifted uneasily. By the wall clock, she had cruised along for an hour without mentioning the accident, the suicide, whatever it was. The old man was so proud, as if the tribute had brought some resolution to his pain. The daughter looked like trouble. "She was in a large class of mine a few years ago, but I didn't get to know her, other than by her excellent work." Defensively, she muttered about the loss of a young life being the greatest tragedy. Sententious. As a comforter figure, she deserved a D for dubious.

"It was sadder for us. That's why I'm bitter. She made her choices, and we had to deal with the consequences."

Choices? Was Dulce hinting at suicide? Maddie remembered the Prozac. "What do you mean?"

"Miss Hundred-and-One Percent. Nothing was ever good enough for her."

"She was a fine student."

"Too fine. What do you think happened at the library? The neighbors are all talking. Thank God I don't live here anymore." The woman stubbed out the cigarette as if she wished the ashtray were her sister's face. "You know, all my life I heard about Cheryl this, Cheryl that. Head in a book, not doing the chores, like me, especially after Mom got . . . sick. Easy scholarships, too. No job wiping up after old people at the nursing home like I had to do."

After a long silence, Maddie narrowed her eyes, taking Cheryl's side by instinct. "Life wasn't that perfect for her. She had some problems. The therapy—"

"What a bunch of crap. Hogging all the attention. And what good did it do? She went out the window after all. Mother was depressed, but in those days it was a nice little family secret. Cheryl was front-page news." She drew back her thin shoulders. "And that school shrink. Nothing but a scam."

"Are you saying that Cheryl killed herself?"

Dulce didn't respond to the question, riding venomous waves. "She was always smarter, prettier. The little princess. You must have heard him, how he treasured her. Suppose he gave you the royal tour."

Without the graceless curl to her lips, the ugly jealousy, Dulce might have been attractive. The father hadn't mentioned a career, nor any grandchildren. Marriage as an escape? "But couldn't it have been an accident? Lots of students sit on those window sills when the weather is hot. And she was taking pills for depression. They can cause unsteadiness."

The woman tightened her lips and picked up the cigarette butt, crushing it until the tobacco dribbled out. She inspected the empty shell as if assessing a spent and futile life. "Call it that. Looks better for the family, don't you agree?"

Chapter Thirteen

Dulce's acrid words about her sister's therapy had a very bad smell, almost as pungent as what Maddie discovered in the kitchen. Nikon had stayed too long at the autumn fair outside, consuming his usual picnic. She hoped it was not a poison mushroom. Try though she might to steer him from those spotted fly agarics, no telling what he had pawed loose in the yard. She cleaned up the mess and gave him a teaspoon of Pepto Bismol, along with liberal water. "You've already had breakfast, and a poor choice it was. Maybe some plain rice later." He lay behind bars, sans edible toys, doing his Uriah Heep "umble" act. Soon he'd better be trustworthy around the house. That cage was cumbersome.

Before leaving for work, she checked into the *rec.dogs.pets.behavior* newsgroup. To avoid server fees, she logged on via the university portal. Headers read: "Dog Obsessed with Light Bulbs," "Six-Year-Old Eats Potting Soil," "Should I Let My Collie Kiss Me on the Lips?" The postings deteriorated into personal arguments, along with profanity and outrageous grammar. "Carin" terrier? Pet degree? Was the Internet Earth's brain or bathroom? As for Nikon, snow would prevent more gobbling, and perhaps by spring he'd forget the obsession. She tuned into *sci.med.vision*, where the main subjects were Lasik or PRK surgery. Complainers with floaters were told to get used to it rather than risk the YAG laser, which blasted the murky protein deposit into a milky way. She squirmed as she read a diagnosis of trematode parasites wriggling across a poor man's visual field. Returning to the prompt, out of curiosity she hit "sho users," a spyglass at Copper. Even at that early hour, "amukherjee," "rconrad," and ten other faculty were cruising the net or sending e-mail.

With Cheryl's dubious therapy in mind as she drove to school, Maddie tried to recall the best gossip route to the Health Clinic. Hadn't Anisha worked there in administration before becoming Director of SWINC? Maddie could deliver the good news about Barney, then pick her brain discreetly about the psychiatrist. It was becoming evident that the police had satisfied themselves that Cheryl's death had been an accident or suicide. Having learned about Mrs. Crawford's problems, Maddie opted for the latter. Genes spoke loudly.

"She's free around four," Anisha's secretary said over the phone.

As Maddie collected a coffee later, Gary slouched across a battered leather chair in the Common Room. "Marie told me what a circus that rally was. Funny Malcolm never made it." Except for the lizardskin cowboy boots and Dr Pepper, he might have been a six-four Tom or Huck, his face freckled and a stubborn cowlick mussing his brown hair. A light sagebrush aftershave tickled her nose. "Check this out," he said, handing her *The Peninsula Register*.

She scanned the article, moving from the objective description of the rally with several action shots to an interview with Stephen Glogore. In addition to complaining about the auditorium, he reviled SWINC's expensive administrative offices. The majority of Copper's students sat packed into crumbling buildings. Leaks in ceilings. Torn carpeting unreplaced. The pictures made the university look like a slum. Technical details about chemical storage had probably come from Malcolm. Her chairman had instituted the Health and Welfare Group (HAWG), a taskforce for a safe work environment comprised of students, staff, and faculty.

Later that afternoon, Maddie headed for SWINC. Anisha's door was open, but the secretary made a friendly traffic-cop motion. She took a seat by the door under a sign proclaiming the new building a fragrance-free zone. What next, a ban on peanut butter? Grabbing a brochure on eye diseases, she had finished absorbing the symptoms of *retinitis pigmentosa*, testing her peripheral vision by fluttering a finger beside each eye, when voices rose inside the office.

An uncomfortable energy charged the air, tones reined in between outrages. Anisha said, ". . . has to be done about . . . classified information from HAWG, too."

"That son of a bitch. And the pictures. My God. The Mayor, Senator Lepke. We looked like gangsters. I could hardly choke down the wine at the luncheon." The sound of a fist pounded on a table. "We have to . . ."

Maddie watched the secretary quiver, then wheel over to the console. The phone rang in Anisha's office, and the talking stopped. Seconds later Reggie stormed out, his dark striped tie flapping against a tailored blue suit. As a student with a white cane tapped along the hall, he braked suddenly, rolled a muscular neck in an ostentatious calming motion, straightened his tie, and strode off. Anisha came to the door and waved, her breathing labored, a spot of color decorating each cheek like a Russian doll. Maddie entered, noting more improvements. Three Dali lithographs decorated the walls, and an elaborate Italian coffeemaker steamed in the corner above a small fridge. Through the burgundy vertical blinds, a bright sun warmed the room. "Would you like a cappuccino?" Anisha asked. "It's quite the little wizard."

Maddie shook her head in polite refusal and settled into a butter-soft leather couch. "I have good news about Barney.

He scored a solid B on his first test. I don't see any problems with English."

With a relaxed sigh, Anisha gave a knowing wink, uncapped a faux-marble Mont Blanc pen, and jotted notes in a firm hand. "Wonderful. I'm sure your excellent instruction was the deciding factor."

"Thanks, but I don't deserve the honors. Grammar I teach on cruise control. Anyway, I will confess a secondary purpose to my visit. It's about the girl who died in that fall from the library."

"So tragic. Yet she might have survived to live a productive life in a wheelchair. That's why we're here." Her voice was almost merry.

Ignoring the strange logic, Maddie continued. "Cheryl Crawford was one of our best students. We're all devastated. Yet some questions have arisen, especially since we've been in contact with the family. It is very awkward." She paused and took a deep breath. "It seems that the girl was seeing a psychiatrist at the university. Cheryl's sister made serious allegations about the treatment. So, with your connections at the Health Clinic, I wondered if you knew the doctor."

She watched Anisha shift in her chair, her mouth rise at one corner. The pen drew a circle, added another with what looked like ears and a tail. "I'd hazard a guess at Glenys Washington, that fraud."

"Fraud?"

"Exactly. She was fired at the beginning of the semester. No ifs, ands, or buts about that ungracious leave-taking. The accountants returned from summer vacation and finally did their jobs. Seems that she had been billing the university for treating students with multiple personality disorders . . . billing them for each personality."

Maddie stifled the urge to laugh as Anisha continued. "And a cat to boot."

"A cat?" Kegel exercises came in handy once again. "Was she charged, then?"

Anisha made a dismissive gesture. "And embarrass the university with the publicity? Using hypnotism to channel into past lives? Over-prescribing medication? You know President Bowdler. He hushed it up quicker than when he packed off that botany professor who traded sex for grades. Smelly fellow, as I recall. Some trumped-up project in the Brazilian rain forest. He'll never teach again."

"That poor man." Maddie could still see the pain in his proud face.

"Pardon me? He certainly deserved what he—"

"Cheryl's father. He'll be at convocation to receive a posthumous degree for her. The accident broke his heart."

The dark, liquid eyes narrowed. "You are far too naive, Maddie. Put the facts together. Why was she seeing a psychiatrist? Was it really a fall?" Anisha's thoughts echoed Dulce's. Yet, meeting people daily with a host of disabilities, the woman had a wisdom born of personal experiences Maddie in her bookish haven couldn't imagine.

Dinner that night was a quick, no-fail supper of tomato soup and grilled cheese while Nikon chomped kibble, apparently recovered from his indisposition. Still, nothing could divert Maddie's mind. Television selection was prosaic, and her TBR pile had dwindled to dregs: a biography of Mrs. Browning, the only amusing chapter involving her frustration in teaching her dog Flush to count or play dominoes. Even Internet connections had gone hieroglyphic in the wind. The newspaper was no consolation. She'd adopted a grim hobby after Cheryl's death, reading the obituaries: clucking at passings over eighty, quaking at the alarming number under fifty-five. So what if she woke up a bit stiff and failed to spring back from the occasional muscle strain? At least she was still steady on her pins, as Grandmother Ethel used to boast.

Dog Fancy had a profusion of ads for electronic training collars. Then she came to the Pet Memorials section: airtight caskets and urns, gravestones of diecast metal, marble, and full-color photos on granite. "You don't have to say goodbye! There is an alternative to burial or cremation. Freeze-dry preservation. Recommended only for animals under forty pounds." She watched Nikon chase his tail again in clownish ballet. Was he obsessive-compulsive, too? "You always cheer me up. Let's take a walk." Stretching off a twinge in her back, she took him for a brief walk in the woods before the shadows fell. Only last week the reliable fall trio of flowers—the pale lavender New York aster, the lush goldenrod, and the pearly everlasting—had finally faded. Everywhere, metaphors for death presented themselves: Hardy's sun chidden by God, and Hopkins' goldengrove unleaving in spirals which Nikon pursued like dervishes. Her life had fallen into the sere, grow-old-along-with-me phase, and yet what had she achieved? Slogging the days, a footnote at a second-, admit it, third-rate university. At least police work would have been more useful and challenging.

She was muttering to herself, stubbing her toes on knobby roots, oblivious to Nikon's investigations. A blur of wings heralded a grouse flying to safety in the feathery embrace of a white pine. The dog dashed off. Seconds later an unmistakable reek filled the air. "Nikon, NOOOOOO!" she screamed. His first canine lesson in woodcraft. Never chase a skunk. You can catch one, but why would you want to? He skulked back, ears at half-mast, and burrowed his oily head into her pants in torment before she could stop him. "Let's get you home. Those eyes must sting, and I know how that feels," she said.

Fortunately, a large can of tomato juice sat in the pantry. Along with a goodly assortment of shampoo, cleansers, and a secret ingredient, Crest toothpaste, the pair soaped energetically together in the bathtub. "It's you and me, kid," she said as he moaned softly, too cowed to try to escape, too mannerly to scratch his nails on the enamel.

She fluffed him with a pile of towels. "Maslow's hierarchy of needs strikes again. There I was contemplating my failure to achieve self-actualization, when I was cast down to the lowest level of survival. We're never far from the cave."

A northern front brought a heavy frost that night, a reminder that balmy falls had their price. When she had been young, Maddie had quaffed the long, hard winters like a tonic, laughed at their challenges, met the bitter climate with the wind in her teeth. But now she could understand her retired snowbird friends packing up for Florida or the hot, dry Southwest. She cracked open the bedroom window for some fresh air, retreating at the blast. "This is no country for old men," she called, the wind tossing her words back, making her jaw ache. And not much of a one for young girls, either. What damage had that psychiatrist done to Cheryl? The diligent hamster running a treadmill in her mind wouldn't rest until she confronted Glenys Washington. Evidence indicated the woman was a charlatan, but face-to-face contact was necessary. If she'd been responsible in any way for that untimely death, she needed to pay.

Chapter Fourteen

Small town Stoddard afforded little opportunity for hiding. A simple check in the phone book located Glenys. Apparently she was still running a practice, albeit a small one, given the fact that she answered the call herself. Maddie booked a personal consultation, drawing conclusions from the speedy accommodation that Glenys was less than busy. Then she strolled next door to Ed's garage, where since dawn she'd heard the familiar sounds of puttering over a truculent lawn mower or Weedeater.

Instead, he was honing the coiled blades of a snowblower, the wing-wing sounds of his grindstone echoing, a tang of fresh oil in the air. "Is our first blizzard that close? I was hoping El Nino would rescue us," she said. "Ed, I need a favor. How good an actor are you?"

He mugged a wild expression, twinkling eyes rolling and his tongue lolling like Nikon's on a hot afternoon. "Played a nut case who thought he was Teddy Roosevelt in *Arsenic and Old Lace*. High school stuff."

"I don't need a maniac, and I'm fresh out of lace. Here's the scenario." She put an arm around his shoulder and winked. "It shouldn't take more than a few minutes."

Back in her bedroom, to create the image of a middle-aged neurotic, she chose her frumpiest dress, a calf-length dark brown wool model strictly for funerals, adding a string of seed pearls. Out of a drawer came a plastic bag with the ravages of a make-up kit. From the caked remains, she applied a deadly kiss of dark shadow under the eyes, covered by a liberal application of palest powder. A shaky composure might help, so she emptied her steel penny collection out of an ancient black purse and substituted a tube of Tear-Gel.

The pleasant two-story brick home on Williams St. Hill had a dazzling view of the bay. In the lockstone driveway stood an emerald green Lexus, gleaming from the car wash. Maddie's patent leather, silver-buckled flats wedded her pampered feet to the pavement, and the pantyhose unearthed from a rag bag made her waddle like a mallard in tights. Standing on a porch which ringed the house, she turned the brass bell crank. A few drips of gel, then dark glasses. Enter stage right, pursued by a bear.

"Come in," a voice called. Maddie entered a hallway of polished mahogany wainscoting from the days when finishing carpentry came without a second mortgage. A heavy curved banister with a ball at the bottom saved the slider from free fall at a price to the coccyx. Above the foyer, a delicate crystal chandelier tinkled gently in the air currents. Like all older houses, this one nursed its identity, a combination of rare woods, cooking, and bygone days of coal fires.

A tall woman, too thin for Maddie's liking, Kate Hepburn bone structure that would snicker at the decades, greeted her with a handshake a tad aggressive. In her late thirties, Glenys wore an apricot velour dress with a cowl neck, a metal mesh belt, and tasseled gold sandals more suited to the Casbah or beach. "Welcome, Ms. Bryce," she said. Maddie doubted that the woman had ever heard of her, much less anyone in the mousy English Department, but why take chances?

Glenys' arm swept them into a large, bright study, where she lowered the lights a degree and pressed a button on a curious white plastic machine. A pleasant floral aroma filled the room. Maddie cocked her head. "Lavender?"

"Designed to relax. Your tenor revealed such inner distress on the phone." She seemed to be assessing Maddie like a piano tuner. "Could you remove your glasses? We will communicate better face to face."

Blinking stoically as the gel began seeping cooperatively from the corners of her eyes, Maddie placed the glasses in her lap and crossed her legs demurely at the ankles, parochial school style.

"Have you been in psychoanalysis before?"

Maddie sighed in a self-conscious defense. "I'm afraid that I come from an old-fashioned family. Tea and sympathy were the traditional remedies."

Glenys uncapped a filigreed gold pen and opened a notebook. "Let's get to know each other first. Set the groundwork, so to speak. Decide whether therapy is your best choice."

Maddie pursed her lips and for the next half hour fielded questions about her age and health (here the pen cruised), marital status (revving at the "un" status), her job as a real estate agent (scrabbling . . . was Glenys planning to relocate?), and Mother and Papa who had "passed on long ago" (circular motion). Meanwhile she surveyed the room for clues, the science of personal artifacts. Eggshell white paint, tan postmodern furniture, taupe carpet. Undisturbing, never committing to black or white, like "Neutral Tones," Hardy's broken lovers burying their relationship at the bleak edges of a pond. Framed diplomas clustered on the wall, shiny pinking-scissored gold seals attesting to certification. Two file cabinets sat in the corner. A cluster of pastel teddy bears on a corner shelf struck a note more ominous than cheerful.

Glenys folded her hands, a glittering diamond solitaire on

one finger, and let silence fill the air, a telling device Maddie used for problematical student conferences. Being quizzed on private matters, even fictitious ones, wasn't comfortable, and she gazed at the floor in honest embarrassment. "I've been having the worst time sleeping lately." All-purpose female complaints were a safe opening.

"Anything particular bothering you? Stress at work?" A pregnant pause. "Close relationships?"

"No, I'm past that silliness." She thought of her New Year's date with Ed and hid a grin with her hand. "It's more like a dream."

"But you said you weren't sleeping."

"A waking dream. Fitful sleeps. So vexing." Oops, vocabulary check. A realtor wouldn't use a word from a penny-dreadful novel.

In Francy Temple's time-honored observation, Glenys didn't bat a mauve-lined eye. "Are you taking any medication? Some prescriptions, even over-the-counter drugs, have side effects that include restlessness."

"Nothing except vitamins. An aspirin at night. I hear it's good for the heart." She rubbed at her neck with a martyred expression. "Helps my morning stiffness, too."

"Do you remember the dreams?"

"A man. A large figure. Threatening." Maddie's fingers trembled like blind moles around the sunglasses, searching for inspiration, landing on the Lady of Shallot. "Shadows. I am half sick of shadows."

When Glenys concluded at last that she might benefit from a program of therapy, Maddie ventured a fretful sniff, pulling a tissue from a container on the desk. "I'm so glad. Perhaps it's the time of life . . ."

A tiny beep sounded. Glenys brushed her wristwatch and put down the pad, floating a smile in the air like a Cheshire cat trial balloon. "I think we've made a good start. Would you like to make another appointment? This time is open for me."

Maddie smoothed a crease in her dress, casting a surreptitious glance through her eyelashes at the large file cabinets. "Perhaps," she said, hesitating. "But I wonder . . . those dreams I can't recall. Do you use hypnosis?" Her voice assumed the naiveté of a child selecting bonbons.

"On occasion." Her voice grew cautious. "It's not indicated in all circumstances."

"But we can try?" With an audible rip, the tissue came apart. She bunched it together and crammed the mess into her purse.

The candystore owner needed to make more Lexus payments, and the voice was seamless silk. "Whatever you wish. The road to wellness has many paths."

Suddenly the bell crank sounded. Scribbling into a daybook, Glenys frowned. "Excuse me for a moment," she said and left the room.

Maddie jumped to her feet, opened the file cabinet drawer marked "A to D," and working with nervous energy, located Cheryl's records. With the speed of an English teacher, she scanned Glenys' notes. "Fixated on her studies. Possible to build on mother's early death. Suicide? Good for at least a year. Hypnosis can open more possibilities." Later entries added, "Says she is thinking of stopping treatment. Advised her to try the Prozac. Should cement our interpersonal bond as she regains spirit." The thin ice between ethics and manipulation fixated Maddie on the disgusting subtext. Patient as cash cow.

Voices rose from the porch. "I told you I don't need—"

"Gutters could use a cleaning before winter sets in, and those old chimneys might not be safe. Friend of mine got a bird down there, and before he could—" Ed's accent came from years of watching "HeeHaw."

"No, thank you!" The screen door slammed. Reaching back to the cabinet, Maddie turned too quickly and tripped over the wastebasket, file in her hands. From the doorway came a gasp.

Glenys stood, hands on hips like a death camp commandant, her face purple, one vein at her temple pulsing. "Whoever you are, you have something of mine." She snatched the file. "Now leave! Before I call the police."

No use pretending. Maddie rose slowly. Measuring her tones like spoons of alum, she nailed Glenys with a fierce and unrelenting stare. "Don't play the innocent. You weren't fired from the university for nothing. Instead of helping Cheryl, you saw only a meal ticket and pandered to her insecurities." Glenys shifted her glance like a guilty dog. "If she committed suicide, you may be responsible."

"Get out!" She reached for Maddie's arm, long purple nails biting into the fabric.

"Tut. Tut. Don't leave any marks. An assault complaint is possible even without contact, in case you were unaware."

Glenys made a spitting sound and released her, retreating awkwardly towards the desk. The swivel chair hit the bookcase, knocking a teddy bear to the floor. Maddie's stomach turned over as she imagined this monster involved with children.

She strode out of the office, the bold front vanishing as she reached the sidewalk. Huddling in the car to quell the nausea, she laid her head against the steering wheel. Finally, she took a deep breath and turned the key. The Probe screamed like a young girl and died.

A face appeared at the glass, grinning as she rolled down the window. "Warned you about those cracked belts."

She gave a bracing sniff and forced a weak laugh. "Ed. I'm sorry. This whole business has me so upset. You've been such a good sport and I haven't even told you . . ." As he drew back into middle distance, she noticed scratches on his cheeks. "What happened? You didn't tangle with Glenys, did you?"

"Never take a cat through a truck wash." He pointed to Peep standing in the passenger seat with paws on the window. Then he had Maddie pull the release lever, and he raised the hood, tinkering for a minute. With a few creative curses, he rummaged in the massive tool box in the bed of his Ford 150, retrieving a belt, which he whirled like a lasso. "This here might fit if I jury-rig the thing."

His expertise got them to an auto-parts dealer and the liquor store for a bottle of Glenlivet. At home, while he installed the new belt, she let Nikon out, changed into sweatpants and a long-sleeved t-shirt with a fading picture of Honey, then joined him. Living in the real world, unlike Copper's stodgy elite, her neighbor was an arrow of common sense aimed at the heart of any problem.

How many times had they talked quietly in this masculine den, a world away from the chitterings of academia? Lining the bookcase no scholarly tomes, but *Reader's Digest* condensations, a shelf of Dick Francis mysteries, and Chilton's auto repair manuals. On the walls, Ed's taste ran to clipper ships or sinewy thighs and quivering haunches of Stubbs' horses and lions. The English painter had studied musculature from a dissectionist in the wilds of Yorkshire.

"Appears like you've knocked down a hornet's nest, Maddie, and all's you're going to get is stung," he said, after she finished her story. He got up to stir the cheerful birch fire. "Fell, jumped, don't seem to make much difference now that the poor girl's dead."

"But surely the law—"

"Not a chance. Them case notes are long gone now. Count on it."

Taking a slug of the scotch he'd poured, she leaned back into the overstuffed chair and let her shoes fall to the floor, rubbing her savaged toes with a relieved groan. "You're right, of course. I'm so furious that Glenys was working under the auspices of our university. Sorry, too, that we didn't see the signs of the girl's distress. Grace hasn't been much help, but at least we have that thesis nailed down." Peep strolled around the corner and sniffed at her pant leg, rubbed off some fur to add to Nikon's, and curled up at her feet, thrumming a tranquilizing blessing.

Ed swirled the amber liquid in appreciation of the Highland smoothness. "You did what you could, Maddie. And more than you should have," he added.

An hour later, she said her goodnights and went home. Nikon had been left free briefly as an experiment, a martial Gottschalk CD for company. Everything was serene in the kitchen. Then she turned the corner. The toilet paper had been unrolled from the bathroom, along the hall and down the cellar stairs. Small lumps of papier-mâché dotted the floor, and she picked up a handful. Her innocent boy was sitting on the sofa like a pasha.

"What's this?" she yelled, brandishing the mess, then making an unsuccessful grab. Off the couch and upstairs he ran. "I saw an electronic collar advertised, Nikon. That's what I'm getting you for Christmas. No, maybe tomorrow by Fed-Ex!" she yelled, her voice cracking. "And I intend to juice it up to max!"

Cooling off as she watched the glowing sun fall through the cedars, she found herself making excuses. Her failure to puppyproof the house. With this fiasco added to the confrontation with Glenys and the car problems, she felt suddenly too old to cope with a teenager. What would he be like as an uncut male, when those hormones started to roar? Maybe she should reconsider plans to breed the man. Anyway, with those long forelegs he might exceed the twenty-six-inch standard at the withers, not to mention that east-west front and the cowhocks.

Ed was right. Over and done. She had a job and obligations to command her attention. Dinner and to bed.

Chapter Fifteen

"So that's it, I guess. More of a whimper than a bang," Maddie said, omitting the distressing details for fear of sending Grace more ghosts than she could handle. "Cheryl was depressed, on medication, end of story. We'll never know what happened." She looked at the delicately pattered bark cloth hanging on the office wall, the long side-blown wooden trumpet with the cowrie shell-decorated bell, a tiny enclave of an unfathomable world. "How's the thesis coming?"

"I altered the introduction to omit the Norris chapter. Nancy ran a spell-check, adjusted the formatting. If anyone ever reads it, they will not notice the omission."

"I'm glad." Maddie felt little satisfaction at the technical closure. Cheryl Crawford with her angel pin, now one of the chorus, would receive her degree, a small comfort for the family and another picture to nail on the wall. A token public relations gesture to demonstrate the university's concern. *The Crucible* and *The Peninsula Register* would gobble it up, welcome relief from the SWINC embarrassments.

A car backfired in the parking lot outside, and Grace gave a tiny cry. "Are you all right?" Maddie asked.

Grace went hesitantly to the window and lowered the blinds. "I have made more than one uneasy peace. But it is not about Cheryl."

"What's wrong? Why so jumpy?"

"Foolishness. I do not like . . ." She peeked through a

broken slat, then turned. "But I must talk to someone. It involves my past."

"Go on."

"An old sweetheart of mine, though that is hardly the word. He was an important officer in the military when I left Uganda."

Romantic revelations from this enigmatic woman took Maddie by surprise, but she shifted to a studied neutral as Grace continued. "He was a monster."

Maddie narrowed her eyes in disbelief, receiving a quick response. "Oh, never to me. Victor Abukha treated his ladies like queens-in-waiting. Very flattering, I can tell you. Expensive dinners, a fine automobile and chauffeur, the manners of a courtier. And of course to my childish heart he was a handsome figure in uniform. But I severed our friendship when I heard what he had done to others. Political arrests. Forfeits of property. Disappearances. At the time, I felt safe. My father and my uncles held high government positions."

"Then what happened?"

"All these twenty years he has risen in power, traded on privilege and death threats. Now he is a general, the most powerful in the country. His forces keep the president in power. And he has always said that he would have me, however long the wait. Patience is a dubious virtue of our people."

"You're never going back, so . . ."

Grace's strong brown hand clasped Maddie's, a rare and telling gesture. Then she nodded toward a small portrait of a thin, dignified man in a dark suit, the familiar shiny curves of the United Nations building embracing him. "My father died last year in New York. It was called a traffic accident, a hit-and-run, but I wondered. Suppose not. Perhaps Victor followed me."

"Way up here? Come on."

Grace laughed bitterly. "Nothing to arouse police involvement. No drama like a bomb or a shooting." She paused. "But he is a clever animal. Entirely amoral. His resources are great. He could hire the best men."

Maddie didn't know how to react at what sounded like a television movie script. African agents in Stoddard? They'd probably freeze to death if they didn't skid off the road in rental cars. She tried a lighter tack. "You need a vacation. Cabin fever is setting in."

Grace picked up a travel brochure from the desk. "You read my mind. I arranged for a trip to Hawaii this Christmas. So warm. More like my native land." Despite a cozy mohair sweater, she shivered. "How I abhor the eternal cold. It saps me. I am outside only to travel to the university."

Back in her office, Maddie diced among the usual topics for the first freshman theme. "If I Had a Million Dollars," "Three Types of Roommates," "Stoddard's Most Interesting Site." Banalities, but better than bromides about capital punishment, abortion, and drugs. Impossible to buy from the essay mongerers, too. Her blood pressure had skyrocketed on her first visit to the "Termies-R-US" Web site hawking billions of bytes of "research." Gary had shown her a twenty-page tome on Walt Whitman's Civil War experience: seventy footnotes and not a single book from Copper's library. Why tempt them to hang themselves? Juggling the basics of an intro, body paragraphs with topic sentences, and a conclusion was Sisyphean labor enough.

She yanked the sheet from her printer and set off for the copier. In the hall, a cheery, unfamiliar face greeted her, probably from English 100. "Oh, Professor," the girl said, framed by two thick pink braids. "Me and Josh missed the last class and wondered if you had any extra handouts?"

Maddie halted in mid-stride. Off-the-cuff lessons. But she had a mission. "There weren't any, my dear. But I must advise you in my capacity as your instructor, so don't take it personally. You are training for a career and should know that the pronoun 'me' cannot be used with that syntax. 'Josh and I' is correct."

The girl smacked herself lightly on the head. "Wicked! Like you say, you're just doing your job for . . ." She paused. "For Josh and I. Thanks anyhow." She waved at another student and rushed off.

"Winston tastes good like a cigarette should" hooked a nation on nicotine. Even Shell gasoline had billboards about going "further" with their gas, and Teacher's Scotch Distillery had never answered her letter telling them that their label spelled "it's" incorrectly. But "wicked"? Somehow complimentary in context. As Maddie punched the code into the copier, Nancy was on the phone, beckoning to her. "Have you seen Malcolm this morning?" she asked, twisting a lock of curly brown hair into a corkscrew.

"No, but I just got in." Maddie selected commands for ninety copies. The usual ne'er-do-wells had already dropped out.

"God, he's pulled a royal flush again. I called him last night to remind him of his nine a.m. meeting. Budget crisis. Told me he was feeling a bit under the weather, the flu or something, but that he'd make it. Dean Nordman's been giving me a tongue-lashing. Not that Malcolm hasn't missed meetings before, but blame that on a hangover."

Engaged in conversation, suddenly Maddie became aware that none of the copies had emerged. She bent down and opened a side door. "Out of paper? What's up? This machine carries a three-foot stack."

Nancy fidgeted, her tone apologetic. "That's what the

meeting was about. Copying's cut off all over the university. The Dean made me lock up the paper."

"Big deal. I'll bring my own. Paper doesn't cost much."

"Copying does. Over ten thousand bucks this year in our department."

"I guess we're spoiled. Anyway, the students toss them into the wastebasket. So do we go back to spirit masters? Talk about substance abuse. I thought HAWG declared that stuff toxic, trucked it up to the Keweenaw Peninsula to be cemented into a mine shaft." She grinned at Nancy, but found her close to tears. "No problem. We can lump along for a while, use the blackboard. If the chalk hasn't been confiscated."

Nancy opened a drawer and placed several fresh sticks on the desk. "But what about Malcolm? It's nearly two, and I've called and called with no answer. I'm really worried." Her soft gray eyes seemed to make an unspoken request.

If there was one necessary friend in the Ivory Tower, it was the support staff. How many times had Nancy gone beyond the call of her job description? "Blessed are the flexible" was her motto. She typed tests at the last minute, switched off forgotten coffee pots, trudged to the far corners of Denney to notify students of cancellations. A classy woman. Kipling's Colonel's lady and Nancy O'Grady were sisters under the skin. "Relax. I'll stop by his house. You're right. He might be sick." Those bulging eyes. A roadmap of red veins straight to apoplexy. "I hope he takes retirement soon and climbs out of this bog."

"Ha. He's been retired ever since he made chairman," Nancy said with an artificial laugh, lining up a row of chalk for the next inquiry.

Malcolm lived in a quaint cottage next to the oldest cemetery in Stoddard. One bright June afternoon, he had given

Maddie a tour of its Victorian grave art. The picturesque little grove dated from the advent of the mines. Surrounded by mammoth oaks and maples spared the woodman's axe, pebbled footpaths ran among the ferns, gravestones poking up at intervals, framed in summer by wildflowers changing with the season. Malcolm belonged to a local society which trimmed the plots and whitewashed the fading lettering. A world and time away from football and rock bands, so many hopeful young immigrant men burrowing after copper, over half the population in 1870. From where she stood beside the car, she could read one tombstone: "Eino Maenpaa, killed in the Bullock Mine, May 13, 1872, aged nineteen years. Lamb of God Have Mercy." The simple beast, legs folded under, had been a popular image.

In the driveway sat Malcolm's black Mercedes, a vintage boat with over three hundred thousand miles, like its owner, he bragged. So he was home. Maddie had second thoughts. This visit might prove embarrassing, were he suffering from excessive infusions of brandy. Along the brick walk, the perennials were in sloppy shape. The monkshood should have been lopped to let the sedum grow, and leaves blanketed the lawn. Plenty of money, just too absentminded and independent to hire regular help, except for his housekeeper. Mrs. Bach, was it? The bell sounded, then resounded. Townsfolk kept their doors locked, but she tried anyway. No luck. Growing more concerned, she circled the house, peering in leaded lozenge windows like a reluctant voyeuse, until she reached the rear yard. Was he outside?

Malcolm's three acres had been sliced from a century farm along with other "estate" lots, his parcel encompassing the remains of an old apple orchard. Far enough back to avoid complaints from neighbors were the tin-roofed wooden sheds of his game pens. She walked fifty feet, calling to no avail.

Then she checked the kitchen door. Also locked, but what about the ubiquitous hidden key? Her eyes scanned the ledges, moved around the garbage cans to a pile of gardening debris, a withered geranium on the compost heap, a row of upturned pottery under a birdbath. Something obvious. "With blackest moss the flower-pots . . ." No, "plots," not "pots." She'd been misreading that line from "Mariana" for years. Still, Tennyson gave her a hint. A key lay underneath one pot, wrapped in a plastic bag.

She opened the door and placed the key on a counter. "Malcolm? It's Maddie." No answer. Probably upstairs in his "garret," he called it, ever the dramatic. "I'd choose to die like Keats, with arterial blood spurting and a plump, warm cat on my chest. But consumption has been cured, and I abhor cats, so I must seek out a modern malady."

The kitchen was small but inviting: gaily-patterned curtains and a low, beamed ceiling, dominated by a gargantuan hutch with proud age scars. Perhaps it had belonged to Malcolm's mother. Maddie didn't imagine an old bachelor collecting the Willowware lining its shelves, though the Toby jugs of Churchill and Merlin won her approval. On the polished maple table, an empty cup sat next to a cold brown Betty ceramic pot and a bowl of congealed mush. Looked like old-fashioned cambric tea: bread, sugar, milk added for an upset stomach. The sink contained a plate with remains of a meal: sweet potato skin, a lone green bean, and fragile bones from his legendary quail, no doubt. Mrs. Bach always left his evening meal. According to Malcolm she was an excellent cook, perhaps something more intimate from the sparkle in his eye.

Faint strains of "Elvira Madigan" led her into the living room, a nook of sofas and chairs, where the radio was tuned to PBS. A bottle of decent Chablis was empty, a wine glass beside a snifter and a half-full bottle of Courvoisier. A couple of *Harper's* and Sunday's *New York Times*. It looked like a quiet night had passed, normal except for the oppressive heat from the gas fireplace. She turned off the control.

Maddie climbed the steep stairs, treading lightly on the worn carpet. At the top were two doors and an open bathroom. She stooped to pick up a small package from the floor, a bubble pack of a popular cold remedy, three capsules gone. In the room on the left, nothing but packing boxes and furniture castoffs. At the other door, she knocked to no response. Probably dozed through the morning like many people with flu, hangovers, or a combination. Those decongestant capsules could cause severe drowsiness. As the door pushed open, she saw Malcolm propped up in bed, looking comfortable enough, though heaped with blankets in a room already stifling.

"How are you doing, old friend?" she asked in forced cheer, placing the cold tablets on a dresser. "Nancy dispatched me when you didn't make the meeting." Walking closer, she noted a glass of water and a leatherbound book open on the night table, gray silk dressing gown neatly folded on the chair. Nothing signaling panic. But how odd that he wasn't speaking. Malcolm rarely shut up. Was he feeling that low? "I've found another poem for *The Stuffed Owl II*. 'The mountain sheep are sweeter,/ The valley sheep are fatter;/ We therefore deemed it meeter/ To carry off the latter.' " Thomas Love Peacock, another dimwit of the period. Not a flicker from the bed. She picked up the book, Johnson in gold leaf on the spine. Vellum pages. "The Young and the *Rasselas*? Never would have suspected you for the soaps." Not even the rise of an eyebrow, and Malcolm never resisted a pun on his idol. In the continuing silence, she approached with growing trepidation. Nursing was not her profession. Caregiver to a sick dog was the limit.

A crust of yellow vomit ringed his mouth, dribbling down his beard onto his striped pajamas, and she shrank to see him so helpless, his dignity compromised. Maybe the bed was soiled. Should she offer to take him to the toilet? Certainly a call to Mrs. Bach would be in order. If the woman couldn't help temporarily, she might know a practical nurse from the community. His bulbous eyes, normally bright and merry, were bees-winged red across the conjunctiva, wandering from side to side in vacant confusion. She moved her hand across his face with no reaction, then felt for the carotid artery. His pulse was stuttery and weak, his breathing shallow, as if he were winding down.

"What's wrong? Can't you hear me?" When she shook him gently, his head lolled against the pillow, the thick white hair wet and matted. Paralyzed? Only then did it occur to her that he might have had a stroke. But what about the symptoms he had described to Nancy?

In the palpable silence, a monotonous sound intruded from a stalwart Seth Thomas grandfather clock in the corner, the pendulum swinging slowly, dragging the seconds. An old song came to mind: "It stopped short, never to go again . . ."

Downstairs at the hall phone, she dialed 9-1-1 and gave the address. Then, after opening the front door, she returned to play reluctant nurse, clasping his gnarly hand, "blue as a vein o'er the Madonna's breast." Browning's Bishop of St. Praxad's in progressive dementia ordering his tomb. "All lapis, all, sons!" The water she offered trickled onto the sheet, and only his frightened eyes moved in unseeing torment. Tick tock. ". . . when the old man died." How long for the ambulance? Her heart threatened to break through her chest, to school the clock to her own fearful metronome and speed the rescue. Then a pounding of rapid footsteps meant help had arrived. "Up here!" she called.

"We thought he had the flu, but it looks more serious," she told the two attendants. A red-headed young man, hardly older than her students, set up the gurney, fumbling at the straps and wiping sweat from his baby face.

"Easy now, Teddy," a chunky woman with muscles of a stevedore said, her voice low and calm. With the efficiency of experience, she pushed aside the bedclothes at Malcolm's throat, taking pulse and blood pressure, flashing a penlight into the eyes. "There's paralysis all right. It's a pretty serious stroke. We'll get him oxygen and a drip, then have him at the General in ten minutes."

Not again, she thought, recalling Ian Macdonald. Today, this very day, she would buy a blood pressure machine, even if they weren't on sale. "What are his chances?" she whispered, fixated at a tiny gold locket around Malcolm's neck. A keepsake, perhaps, but strange jewelry for a man.

The woman patted Maddie's arm. "Recovery comes pretty quickly if it comes at all. The first week tells the story." Then she and Teddy moved off, maneuvering down the narrow stairs so carefully that a crystal goblet could have been safe on Malcolm's chest.

Maddie went into the bathroom to wash her hands, noticing signs of sickness in the toilet and the sink. How did that jibe with a stroke? But she wasn't a doctor, and besides, recalling the liquor and pills, she knew events rarely had a single cause. Her lecture came to mind: "Suppose I am driving home at dusk. It's rush hour. Snow begins to fall. The car ahead has no brake lights. Perhaps I'm going a bit fast, following too closely. Then a deer runs onto the road. The car in front hits the brakes. Remove one factor and perhaps the accident wouldn't have happened."

"Sure, but you'll still get charged," some wise guy always quipped.

Shaken, she sat for a while in the kitchen, sipping a glass of water, contemplating the evidences of a soul. Strange that so few minutes had passed for such a great reckoning in a little room. Only four o'clock. Time for Mrs. Bach to arrive? Leaving a note would be crass. Perhaps a few minutes more.

As Merlin and Churchill watched from the sideboard with a mute wisdom of two disparate ages, a roar in the driveway as loud as an incoming Apache helicopter was followed by a tinny door slam.

The front door opened. "Sir Fopling? I saw your ebony steed. Mrs. Loveit's got a special delivery for you" called a jolly voice. Into the kitchen sailed a stout figure in an astrakhan coat with a fur collar, white sausage curls escaping from a paisley scarf. She did a double-take at Maddie, but merely deepened her plummy tones. "Oh, I don't believe we've . . ."

Feeling like a secondary character in a Restoration comedy of manners, Maddie stood. "Mrs. Bach? I'm Maddie Temple, a colleague of Professor Driscoll. I'm afraid he's been taken to the hospital."

Bags of groceries crashed onto the floor, oranges rolled like billiard balls on a lazy break, and the sharp smell of disinfectant filled the air. With one hand on her crepey throat, the woman groped towards a chair, suddenly pale and shaky. "My God. The old ticker. All that rich food. Cream sauces bubbling with butter. I warned him. Tried that *Heart-Smart* cookbook last Christmas, but he'd have none of it. Took one bite and walked out the door to a common restaurant. That broke my spirit, I tell you."

Maddie helped her out of the bulky coat, grabbed a dish-towel and swiped at the spillage, then set the items on the counter. "No, no. It might be a stroke. There was paralysis. He couldn't seem to talk." She bent carefully to round up the fruit.

Mrs. Bach paced about, shaking her head, rubbing chubby hands together as if kindling a fire. "Last night, just last night." She pointed to the dishes in the sink. "I prepared his favorite supper. A triple brace of quail, he called it. That's six. I served them with my special Cumberland sauce. Tucked in right in front of me. Gobbled it all up, he did."

Maddie narrowed her eyes in thought, recalling the bathroom with a shudder. "But he complained of the flu later when our secretary called. Perhaps it hit after the meal."

Mrs. Bach stiffened, twisting a white curl with her finger. "Nothing to do with my cooking. Fresh as you could get. He cleaned the birds himself. Had them all ready. None of that messy feather plucking for me. That's our rule."

"Of course. And the flu's going around. How was he when you left?"

"Top of the world. Reciting limericks like a mischievious schoolboy. I started to clean up. Told me to go on home. He was expecting company later. Didn't want any kitchen clatter."

"Company?" Maddie turned her head, shutting off the extra "mischievous" syllable. "Do you know who?"

"He didn't say." Out of habit the old woman rose unsteadily and began tidying the kitchen, scraping the leavings into a garbage bag and washing the dishes. "I'll go on over to see him." She paused and yanked at her girdle with a groan. "Grandson's expecting me to take him to the movies. Guess I'd better—"

Maddie put a hand on her shoulder. "They'll want to stabilize his condition first. He'll probably have no visitors until tomorrow, not even relatives."

A tear furrowed its way down the powdered face. Mrs. Bach sniffed. "The man's alone in the world. Not even a brother or sister. Bachelor, too. What woman in her right mind would put up . . ." She excused herself, and Maddie could hear her softly weeping in the living room.

A quick call reached Nancy just as she was about to lock the office. "So he's at the General, and that's all I know. You'd better tell Flo." She'd be in her glory. Lord help the English Department.

Chapter Sixteen

Next morning Maddie made a commitment to get to school early to arrange her lectures before sandwiching in a visit to Malcolm. At her desk she sat for an hour leafing through notes to Tennyson's "In Memoriam," dedicated to Arthur Hallam, a friend whose premature death had sent the poet into a decade of writer's block. The ponderous 131 stanzas of grief therapy contrasted starkly with the gemlike poem "Break, Break, Break." Sixteen heart-hushing lines: "But O for the touch of a vanish'd hand,/ And the sound of a voice that is still." She recalled Malcolm's cold fingers laced through hers, the emptiness of the room echoing louder than Hell's worst screams.

Heading for the department to check with Nancy, she spotted Flo's French roll nodding at the secretary. Queen at last, all but the scepter in her hot little fist. When Malcolm recovered, he'd probably take retirement, but Flo's interim position would gain her the chairmanship by default, especially with her golf buddy Nordman's approval. She bit her lip, wondering if she could avoid the woman by backing out of the office and returning later.

Flo accepted a tissue from Nancy, turned slowly, and fixed on Maddie like a long-lost friend. Instead of preparing for an annunciation, she seemed poleaxed. The burgundy plaid suit clashed with the pea green blouse, as if she had chosen in the dark. For once, her face revealed a strange fragility, a trace of mascara dripping from one eye.

"Any word?" Maddie asked. Perhaps his condition hadn't been as serious as it had appeared. Perhaps there were miracle protocols for strokes. Perhaps Malcolm was wolfing a longshoreman's breakfast and had already phoned the department between slurps of coffee. Perhaps even for eighteenth-century rationalists, there was a God.

"Nothing. I plan to go over after lunch," Flo said in a rare whisper. "Nancy said that you were, you saw—"

"Yes, I found him late yesterday afternoon." The minimal details she recounted seemed to pierce the woman like a thousand cuts. Once Nancy had recounted Flo's devastation when her mother died. Watching the padded shoulders slump, Maddie wondered if those sad memories had been reawakened.

"Couldn't talk. God, what a blow." Flo drew a tremulous hand across her pale face. One feature in painfully obvious contrast to her personal care and exercise was her nails, gnawed to the quick, the cuticles swollen as if on the verge of infection. Biting them in secret, like a wary child, Maddie thought. Yet what did she have to worry about other than husband Bruce? "He wasn't that old," Flo murmured.

It seemed only decent to offer practical help, colleagues rallying around the fallen leader. "Malcolm may be away for a while. If you need someone to act as coordinator, I guess I could stand in," Maddie said with weak commitment, knowing that essays would soon begin multiplying like fleas on a hound.

"The Dean has approved my temporary appointment as chairman." Flo straightened and consulted her clipboard. "The class lists will have to be collected for a head count." Each department claimed its spoils from basic funding units, aka students. Allocations came a few weeks into each semester. She scanned a page which made her frown. "Midterm marks for non-English majors should be sent to the appropriate departments. Textbook orders are due by the end of the month. And we need to hire someone for a remedial night class Athletics has requested."

"I'll send a reminder to the faculty. Let me know any other details."

Momentarily tuned to the siren music of administration, Flo pulled a pile of correspondence from Malcolm's box, kneeling awkwardly to collect the falling papers. A small fart erupted from the efforts, but she merely gave the two women an accusative look as she clicked her three-inch heels into his office, closing the door.

"I'm going to the hospital, Nancy," Maddie said. "Visiting hours probably start about now."

"That poor old man. I can't believe it. Flo's sent flowers from the department." Nancy blew her reddened nose, topped up a wastebasket brimming with crumpled tissues. "Out of her own pocket, if you can believe."

That is a miracle, Maddie thought, back at her desk as she calculated marks and scrawled a memo. Quick work with the Dean. Those putting lessons paid off. Flo gets her wish. I get a salary increase. Aruba on March break, with its quaint Dutch resorts and *rijstaffel*. Then she stopped in reflection, feeling selfish and mean-spirited. Malcolm was lying in a hospital bed, and she was plunging her toes into hot sand. At the very least, she'd make damn sure Rita got that remedial class. Administration had its perks.

Stoddard General had been built in Grover Cleveland's second term, remodeled so many times that it resembled a Victorian birthday cake designed by a bunch of chimps working with a viral copy of AutoCad. Sandstone and pressed brick on the bottom floors, the stamped metal frieze below the cornices showed evidence of a Renaissance revival. The grotesque effect was doubled by a layer of stained aluminum siding from the Fifties and a recent cement block addition. Despite the ugly façade, the care was excellent and people were happy to avoid driving hours for treatment. The General didn't attempt anything tricky like heart surgery or transplants, but it had a solid reputation for basic medical care as well as obstetrics and pediatrics. A helicopter unit with a pad on the roof airlifted critical cases to Grand Rapids.

The admissions area, a turquoise plastic monument to tastelessness, was typically quiet for a weekday morning in a small town. As Maddie entered the lobby, limp Muzak buzzed her ears, a thousand and one inoffensive strings. A teenaged girl with a bandaged ankle sprawled in a row of rigid plastic chairs linked in a galley-seat effect. Hand nuzzling a bag of chips, she stared at a game show on a television attached to the wall. Thankfully, the sound was off. Better than nothing, her expression read. At least she could follow the questions and answers on the boards. A nurse nodded over a copy of *The National Enquirer*, tucking it under the desk as Maddie cleared her throat.

"I'm visiting Malcolm Driscoll. He was brought in late yesterday afternoon."

The chinless woman with a lacquered burgundy bouffant yawned so broadly that Maddie could see her wiggling tonsils, checked a chart, then blinked. Two bovine eyes bounced around awkwardly, as if in search of a heavenly rescue chopper. A clumsy tongue moistened her lips, meaningless syllables spilling from her mouth like Scrabble tiles.

"Well?" Didn't people understand English?

"I'm afraid he . . . he—"

"He what?" Had this short-circuited person graduated from an accredited nursing program?

With a choke, she blurted out a response. "He passed away. Are you a relative?"

Caught between cold logic and emotion, Maddie answered on instinct. A relative. A relative clause. Her legs weakened, but her voice assumed the even tone afforded a freshman needing special guidance. "Close enough. I want to speak to his doctor. Right now."

While the nurse punched buttons as if her life hung in the balance, Maddie sank into a chair. It didn't make sense. Death should have come sooner or not at all, from what she imagined of strokes. Still, maybe a fast exit was merciful. If he'd been paralyzed, thoughts exploding across his magpie mind, rotting in a nursing home would have been a living hell. The department would be shocked, not devastated. They were too rational and disciplined. Old retirees passed on from time to time. Still, no one had actually dropped dead in leather harness, like an overheated ox.

In distraction, she ran shaky fingers over the selection of magazines, constructing a historical collage. Bill Clinton on *Newsweek*, Princess Di on *People*, and even Gorby grinning on a greasy *Time*. The clock on the wall death-marched nearly an hour. She debated calling Nancy to cancel her classes.

"You were inquiring about Professor Driscoll?" A slim man with jet hair and a neatly trimmed moustache moved in front of her, a chart under his arm. Dr. Abourbi, the nametag read.

She extended a hand and introduced herself. "I discovered him quite ill yesterday and called the ambulance."

"Ah, yes. I am so very sorry. He died early this morning. We have been as yet unable to locate any relatives." His grip was firm and reassuring, his shadowed eyes intense.

Died. A monosyllable. Pure and final. Without the embroidery of "passing on," "expiring," "succumbing." But

140

succumbing to what? Maddie felt her eyes moisten, a lump grow in her throat. "It was a fatal stroke, then? The paralysis . . ."

He looked pensive. "There was paralysis, but—"

"The flu? A raging virus?" She wanted clinical proof of the horror that had turned a pleasant little house into a mortuary. Wasn't science exact?

"His white cell count was normal, and the MRI found no sign of a stroke."

Maddie rubbed cold sweat from her upper lip. "What, then? The brandy? The cold pills? Some complication?"

He sat down beside her. A fresh crimson smear on his white coat meant that he might have stolen valuable minutes to deal compassionately with the mourners of a man beyond his abilities to heal. "I am saying only this. We have a collection of very strange symptoms. Paralysis without stroke, without injury. Quite rare."

"He was so sick. Vomiting. Diarrhea. But he couldn't talk."

Abourbi took out a pen and consulted the chart, thumbing through the pages. "The report said only that a woman found him. I have been hoping to learn more about his last hours. Please tell me everything you noticed. Were there any signs, gestures?"

She spread out her hands in beseechment, aware of the inanity of words. "His eyes were open, but they weren't seeing anything. I was standing by his bed. He didn't react . . . except to my voice and touch."

Abourbi raised an eyebrow, then scribbled a delicate lacy line.

Maddie couldn't help peering. Wings of a smile crossed his smooth, light brown face. "Arabic. I am Egyptian, born in Cairo. I think faster in my native language."

"No hieroglyphics?" A giddiness prompted the silly question.

"Thank God, no. Can you imagine the computer problems with ravens, crocodiles, and ibises?" Tension relaxed for a moment. Then he shook his head. "More detailed tests might solve this mystery. But our lab is primitive. Perhaps the forensics people in Detroit will have some answers."

"Any guesses?"

"It is the sudden blindness that confounds me. The apple is tempting, but inside hides a small worm. Very fortunate that you noticed the condition before he entered a coma."

"What does it mean?"

He met her eyes with no mistake in the message. "Ingestion of a toxic substance."

"Toxic." Her hands trembled as she watched Mrs. Bach stop at the desk, a stricken look on her face. Maddie turned back to the doctor. "Translation: poison."

Chapter Seventeen

Sitting in the Common Room, tallying textbook orders for January, her eyes boggling at the endless series of numbers, Maddie looked for relief outside the large, vaulted window to the Oval as a cold wind swept desultory flecks of snow over campus. The flag at the obelisk was at half-mast again. Copper's losses in both World Wars, then Korea, Vietnam, and the Middle East. First for Cheryl and now for Malcolm, as if one more guttering candle had flickered out, drawing the darkness of the corners into an ebony cavern.

With the initial shock over, the faculty turned to black humor as comic relief from the tension. "*Journal of the Plague Year,*" George said as the banjo clock over the mantel chimed the hour. "Struck down in his prime."

Marie shook her jowls as she nibbled an oatmeal cookie. "A long and active life to the last. Couldn't ask for more."

Rick growled, pulling out his cigarettes and smelling the pack fondly as he pointed to the No Smoking sign. "I could use one of these. Flo's jerking us around already. A five o'clock meeting in the middle of the semester. Malcolm only had one a year. And look, no muffins."

Nancy took a few slugs from her water bottle, then opened her notebook. "And don't expect any. She tried to get me to bake some at my own expense. Told her it wasn't in my job description. And I'm not bringing anything at Christmas either. Last time she took home half my brownies."

Following Grace, who slipped in without speaking, Flo arrived ten minutes after the hour, narrowing her eyes at the group as if they were felons and dropping a large exercise bag onto the floor. A dark blue suit with gold epaulets lent an appropriate military appearance. She sat conspicuously at the end of a rectangular table instead of the round table Malcolm had used and did a conspicuous head count. Maddie passed in the class numbers and book orders, receiving only a papal nod. "Where's Gary?" Flo asked in acid tones.

Nancy shifted defensively. "At the dentist for a root canal job. The man was in terrible pain, his face swollen like a potato. He waited until four when his class finished."

Flo pointed her pen like a rapier. "Make a note that he takes a half day of sick leave. And tell him to bring documentation. The same goes for all of you. Leaving early on Friday or arriving late on Monday is suspicious as well. No alcoholic's weekends."

She ignored the incredulous expressions and placed a clipboard on the table, removing a thick sheaf of pages. "There are twenty-five items on the agenda," she observed with a spidery eyebrow arched nearly ninety degrees, and the faces looked as constipated as her list. "Number one: proper attire." Her glance moved from Maddie's jeans to Rick's Grateful Dead t-shirt bearing a tri-colored coffee stain.

Driving home at half-past eight, Maddie chewed her nether lip. Flo was turning the department into a penal colony. A peanut colony in studentese. Their supposed sins would be etched upon their bodies with the exactness of Kafka's infernal harrowing machine. She took a deep breath, held it, and exhaled in a relaxation strategy. What substance of power lay under the padding? How far would the Dean support his golfing partner? The carps about clothing were sheer bluff. No one could be fired for wearing jeans, or could they?

144

Scarcely had she arrived home and dished out Nikon's food when the phone rang. It was Grace, her voice weak and shaky. "I am sorry. I did not know what to do."

"What's wrong? Where are you?" she asked.

"In my office. I stayed after the meeting to prepare Monday's exam. Minutes ago, I heard strange noises in the corridor. I am afraid to leave."

There was a garble of static, several clicks and buzzes. The new voice-mail system was forever connecting the wrong people. "Can you speak louder, Grace? Why are you afraid?"

"My past follows me like a bird of prey. This afternoon my car was damaged. A sharp stone or similar object dragged along the side."

Conscious of the Probe's precious original paint she protected with Carnauba wax, Maddie winced. "Come on. The old key trick is typical of lowlifes. It could be a simple hate crime." Like before, she hesitated to add.

A buzz, a sound of breathing, another click. "Victor always told me he would find me when the time was ripe. He has the resources of a pillaged nation. Never would he forget the humiliation of my refusal. He feeds upon revenge."

This desperation led Maddie to wonder if she should recommend therapy. Certainly Grace's distress was reaching the breaking point. Still, she shuddered at the word "revenge" and decided to humor her. "You mentioned a trip to Hawaii at Christmas. How about staying with me until then? I have a spare room and Nikon's a great guard dog."

Grace choked back a sob. "In my country fate rules our destiny. You recall the appointment in Samara. If Victor wants me, he will have his way."

Remembering the time of year, Maddie grasped at another idea. "Did you turn in any failing grades at the midterm?"

The question acted like an adrenaline shot. Grace's voice

strengthened at the affront. "Of course. Every class has its malingerers, those who do not belong at a university."

"How about athletes? They need a solid C average to stay on the team. I've had calls from more than one anxious coach."

"You may be right. A certain Dartmore boy complains in a rude fashion. He wears a team jacket."

Pointing her finger like a gun, Maddie said, "His mother has been lobbying against the SWINC Project. Probably high pressure in the family for favorite son and heir to succeed. Sounds like he might be a good guess. Just hang on. He'll flunk out or get fresh problems with new teachers in January. And for now, call Campus Watch at 8111. An escort will be right over." As Grace hung up, for the moment reassured, Maddie wondered if she were shortchanging her friend. Yet what could she do? With her vision problems, driving at night was impossible. Why couldn't the woman have used a taxi?

Early Monday morning, Nancy motioned Maddie over, a cautious apprehension in her voice. "Something's up. The police came in like gangbusters and set up a command post in the Common Room. Everyone has to be here at ten, classes or not. They'll be questioning us separately. Why all the trouble over a stroke?"

"Maybe it's not that simple." So Abourbi had the right idea, she thought. Poison. But how? In the food? Mrs. Bach prepared his meals. Suspects began to emerge from the bushes of her mind. Anisha and Reggie at SWINC. Flo's shortcut to the chairmanship. Then the question of his estate. An old man working at a good salary all his life, no apparent relatives. Or was Mrs. Bach wrong? A lurking cousin with debts? Illegitimate child? She scoffed at her dramatics. But who was the visitor the housekeeper had mentioned?

146

Already on campus, she was the first summoned into the Common Room. Alone at the long teak table sat a man pushing sixty, wearing a rumpled brown suit with a knit tie. His thinning hair was artfully arranged over a balding dome. Briefcase open, revealing a large bottle of Maalox, a tape recorder at his side, he looked up and gestured to a chair.

"I'm Detective Rob Phillips. We spoke before about that accident at the library." He took out a pencil and leafed through his papers with the eraser end, a flash of pain on his face as he rubbed his stomach. "We'll be taping this, Professor Temple, if it's all right." He didn't wait for her answer. "You were at the crime scene. Let's start there."

Crime scene. Yellow tape, cipher-like figures in white suits scurrying about dusting for prints, dropping dustballs into tiny plastic bags. Surely the police didn't suspect her. Measuring words in paranoid fashion, Maddie reviewed the terrible afternoon.

His voice interrupted her description of the kitchen. "And you saw the remains of the meal?"

She frowned and searched her memory. "His quail, sweet potato, green beans, that's all. Except for the wine and brandy in the living room. If you think he was poisoned—"

"Who said anything about that?" He mashed the pencil point on the pad.

Maddie clenched her teeth. Better keep quiet about Abourbi, not compromise his professionalism. In a counterattack, she firmed up her tone. "Isn't it obvious? You're asking about the meal. Didn't you get samples of the food?"

He opened the Maalox and drank a quarter of the bottle, licking his lips more from custom than delight. With a sigh, he waved his hand in a gesture of uselessness. "It's in a landfill by now. Mrs. Bach was very efficient."

"My God. Do you suspect her?"

"At this point, it's our job to suspect everyone. Certainly she had the opportunity . . . and obviously the means."

"And the motive if he left her his money," Maddie said more to herself. "What does the will—"

"If you want to work at the police department, fill out a job application. You'll answer the questions, please, not me." He narrowed his eyes at her in an unconvincingly gruff manner.

Ignoring the pronoun error, Maddie asked with shameless curiosity, "What kind of poison was it? Arsenic? Strychnine?"

His large hands roamed his notes while one raised corner of his mouth belied the serious tone. "Victorian literature, that your specialty?" She nodded as if that, too, were a felony. "You're a century off, Dr. Temple. People have been known to use all sorts of chemicals. Heavy metals like lead, mercury, or thallium. Tricky stuff like aniline or benzene. This was an old devil. Hemlock. Just got the scans back from Detroit."

Maddie leaned forward, hardly believing that she had heard correctly. "Hemlock? Like Socrates used?"

He paged through his notes. "Socra—"

"The Greek philosopher. For supposedly corrupting the young, his political enemies forced him to drink hemlock." She warmed to the puzzle. "So you found that in his stomach contents?"

"No luck there. Apparently he vomited it up. But traces appeared in blood tests. Along with small amounts of alcohol and a common cold remedy."

Maddie recalled Mrs. Bach cleaning the kitchen. How had the poison been administered? In powder form? Tincture? Could it be purchased easily? Surely it must have tasted bitter. She watched Phillips make a final tick with his pencil and consult his watch. Quietly, she asked, "I don't want to be forward, but have you considered suicide? Was he ill? Perhaps he didn't want to go gentle into that good night."

"No, the doctors are clear on that. Moderately good health. Some fatty liver tissue, but safe for another five to ten years. Let's follow your suggestion, though, and suppose for some odd reason he believed he was dying. Wouldn't the man have left a note? And telling the secretary that he was sick. Taking those cold capsules. Gimme a break." He paused. "His death was pretty ugly. Hours of paralysis, the mind alert. Nothing planned about it."

She groped for an answer. "But if not the housekeeper, who? The place was locked. I found the key outside."

"So what? The doors locked on closure. Not rocket science. Let's move on, please. I have a lot of people to interview, and if they're all like you, I'll be spending Christmas at this table. Tell me who disliked Professor Driscoll, or who might have wanted him out of the way."

Maddie considered for a moment. SWINC and Flo. Flo and SWINC. The mysterious visitor wild card. She felt strangely empowered, asked to choose a sacrifice. No use hiding anything. Let them sort it out. "Well, there are several . . ."

Nodding to George and Marie waiting in the hall, Maddie returned to her office, flopping into the mammoth leather armchair, her arm resting on a strip of duct tape repair. From the corridor, she could hear the drones of conversation, the opening and shutting of doors. The human ramifications began to sink in. Imagination was the stimulus of great literature, the ability to put a reader into another's shell, to connect the joints and bones, knit the nerve ends until sensibilities married. She'd tried to bury the terrors of sight, sound, and smell, but found herself reliving the nightmare. Malcolm was no pompous bishop scripting his final minutes in self-aggrandizement, changing the tomb from basalt to black marble to jasper the color of pistachios to all lapis lazuli. Alert the whole time. Behind his poor blind eyes, the old man had felt the paralysis creep through his body. By the time Maddie had found him, nearly a punishing day later, his mute mouth couldn't form a single word to respond to her touch. She shivered, cursing her stupidity, wondering if she could have helped. What a way to go, some fool babbling bad poetry beside your deathbed. She made an involuntary sound halfway between a strangled laugh and a sob.

Chapter Eighteen

No doubt about it. Barney was struggling to make eye contact as he spoke, pupils darting like fussy bees behind his horn-rimmed glasses. Maddie reconsidered the Asperger diagnosis as she checked the outline for the first essay. Most students disregarded her advice to plan carefully, but for him, direction was gospel. She squinted at the crotchety handwriting. The topic involved describing a local place where an observer could learn about Stoddard and its inhabitants. Most students had chosen the shabby bus depot, the library, a favorite restaurant, even Creswell Park. True to eccentricity, Barney had fixed upon the Old Bonanza Mine. He had taken the tour fourteen times and described in ponderous detail the artifacts as well as scientific information about mineral deposits and early copper mining.

"Your analysis doesn't have much to do with people," she observed, taking off her reading glasses.

One shoulder twitched, and the motion rearranged his skeleton section by section, like an itchy trilobite. "But I do not find people very interesting."

"I see. So that's why you chose the mine?"

He scratched one pointed little ear, ducked his head like Nikon under scrutiny, a long hand-knitted scarf around his neck, perhaps Mother's work. "I ride over every week. They do not even make me pay anymore. Doctor, do you know that in 1920, thousands of gallons of whey from a cheese factory got dumped into the deepest shaft? They say that you can hear Old Bonanza's guts still—"

"All right, Barney." She had missed lunch, and her stomach was reminding her. Personal tutoring was the job of the Learning Center, and Maddie was glad not to have one hundred Barneys knocking at her door. She pondered for a minute while he stood, shifting from one foot to the other, stuffed rabbit with a CU sweater riding in the backpack. Parked in another dimension, his different drummer was pounding out paradiddles unheard by normal souls. Why not let him try? Writing was the goal, and inspiration an obvious bonus.

Suddenly his wavering elbow triggered a switch and a song began to play: "Easter Parade." Out of instinct, forgetting that he needed more verbal directions, she arched an eyebrow and, to her surprise, he responded instantly by turning off the noise. "Describe what you saw, heard, smelled, touched. Use all your senses. Fatten up the outline and show it to me next class." Barney's eyes lit up, and his angular body lurched toward the hall as the phone rang.

"It's June Bach. Are you busy? I hope I didn't call at a bad time."

Maddie wondered if the housekeeper had been distressed by the interrogation. Official sources were being so guarded about the investigation that even Jerry hadn't been able to ferret out information. "It's fine. I'm sorry that we didn't have time to talk at the hospital. How are you?" she asked. Late for class that sad afternoon, she'd given the old woman only a brief hug before leaving her with Dr. Abourbi.

A sigh echoed over the lines. " 'To everything there is a season,' Malcolm always said. I'm getting organized. It's those damn quail, and one partridge in search of a pear tree. Been feeding them until I figure out what to do. No use wasting good eating. But I have to go to the Sault for a couple of days to visit my baby sister. Gallbladder surgery, a regular epidemic these days. Fat, forties, and female."

"Do you want me to stop over?"

"Would you be a dear? Back of the house, you'll find the pens. Not fussy, my birdies aren't. Water from the tap and crushed turkey pellets in the barrel in the shed."

Maddie gulped. "They eat turkey?"

The old woman chortled. "No, sweet. Same concoction as turkeys get, according to the feed store. Two cups a day will do it. Thank God he didn't raise horses."

After Maddie locked her office, Flo's voice followed her down the hall. "I hear that you gave Rita the remedial class. She wouldn't have been my first choice, an extra two dollars an hour, but trust you to be a bleeding heart." She tapped her teeth together as if testing a bear trap.

Maddie turned reluctantly. "Nancy mentioned the HAWG meeting next Tuesday at four. I guess that's also my responsibility. Sounds like a colossal bore."

Flo seemed to take personal umbrage at the statement, her eyebrows forming a perturbed vee. "The committee does very important work. Checks air quality. Working conditions. Proper storage of chemicals."

"Ho hum. I'll bring a book. *Great Expectations*. No, with the financial climate, maybe *Bleak House* would set a more appropriate tone."

After mining a cuticle with a determined look, Flo paged through an appointment book. "You have the wrong attitude. I'll stay on the job there. It's one of the Dean's special projects."

Outside at last, passing Maxwell Auditorium, Maddie saw colorful posters advertising upcoming plays. *Little Shop of Horrors* and *Romeo and Juliet*, something for everyone. Her father and Billy enjoyed an occasional diversion from their nightly television bouts. She hadn't given Stephen Glogore a thought since that rally fizzled like a dud firecracker. How curious that Malcolm fired the first blasts against SWINC, organized the forces, then failed to show up. Now he was dead. Was there a connection? What did Glogore know?

As she entered the old auditorium, fusty-cold from a heating system laboring overtime with leaky doors and huge spaces, she sensed excitement. Students were scurrying about with props and scenery, a jovial camaraderie energizing each step. Literature brought to life the way it should be.

At the front of the shabby stage, wrapped in a huge woollen cloak, Glogore posed with one long hand on a bony hip, the other brandishing a laser pointer like a *Star Wars* knight. "No, no, not that gel, you ninny." He flashed the illuminated dot toward the back of the set, where a woman in black leotards, an oversize mohair sweater, and a floppy beret sat enveloped in a beanbag chair. She took intermittent puffs from a cigarette in a foot-long holder sparkling with jewels. "That light green makes Wanda look like a corpse."

He turned to Maddie with a welcome grin. "Come to volunteer? I knew the English Department wouldn't fail." He cocked his head, ran appraising eyes over her face. "A few crow's feet. Not quite old enough, but with the miracles of makeup and a wig—"

"Volunteer for what?" She laughed nervously at the scrutiny.

"My nurse ran off to San Francisco, too young to remember to wear a flower in her hair." He spread his long, wiry hands in a helpless gesture.

"Your nurse?"

"For *Romeo and Juliet*. Greenwich Village, 1960. It's a choice role. Steals the show every time."

"God, no. In high school I never got past the prop crew. Too afraid of memorizing lines." She eased into an ancient folding seat, the wood veneer creaking. "It's about Malcolm."

He grunted in contempt. "Fine ally he turned out to be. Damn tragedy he's dead, of course, but the bugger backed out in the thick of battle."

"What do you mean?"

"Malcolm spearheaded the movement, got us suckers involved. Cynthia, that flake, had a high profile in town, but he was our cornerstone. Provocative letters to the paper, a killer speech for the rally, so he promised. Then phhhht." His hand waved goodbye.

"He changed his mind."

"Hardly that simple. It was the most outrageous one-hundred-and-eighty-degree turn since Judas Iscariot kissed Christ. When I called his office to find out why he hadn't been at the rally, he utterly refused to explain. Hung up. For a minute I thought he had gone senile, or was being disciplined by his Dean for the bad publicity. It was that strong a betrayal. Never spoke to the man again." His piercing eyes trained the beam on a white wooden cross at the back of the set. "The oddest thing. He seemed to be weeping. In the theatre, one is sensitive to tones."

Starting up the aisle, suddenly she stopped and called back, "Say, for the nurse? I have the ideal person."

Maddie drove to Malcolm's later that afternoon. The small cottage seemed lonely without its master, a few cracks in the delicate Tudor windows and broken tiles on the gabled roof. The late October day was brisk, the wind flexing muscles to tease the fallen leaves into dizzying swirls. Tempted by a bright maple grove which bordered his property, she took a roundabout path to the pens, winding along a mossy path through the second-growth hardwoods. The red-jeweled berries of Solomon's seal hung pendulously at the end of the large, yellowed leaves. Scrubby striped maples struggled under the canopy of sugary big brothers. Turning back, she entered the old orchard, then stopped abruptly as she watched a small deer nibbling lunch. The snap of a twig flicked brown ears into action, and it bounded off into the brush. Under the wizened apple trees lay tiny fruits. She picked up one, bit into it on a whim, and winced. Too tangy and tart; perfect for applesauce, though. Probably some pioneer variety long abandoned for tasteless but durable supermarket strains.

Then she came to the partridge pen, one lone bird pecking forlornly at the ground, blinking hopefully at her. Scanning a new corral fenced with chicken wire, she couldn't locate the quail, thought they had gone inside the shed through a small door. Instead, they were hiding under tall, feathery plants, which had dropped tiny seeds. Attractive, resembling Queen Anne's lace. Flowering so late, it might add interest to her garden. She broke off a stem and tucked it into a pocket to identify later. Rousted from cover were twenty quail, wee souls, hardly two mouthfuls each. They cooed peacefully, accustomed to humans. She filled the water bowls, then searched the shed for the barrel and scooped out a pan-full. Distributing the pellets, she felt like Tess of the D'Urbervilles in a bucolic reverie over a dashing officer.

On the way home, she stopped by her father's. "Look at this," she said, reaching into her jacket for the plant. "I can't place it. Maybe Billy might know."

"He took the bus to Lansing to the Vets' Hospital where he gets his check-ups. Make sure the old Big C doesn't come back. The guy's always joking. 'It's not the cough that carries you off. It's the coffin they carry you off in. Consumption be done about it? Of cough.' What a card." He lowered his voice and met her eyes. "I think he's scared sometimes."

"We all are," she said. "Lucky the Temples are tough Scots."

"Now, Madeline," he added, rubbing a hand over his crewcut, "this might be a good time to tell you . . ."

Her heart skipped a beat or two or three. Bad news? Not about Billy, not yet. But her father?

"I've been to Doc Granger about that peeing. Damn nuisance to hit the john seven times a night. Might as well sleep in the bathtub."

"And?" She reined in the fear nuzzling her chest.

"Wants me to get a prostrate test. Some ultrastuff. Drink water 'til you bloat up like a pig. Could be I'll need one of them roto-tooter jobs."

Prostate. "I'm sure you'll be okay. Prevention is the best medicine." How stupid that sounded. She felt her ears flame with alarm, an embarrassing barometer. Was it her blood pressure? Never had bought that damn machine.

Her father seemed inclined to talk. "I don't know. Mel Stewart, our top bowler, bought the biscuit. Had his funeral last month. Lost the whole shebang down there and for what?" He shifted awkwardly. "All these years, kind of get used to them. Understand how that dog of yours might feel."

Chapter Nineteen

In true Age of Reason style, Malcolm had left explicit instructions for his funeral. Cremation, a simple ceremony in the Episcopalian Church in the Wildwood, and a dinner catered by Mrs. Bach, her final duty. Or so said his lawyer, Bridie Pedderson.

"I have to read what?" Maddie spilled coffee over the table. Nikon jumped back in alarm, crashing into his water dish.

"Nothing elaborate, Dr. Temple. The Professor specifically forbade tedious serial eulogies. For him, as you perhaps understand from your similar perspective, literature alone spoke better than vacuous personal tributes." The woman's voice on the phone was reassuring but professional. "You'll go on right after Reverend Baines."

Maddie shrank like a worm under probe at the words "go on." It sounded like a variety show. Yet how touching of Malcolm to honor her. Had he in mind a tender ode or two? Christina Rossetti? Shakespeare? She searched her brain to recall the masters of his period but, with her prejudices, dredged up only pompous pentameters. His age bespoke prose and drama, not poetry. "What kind of literature?"

A rustling of paper engendered a long pause. "A month ago he left me a copy of a poetry anthology that he especially prized. The selections are marked. I'm at the university tomorrow on another matter. I can drop it off."

Hunched balefully in her mailbox the next day was *The Stuffed Owl*, the book that wouldn't die. Maddie paged through the pencilled choices, snorting like a restive mare. Not that she couldn't recite verse with easy grace, but this performance would make her look like an idiot. The department, effete snobs under the surface, would snicker at every awkward syllable, each hackneyed phrase. And how would the more innocent mourners react? The best course was to act as serious as possible, use offense as defense.

That Saturday Nancy drove Maddie to the church, her rusty Taurus station wagon coughing clouds of burning oil beneath a bumper sticker reading: "A Woman Is Like a Teabag. You Don't Know How Strong She Is Until She Gets Into Hot Water."

"God, I haven't been to services since I had to lasso my kid," the secretary said. "Gave up on that when the smart aleck ran off into the woods."

"When it comes to organized religion, I prefer Clough's 'The Latest Decalogue,' " Maddie said. " 'Thou shalt not steal; an empty feat,/ When it's so lucrative to cheat.' Or better yet, 'No graven images shall be/ Worshipped, except the currency.' "

"Speaking of currency, wonder who'll get the pot?" Nancy chipped in. "Thirty-five years here at Copper. Never married. Tidy house, but no mansion. Once I saw him chuckling over the Dow. Told me he popped his cash into mutual funds a dog's age ago. Lots of fun and less risky than stocks. And as for relatives, he was quiet as a mouse."

"So his housekeeper said. *Cui bono?* I suppose we'll find out when the will is read."

The Church in the Wildwood was a fieldstone building with a miniature Gothic grace, scarlet ivy nipping at the clerestory windows, a lead spire visible for miles, and pastoral countryside framing the scene like a Constable painting. All it lacked was a drooling glebe cow. Instead of parking near the church, Nancy picked a remote area off the asphalt. To Maddie's surprised look, she explained, "Reverse doesn't work anymore. I'm limping along until another two paychecks."

"For heaven's sake, Nancy. I can let you have—"

"No way. I'm stubborn about that. But thanks for the offer."

Over one hundred people had come to pay tribute to Malcolm. Some she didn't recognize, neighbors, perhaps, or members of his historical society. Copper University was represented by President Bowdler, Dean Nordman, and other administrators. Rick, George, and Gary formed a stoic departmental male bastion in the second row, Marie behind them, passing a handkerchief to Mrs. Bach, dressed in black bombazine widow's weeds and an enormous gauzy hat with a foot-long feather. Grace sat alone in a corner, her head bowed. Not surprisingly, Anisha and Reggie hadn't come. SWINC had voted with its feet.

Maddie and Nancy eased into a pew, raising the padded kneeler for more foot room. "I'm only following instructions. Bear with me," Maddie said, briefing the secretary on her reluctant role. She distracted herself by leafing through the prayer book, gratified to find that the original Cranmer prayer book was still in use: "We have left undone those things which we ought to have done, And we have done those things which we ought not to have done, And there is no health in us."

A roseate kaleidoscope of light streamed through the stained glass windows of the small church, flashing jewels from a Jacob's ladder scene across Maddie's hands. The fan vaulting with fluted Ionic columns of gray stone led the gaze heavenward with the illusion of space and height. Carved oak benches and intricate woodwork on the choir screens focused on the pulpit, fashioned from the bow of the *Iron Maiden*, a fishing boat which Superior had claimed the year the *Titanic* went down.

Dr. Baines, a senatorial man of seventy, delivered an all-purpose eulogy laced with customary scripture from Jeremiah and Revelations: "Weep ye not for the dead, neither bemoan him." He followed with the assurance that "they may rest from their labors; and their works do follow them." Maddie felt a twinge in her heart for Malcolm. He had steered the department through the choppy waters of feminist lit (later women's lit), black lit (later Afro-American lit), native lit (later Aboriginal lit), gay lit (later alternative lifestyle lit), and finally Upper Peninsula lit (later Youper lit). True to another prophet, Josiah, these courses had gone "the way of all the earth" as their more militant supporters graduated and other splinter groups arose.

Introduced by the good doctor's sepulchral tones, Maddie rose with knees watery as the *Iron Maiden*'s grave. Funerals were not her forte, though if she continued monitoring the obituaries, she'd might as well join the jovial survivors' club which her father and his cronies used as an excuse for bingo and bowling. "In addition to bearing the sterling qualities Reverend Baines has so well documented, Malcolm Driscoll was a man of wry humor," she began, suppressing her soprano into an alto. "His wit will be missed. I have been asked to read from his favorite poems, those which gaze upon death with a lyrical fortitude long gone from our material century." With an earnest expression, she firmed up her shoulders in a charcoal gray double-breasted light wool suit, silver leaf pin on the lapel. Everyone shifted in their seats, expectant. Pray God she wouldn't mix a metaphor, dangle a modifier, or utter a Spoonerism like the "queer old dean" instead of the "dear old queen." Patrick Nordman exchanged a glance with Flo, who sat next to her husband. Madame Chairman was dressed in jet black chiffon, her blonde hair gleaming like a tiara at an inaugural ball.

"John Dryden was the leading light of Malcolm's beloved Restoration period, so I will begin with 'The Faculty at Work,' concerning the death of Augustus Caesar." She recited a series of rhyming couplets, ending with: " 'No racks could make the stubborn malady confess.' " The room was silent. Outside, a lone chickadee warbled optimistic notes in proof against the raw October day.

Few were spared the lash. It hit the seventeenth century hard with Crashaw and Vaughn, skipped more lightly through the eighteenth century except for Colly Cibber, receiving his just desserts, nipped at Keats and Burns, flogged the Victorians, Tennyson, the Brownings, then jumped across the pond to snap at Longfellow and Poe.

" 'Tis all the same with Harry Gill;/ Beneath the sun, beneath the moon/ His teeth they chatter, chatter still.' " Wordsworth passed the crowd without a blink. Then she read lines by Alexander Smith: " 'My heart is in the grave with her—/ The family went abroad.' " Flo's right eye began to twitch. What was her problem? Shakespeare had missed the blast.

Rick seemed to be nodding off, chin dropping over a crooked clip-on tie. Time for a few biting consonants from Alfred Austin, poet laureate from 1896 to 1913: " 'Then I fling the fisherman's flaccid corpse/ At the feet of the fisherman's wife.' " A certain brio, she thought, bracing herself in the prow of the ship as a slight cough came from Marie's direction.

She checked her watch discreetly. "Closer to home, I'd

162

like to conclude with the words of Julia Moore, the Sweet Singer of Michigan, a prophetess without honor and recognition in our own Great Lakes State. Her first volume of verse in the 1870s went into three editions. Violent death was her calling: the Civil War, the yellow fever epidemic, the Chicago Fire. Those of us in the English Department involved in publication will sympathize with her trenchant observations as Julia fought back bravely against her critics with the modest confession, 'Literary is a work very difficult to do.' " Maddie watched Reverend Baines nod understandingly, his sermons notorious for turgidity. She launched the final offering: " 'Ashtabula Bridge disaster/ Where so many people died/ Without a thought that destruction/ Would plunge them 'neath the wheel of tide.' "

Closing the book, she flashed a beatific smile at the audience, rolling the cadences like a television evangelist. "And I know, yes, I know, dear friends and colleagues, that Malcolm is looking down on us today with a grin on his face and a warmth in his heart." Damn right. It was his finest quarter of an hour.

The organ segued into "Lead on, O King Eternal" as Maddie took her seat. Nancy flashed her an OK sign. Minutes later as they were filing out, Florence sidled up, face mottled as the onyx on the baptismal font. "I don't care if it was his last wish. You should have had better sense. We'll be the laughingstock of the university."

Sticking out her tongue at Flo's rapidly disappearing back, Marie took Maddie's arm and squeezed it with surprising power. "A verray, parfit send-off! I'm offended that you left out Chaucer, or wasn't Sir Thopas bad enough?"

They stood for a moment in front of a pebble path winding from the church along a row of fragrant weeping cedars. "Malcolm loved the wildflowers in that cemetery near his

house. I'll transplant some day lilies by his grave next spring,"
Maddie whispered.

A tall woman with prematurely white hair approached as
Maddie wove her way toward the group. "Dr. Temple," she
said, extending a firm hand, long and slim as her swan neck.
Her makeup was understated, without the garish red lipstick
that might give a sepulchral cast to her alabaster complexion.
"I'm Bridie Pedderson. You were marvelous. Frankly, I'd
rather read a city parking statute than dare poetry." She never
cracked a smile. Was the woman serious?

Thanking her, Maddie held out the book, but Bridie shook
her head. "You earned it. And now that we've met, I should
tell you that Malcolm remembered you in his will. All the
beneficiaries have been invited to my office on Swardson
Street at six o'clock this coming Monday."

Mentioned in the will? In astonishment, Maddie tried to
rise above the cliché. And who were the others? Some un-
known relatives? Mrs. Bach? She joined the mourners at
graveside, where a metal box waited on a blue velvet cloth beside a simple bronze plaque with the meager statistics of a
life. After a blissfully brief committal from Reverend Baines,
the male members of the department stepped forward. Elbowed by Flo, a smug look on her face, Bruce Andrews cast
the first dirt in a symbolic gesture. Maddie had seen him only
slenderly at faculty parties, a man sucked dry of life. He
looked to be in constant pain, as if an ulcer or some wasting
gastrointestinal disease gnawed at his core. Rumors circulated that his father had owned a string of hardware stores
but, shortly after Bruce's marriage, had lost his fortune in a
gold mining fraud in Northern Ontario. "Dust to dust, ashes
to ashes," he whispered, and Flo lip-synced the words. His
legs buckled as he passed the shovel to Gary.

"Into the tomb the old Queen dashes," Maddie added to

herself, an ode by a Babu poet on the death of Queen Victoria. She had grown rather fond of *The Stuffed Owl*. Laughter was a logical extension of common sense, and a healthy antidote for misery.

As the crowd turned away, Reverend Baines sniffed her out like a bloodhound, his eyes drooping and rheumy. "Your readings were most inspirational. I appreciate the classic poems. Nothing seems to rhyme these days. Professor Driscoll was reputedly a dab hand at verse as well. Too modest to have wanted his efforts made public, I suppose."

Apparently he, too, had received her performance in a straightforward manner. If that were true, likely so had the others. Only the department would appreciate Malcolm's last jest.

"I've been admiring your windows," she added out of politeness, "that handsome depiction of Jacob's ladder, the fire swirling upwards to heaven. On my travels to England, I visit the cathedrals. York with its Five Sisters masterpiece is my favorite. The resemblance of that variegated green glass to tapestry is uncanny." Maddie considered the established church an anachronism whose only positive contribution to civilization was medieval and Renaissance art, along with Mozart requiems and Bach cantatas.

"Then you must certainly join us when we dedicate Malcolm's window, a generous bequest." He blushed bright pink against his lacy white surplice.

"Really?" She hadn't regarded her chairman as particularly religious. Perhaps he nursed a traditional side. "What's the subject?"

Reverend Baines beamed at her interest. "Our Jacob's ladder from the Old Testament is rare. Most depictions expect earthly eyes to focus on the Redemption and Resurrection. Or the genealogy, the tree of Jesse, for example. No, his window has an unusual Marian theme. A photo or sketch serves as a guide. Often the benefactor, a lord or lady, wished to appear in the scene."

"Marian? Good heavens, don't tell me Malcolm is supposed to be Joseph."

He laughed softly and looked around before he spoke. "Few men would choose Joseph's role, noble saint that he was. Actually, it is Martha along with Mary."

"Who will do the work?"

"One of the talented Fine Arts professors at your university. As part of our arrangement, Professor Driscoll gave me a small picture to work from when the time came. Took it over to Theodore Birchem last week." At the curiosity in her face, he continued. "Pretty little girl. Quite an old photo. Never explained. Wouldn't have presumed to inquire. No doubt a loved one who had gone on before."

So Malcolm had a past before the dalliance with Mrs. Bach. A lively man with many layers. She would miss him. She paused near an ornate tombstone where a skull grinned at her. "Leonard Mandeville, Professor of Victorian Studies at Copper University, 1840-1910," one of many predecessors. What did one cynic say about an old friend? He could be dead or he could be teaching English.

Finally, the mourners pulled apart and began to file out of the churchyard, drops of freezing rain spattering on the grass to end their chats. A familiar figure in a tan overcoat approached from the parking lot. Lieutenant Phillips. She hadn't noticed him in the church. Maddie saw a police car beyond, idling its motor, clouds of exhaust in the heavy air.

"Florence Andrews?" Phillips read from a small card.

Detaching herself from Bruce, Flo turned abruptly with an annoyed look, as if confronting an encyclopedia salesman. "Yes?"

"You have the right to . . ."

Maddie heard little else as she watched the woman escorted away, shock and amazement on the faces of those who remained, a cartoon scene which clashed with the dignity of the ceremony. One by one, cars drove off, faster than suited the occasion. Oblivious to the drama, the church bell was tolling. For Malcolm or the rest of them?

Chapter Twenty

The next morning at dawn, Maddie got a call from her father. "Jerry has his ear to the ground. That gal in your department's been taken into custody. Grilled her like a hamburger all night. Seems like she'll be charged. With murder."

Maddie sat down abruptly at the breakfast nook. "On what evidence?"

A guffaw exploded, and she pulled the phone from her ear. "The babe was at the house, and no mistake. Mealy-mouthed husband lied like a trooper, but can't argue with fingerprints on a glass. Caught her red-handed. Your mother was right. The female is deadlier than the male."

The cozy con artist. Flo's stricken demeanor the day Malcolm died hadn't been honest grief but well-disguised fear. "Poison," she said abstractedly. A classic Renaissance ploy. But how ever did she get Malcolm to drink it?

"Jerry said she belonged to that death society. All adds up. Open and shut." He whistled the notes of the "Dragnet" opening. "Boy oh boy. Wish I could have been there when they nabbed her at the church. Should have gone to that funeral with you."

When she got to work, Nancy waved at her, her animated face matching the excitement in her voice. "Dean Nordman just called. He wants to see you toot sweet in his office." She paused and stapled some pages with satisfaction. "My guess is that he's going to ask you to take over. I mean, you've been

168

acting as coordinator. God, can you believe that Flo would go that far? The old man was a year away from a golden parachute."

On the way to the Administration Building, Maddie put one slow foot in front of the other, trying to build a convincing resolve. She had no ambitions for bean-counting, yet who else would want the job?

"Dear Maddie," said the Dean in his office. With a dazzling smile, he took her hand as if to raise it for a kiss, then enclosed it with his other hand, topped by a heavy diamond ring. "How kind of you to come so quickly. Do get comfortable." While he seated Maddie in one of two love seats, his secretary slipped silently across the thick broadloom with a service of coffee and muffins. To the impartial observer, the Dean was a plug ugly man, heavy lips and a bulbous nose, but a charming chameleon who could mesmerize women of any age with his resonant voice and magical demeanor. A charcoal suit boasted European tailoring alien to Stoddard, French cuffs recalling a more fastidious age. As he bent to pass her a bone china cup, a light scent of 4711 drifted in the air. "As you know, we have a problem."

No, *nein, nyet,* and *non,* she thought, steeling her backbone as she stared out the picture window to Superior's roiling waves miles in the distance. Administration had been an uninspiring burden. Houston, all the blood has been squeezed from the stone. "And?" she said, meeting his eyes, deep and slightly devilish, those compelling eyebrows.

The quicksilver voice matched the graceful scallop design of his cufflinks. "I'll get right to the point. Your department is in crisis. First poor Malcolm. Now this disgrace with . . ." He eased one finger around his starched collar. "A number of tricky budgetary challenges come up in the new year, and we need a capable leader. Funding has shrunk to a trickle. President Bowdler, and I shouldn't tell you this, has urged early retirement on the senior staff."

"If I sense the direction, I don't think I can help you. My teaching and research come first." Even though I may soon be an armchair traveler, she added to herself. No doubt the PD disbursements were on hold until the next millennium.

Stepping away, he buttered a muffin with the care of an artist and took an assessing bite, wiping his mouth neatly with a linen napkin. "There may be layoffs, even program cuts. Bowdler's combining departments right and left. Someone should man the barricades to protect the English faculty." An elaborate sigh sounded like a veiled threat. "If need be."

Maddie thought for a moment, her blood pressure rising. Who else? Marie had her family. Trust this to Rick? Pill-popping George? Gary had no tenure. Surely not Grace, haunted by personal anguish, real or imagined.

Silence filled the room as a tiny gleam ignited the Dean's eyes. He watched her carefully, then consulted a sheet. "I think we could see our way to an extra . . . two thousand a month."

How many bitter winters ahead until retirement? The Probe had over a hundred thousand miles. November to April, its seats felt like plywood. And the heater hesitated like a petulant diva, even though the squirrel's nest had been removed. A couple of months for a down payment on a comfortable Buick?

She surveyed the row of shiny golf trophies on his shelf, drained her cup and deposited it precisely on the silver platter, then raised an index finger. Dean Nordman watched with the corner of his mouth curled into a cautious smile. When Maddie cleared her throat, from a drawer he drew out a page of gray bond paper flecked with dark threads. Uncapping a pen, he prepared to write as Maddie spoke with assurance. "On the following conditions . . ."

Back in the department, Nancy flashed an inquiring look. "Until June," Maddie said. "I'm not cut out for this. And stop grinning." The Dean had offered carte blanche. And by God, she'd keep both classes as well as figuring out a solution to the enrollment problem. How much would a web page cost?

In Malcolm's office, she sat for a while, the third occupant in hardly as many weeks. Flo's Renaissance library lined the bookcase, and a balding bust of Shakespeare faced a statue of Queen Elizabeth I. The carpet bore scuff marks and the scars of the cigarettes and pipes of chairmen past. At least his windows got a thorough cleaning. Still, she preferred her little warren far from the madding, or maddening, crowd. For now, she'd shift only the necessities. It was all temporary, she told herself as she collected the files the Dean had mentioned. Expenses, due dates, eternal meetings.

Out of curiosity, she explored the in/out basket. Only one letter, unsealed. Addressed to *The Chronicle of Higher Education*, it advertised a one-year nineteenth-century American literature post to begin in the fall. Flo was sending out feelers before Gary's tenure had been discussed in committee. "Underhanded snake," she muttered, and tossed it into the wastebasket. Searching for a pencil in a drawer, under some folders she unearthed a pack of letters with a rubber band. "Dearest Froo-Froo." Gray-flecked bond stationery, the Dean's angular handwriting. What could, should, and would she do with this? It merely confirmed what she already suspected, and Flo was in enough trouble. Let sleeping dogs snore.

Chapter Twenty One

Sunday morning, Maddie watched a pewter sky lace the deck with the first snow. No major dump, just a petticoat for the cedars in her yard, the old woman plucking geese as the locals said. How like human nature to rhapsodize over the maiden blush of winter, ignoring the hell to come. She made a mental note to fill the bird feeder. Too late to rake leaves now, she thought smugly. Cozy as a pampered chickadee in her favorite armchair, a Telemann suite playing, a third coffee at her side, she was absorbed in a *Victorian Studies* article about pantheism in Meredith's "The Woods of Westermain."

When the doorbell rang, Nikon dropped his peanut butter rawhide bone, came to sudden attention, and roo-rooed, hocks wavering like Olive Oyl's knees. Poor mannie's frame was growing too fast for muscles to master. She put him into his cage and went to the front door. A figure stood in a clear plastic overcoat, snow coating the brim of a felt hat, features blurred, as if collecting for some underwater charity. At first alarmed, then embarrassed, Maddie removed her reading glasses. "Bruce, come in. You look frozen."

Head bowed, Bruce Andrews shambled into the house, depositing rubber overshoes neatly on the mat. Maddie took his coat and sat him by the gas fire, bringing a cup of hot coffee. His face was chalk-white. A cipher of a man, married to a frustrated overreacher, in his position as househusband, he had endured his share of humiliations.

Bruce nodded mute thanks as he cradled the cup for warmth, spidery fingers with pale, ribbed nails trembling around the handle. Blinking watery blue eyes, he tried to speak, but a consumptive cough sent him searching for a handkerchief. After apologizing, he began in halting tones. "Florence's asked to see you."

"To see me? I beg your pardon?"

Moisture dripped down his face, and he blotted it with his sleeve, pouches of puffy dark skin making raccoon eyes. "We didn't know where to turn. And since you're such a good friend, and you found Malcolm . . . and you're chairman now . . ." Bruce struggled for words, rubbed his bony hands together as if preparing a charm. What pathetic circumstances had tossed these two together, Maddie wondered. Perhaps with sound but selfish reasons, Flo had turned to the charismatic dean.

"Could you go over this afternoon?" The desperate tone left little room for a refusal. Another spasm shook his shoulders, and he clutched at his narrow chest.

For a moment Maddie wondered if he had a heart problem. "To the jail? I suppose so, but I don't know what—"

"If you see her, Florence will think of something. She always does," Bruce said. Mentioning that he had to drive his daughter to a dance lesson, he retrieved his soggy coat and clutched her hand as he fumbled out the door toward a white Jeep Cherokee. His clasp felt like cold tendons on an uncooked turkey, alive enough to have strength to die.

All concentration interrupted, Maddie settled her notes for later and donned her parka. Friend? Not under the most inflated definition. Flo had no friends, only tools. Did she expect Maddie to lie? Furnish some trumped-up excuse?

The snow was turning to rain. She scooped muck from the windshield and started slowly out of the drive, insured by four snow tires. Ed laughed at the unscientific concept for a front-wheel-drive. At a stop sign, she watched an idiot in a TransAm with Tennessee plates skew onto the road, spinning his wheels. Fishtailing, he nearly blindsided a lady propelled across the crosswalk by a golden retriever. Motorists with heavy feet were as bad as those who lumbered onto the street without defrosting their windows, maneuvering ten miles under the speed limit like a tank with a tiny window.

Years had passed since she had visited the old city police building. It crouched like a brick bulldog in the middle of downtown Stoddard, quietly sorting out the drunk and disorderly, the shoplifters, the untidy marital broils. When her father had worked there, handouts from the staff were a bonus: jellybeans, pop, and the ubiquitous doughnuts. As she entered, a trout-faced man in a rumpled brown suit lurched past, leaned against a wall, and vomited discreetly into a trashcan. Just getting released from the drunk tank? He reeked of gin, the battered briefcase a puzzling addition.

Inside, efforts had been made at modernization. The huge oak desk on a platform for the duty sergeant anchored a clean, bright reception area. Long oak benches had been replaced by pastel molded pods, planking covered in easy-clean tile. A teenaged girl in a leather mini-skirt and knit top exposing four inches of concave belly sat listlessly sipping a soda and nodding at a tall man with a crown of gray curls framing a bald spot.

As he turned, his lined face lit up. "Hi, Short Stuff." Jerry Horowitz made a motion to pat her head. "Should have drunk that milk."

"I still hate it. Thank God for cheese." She explained her purpose in coming.

At the desk he pulled out a form for her signature. "Yep, we booked the little woman. What a hard case. Would have been out sooner if she hadn't flapped her gums about legal aid eligibility. Fat chance with that job at the university. Then she kept dickering with lawyers to find the cheapest one in the whole damn peninsula. Ralph Pool, an old rummy. Left a minute ago."

Protocol wasn't big city style in Stoddard. No body searches, no metal detectors. Down a dingy hall lined with bare light bulbs dangling from the ceiling amid crumbling asbestos-coated pipes, Jerry escorted her into the conversation room, leaving a guard yawning outside the door, reading a *Playboy*.

Maddie brushed white flakes from her shoulders, trying not to inhale, then waited in a plastic stacking chair with a suspicious dark stain. Minutes later, Flo shuffled in so slowly that Maddie checked for manacles. Ms. Chairman seemed to have aged a hundred years, like the elephant George Orwell shot, primal knowledge of the deadly bullet entering all cells at once. She wore a dark blue jumpsuit with a bright yellow SPD stenciled on the back. With a whimper, she sank into the opposite chair and put her head in her hands.

"So you were Malcolm's visitor. Why did you lie?"

The woman swallowed heavily and wiped a shaky hand across her brow, bloodshot eyes bleary with fatigue. Without makeup, hair straggling from a few clips, she was a poor thing, a plucked bird. "My God, Maddie. I was the last one to see him. Now they say he was poisoned. That frumpy Mrs. Bach is hardly a prime suspect. What's your conclusion, or shouldn't I ask? I know you've always hated me."

Maddie waved off the self-pitying ploy. "How are they treating you?"

"Would you, even you, like to wear these abominable clothes? I'm getting a vicious rash." She rubbed at the coarse denim with a groan. "And the food. Grilled cheese, hot dogs. Not to mention facing the electric chair."

"Rather dramatic. We don't have capital punishment in Michigan any more."

"I didn't vote for the left-wing weaklings that changed the law, but God grants small favors." She nodded listlessly, blinking back convincing tears. "This will kill Bruce. What will the children do without me? Melanie's dance lessons. Thirteen-year-olds bleed you dry. Little vampires in Nikes and Tommy Hilfiger. Jason is starting college next year."

Not in my class, she hoped. Five Argonauts already, along with a conflagration of Ashleys named after a soap opera character when their mothers were teens. "Let's start over. What were you doing at Malcolm's?"

"This isn't going to look good." She shifted in her chair, ran a shaky hand through her greasy hair, fumbled with a loose strand, and tossed the clip onto the floor.

"Get to the point. I'm as eager as you to leave this place." The stale, windowless room was stirring her claustrophobia.

"Then listen carefully. In September I borrowed some departmental cash to pay for Melanie's orthodontistry. Do you know what that costs? Four thousand dollars. And our miserly family health plan doesn't cover so-called elective procedures. I didn't want my daughter chewing like a rabbit. To cover the shortfall, I planned to cash in some savings bonds due in October."

"You took that much?" Maddie gave a small gasp.

Gnawing a corner of her thumb, Flo caught herself and stopped. "Only five hundred for the down payment. Pin money. Malcolm called me over to his house to twit me. Some joke, the bastard." Her tones gained confidence as she straightened in the chair. "If you doubt me, ask Nancy. I'm no embezzler. Paid it back with interest. This is a stupid technicality."

"What did you tell the police?"

"Nothing about the . . . loan, certainly. I wasn't going to cut myself off at the ankles." She crossed her legs as if illustrating the point. "Said that we talked about some budgetary concerns. I stayed long enough to drink some wine. Doesn't that prove what I said, that Malcolm was kidding? Damn that glass."

"So there weren't any bad feelings? No argument?"

"Mellow as an old pillow, well into the brandy by the time I got there. What's new?" She glared at Maddie. "This has to be a hideous accident. Maybe he had something clinically wrong with him. God knows he looked like an ad for Norvasc. Could we get a second opinion? Doctors up here in the Gulag are such hicks."

"The autopsy was quite conclusive."

"So maybe he committed suicide after contemplating the ravages of age. I admit that I was a fool to lie about having been there. Destroyed my credibility and when they got to the hemlock, it was all over." For the first time, a look of honest pain crossed her sharp face. "My mother suffered incredible horrors from cancer. I joined the society, bought her that book, but she died before using it. Besides, hemlock isn't even mentioned. Just combinations of pills."

"It is an odd poison."

"That classics course I taught years ago: *The Dialogues.* Then Mother. Even our village idiots can connect the dots." She narrowed her eyes. "I'm sure someone put them onto me out of spite. A serpent in our own department."

"Your face is on everyone's dartboard. Even before Malcolm died, you arranged for Marie and George to lose

177

their classes, denied Rick his PD allotment, and then attacked Gary." Her voice turned accusative, underlaid with disgust. "He's a great teacher. Why are you so vindictive about where he publishes? And you planned to sabotage his tenure, didn't you? I saw that letter to the *Chronicle*. A bit premature, wasn't it?"

Flo squirmed in her jumpsuit as the pants rode up the trim ankles. "Richard III had it right. How have I offended unless by my leniency? Gary's a lightweight. Rick's a lazy doper. As for Marie, we have to face facts, move on with the times like living languages do. The last speaker of Dalmatian died in 1895, and who's crying? I would have retired her, not let her muck on with those Lit Survey courses. Malcolm was too soft. Yesterday's man, an administrator who wanted to be loved. Now the crunch has come, and a pragmatist is needed."

"But Shakespeare is still popular, lucky you."

Flo thrust out her chin with a satisfied smirk lighting her face. "We all make our choices and have to live with them. At least it's still intelligible."

"So you saw yourself as the Avenging Budgetary Angel who had to do the dirty work Malcolm avoided."

"Exactly. And now I'm paying the price for my candor. But I didn't kill him. That's why I wanted you here. My lawyer's an idiot. We need answers. Who hated the old man? What about those slimeballs at SWINC? He caused them enough grief. Maybe they framed me." Her thoughts tumbled out full of B movie slang. Worse yet, the choppy syntax was starting to sound like Barney's.

Maddie tightened her lips in reluctant resignation, against her better judgment feeling a rare twinge of sympathy. If Flo had killed Malcolm, why not with more aplomb? An obvious visit. Tell-tale fingerprints on the glass. Or was it a double-blind? Make herself look so guilty that . . . No, without New York City-style lawyers, too costly a gamble for pitifully small stakes. The dubious prestige of chairman of the English Department, a *Titanic* placing matchmaking ads for an iceberg. Malcolm had been cruising toward mandatory retirement, and everyone knew that the Dean was in Flo's pocket, or in some warmer place.

"Okay. SWINC deserves a look. Anything else?"

"Cover everything. Check his files. Maybe he fired someone years ago, though I doubt it. What about a spurned lover? An illegitimate child? Even a crazy neighbor?" She paused, massaging a wormlike pulse at her temple. "There is something else. I didn't consider it important at the time, but cleaning out the drawers, I found a note. Some inane thank-you. It's under Unfinished Business, in case a tax write-off is involved."

"That's all? Doesn't sound very promising."

Flo pounded the table, her face a thunderstorm. "I don't care. I'm innocent. And you're chairman now. Where's your loyalty?" Despite the bravado, she applied herself to a bleeding cuticle.

A knock sounded at the door, and the guard pointed to his watch. Maddie stood. "I'll do what I can. If you're really innocent, the truth should present itself. Is there anything you want? *De Profundis,* perhaps? Oscar might be some consolation."

Flo grew quiet, fixing her eyes on Maddie like a basilisk. "Tell Bruce to bring my Shakespeare, the leather one Mother gave me in high school. I'll read *Timon of Athens*. An outcast. That's what I am."

Chapter Twenty Two

A vicious sleet storm and a traffic advisory had followed Maddie home from the jail, so it wasn't until Monday that she checked Malcolm's cabinets. Surprised to find the department door still locked at nine thirty, she recalled that Nancy was having a "minor medical procedure," in womanese, a D and C. Later she'd verify the claim about the petty cash.

The office could have harbored ice cubes, more signs of budget cuts. Over the weekend, heat was turned to "keep moving." She pulled on an Icelandic sweater from the coat rack, reminding herself to tell her poetry students that the Crimean War generals had furnished names for two excellent designs to the woollen industry, the cardigan and the raglan sleeve. "Into the valley of death," she said through chattering teeth, warming her hands at the steaming coffeemaker. George zipped by to check his mail, and Marie kicked the empty copier and swore an archaic oath full of gutturals. Maddie said, "I ordered a load of paper from the Biz Whiz at my expense. It should tide us over."

Malcolm's files were as disorganized as a kindergarten birthday party. "Unfinished Business" occupied three drawers. It took an hour and a gut-churning ocean of coffee to locate the note. No envelope or return address. Handwritten on ordinary paper. Nothing but a date, October 12, a week before he died. "God's thanks for your generosity. We thought that you might treasure one of his works." It was signed by a scrawl unreadable even to an English teacher accustomed to deciphering freshman garble. His works? What generosity? It sounded like a charity.

On the windowsill, a Christmas cactus shot forth optimistic blooms. The sole plant in the office, it never failed to distribute early cheer, riotous red-orange multiple lipsticks with a single antler emerging from a host of white stigmas tipped with yellow pollen. Nancy claimed that it thrived on neglect, a necessary quality at Copper. From a gallon of the secretary's drinking water, Maddie poured an oblation to its patient roots. "Hope springs eternal, Malcolm, despite your hatred of Pope."

After classes and an asinine meeting with two crabby chairmen about a policy on transfer credits from junior colleges, she ran her finger down her daybook, stopping abruptly at six o'clock circled. "Will," it read. William? No, Malcolm's will. Was she being included as administrator of a scholarship fund? Oddly enough, why hadn't Flo been tagged for duty? She'd been chairman at the time of the funeral.

With only half an hour to spare, Maddie decided that corduroy pants and the sweater would have to suffice. Downtown, she parked on Swardson Street. The Elliot Building had once been the city's premier hotel. Its Art Deco façade evoked a graceful and spirited period. Inside each floor were two concentric squares of rooms, the interior facing a five-story solarium complete with Boston ferns and elegant weeping fig trees. Dignitaries from Stoddard's more productive decades had stayed there. Even President McKinley had cruised through the year before he had been shot. Following the Crash of 1929, when two brokers had swan-dived from the upper floors, the venerable landmark had remained vacant until a canny entrepreneur with a generous heart for classic architecture had restored its patina and sublet to specialty businesses.

Watching Mrs. Bach exit a taxi and enter the building, Maddie did a double-take at a nearby pink limo with wheelchair logo, the driver lounging against the door, his hand flicking a cigarette. What was SWINC doing here? Suing the estate for libel or slander?

Inside the creamy marble foyer were entrances to a popular upscale restaurant and a wine bar. The fragrant wares of a premium tobacconist filled the air, along with arcade stores selling European kitchenware and fine leathers. Doric pillars, crystal chandeliers, and a sweeping staircase spoke eloquently of the glory days of high-flying copper magnates. She tossed a coin into the shimmering pool of a bubbling fountain centered with a replica of Michelangelo's *David* wearing a discreet maple leaf. After checking the board and ringing for the elevator, she found herself in a room with mirrored panels and ceiling, mahogany trim, and brass fixtures. A smiling octogenarian in a crisp brown uniform with gold braids asked in a cracked voice, "Going up?"

"Four, please." The circular control swirled expertly, bringing her to a carpenter's bubble-bead level at the landing. Opening the door with a flourish, the operator winked proudly.

Down the hall, Maddie opened the frosted glass panel marked Pratt, O'Brian and Pedderson. Inside the reception room, Mrs. Bach, dressed in dark purple, black scooped hat with veil, sat to one side on a love seat. Anisha, in a pure white sari, and Reggie, wearing an Armani suit, whispered conspiratorially in velvet wingback chairs, exchanging glances in apparent unease. Anisha turned a suspicious face to Maddie. "This has to be a cruel joke. That hateful man fought us at every step." Unable to disabuse her of the possibility, wondering if Malcolm had one last chortle up his heavenly sleeve, Maddie pursed her lips and took a seat next to Mrs. Bach. The old woman smiled weakly and gave a stoic sniff.

After a few words on the intercom, the secretary showed them into Bridie's office. An Aubusson carpet graced the shiny hardwood floor, along with fine antiques likely plucked from local estate auctions: a walnut and burl bookcase with teardrop pulls, a roll-top desk with a hundred tiny drawers, and a sideboard with mirror, scrolled fretwork, and a marble top. Heavy curtains framed the windows, flanked by large ceramic vases. With words of welcome, Bridie seated them in Eastlake side chairs with leather seats. Then as the room quieted, she read from a sheaf of paper. "To begin, Malcolm Driscoll wished to endow a scholarship fund for a senior English major doing a thesis on Pope. As I understand that you are now chairman, Professor Temple, you will oversee that gift."

Maddie nodded soberly, but with an internal somersault at the mention of Pope. Malcolm loathed the man who delivered biting satires from his groves at Twickenham, complete with artificial grotto and salaried hermit. No one raised an eyebrow, nor did she expect it. Who read "The Rape of the Lock" except for criminology students misdirected by the title?

Bridie continued. "Mrs. Bach, for your faithful service, you will receive fifty thousand dollars and title to his car and residence. He wanted me to tell you that you were the finest actress since Sarah Siddons. I can't place the name, but perhaps the meaning is personal," she said with a wry smile.

Mrs. Bach's wrinkled lips quivered bravely, and she raised her veil to honk into a handkerchief.

Bridie's graceful neck turned again to Maddie. "Dr. Temple, Malcolm also wanted you to be able to take your annual trip to England this year, despite the freeze in professional development funds. He has left you five thousand dollars. And his Toby jugs." Maddie relaxed her grip on the chair arms and imagined the bright July sun of York gleaming through the Five Sisters windows. Jugged hare and nut-brown ale at the Piebald Mare. The old dear.

As all eyes focused on them, Anisha and Reggie shifted. He took her hand and whispered into her ear. The lawyer tapped a pen and cleared her throat. "And along with the scholarship, there is another recent change, made the week before he died." The room grew silent, as if savoring the last prayerful moments before an astral impact. "The bulk of the estate goes to the Students With Individual Needs Center at Copper University."

Anisha gasped, and Maddie watched Reggie adjust his silk tie under a bobbing Adam's apple. Were they calculating how much was left? Perhaps they thought that Malcolm had whittled it to a penny as a final insult. But Nancy's hints about investments indicated that the remains of the day were considerable.

Leaning forward, the pink tip of his tongue probing in adder fashion, Reggie asked, "And how much is that?"

Bridie folded her hands and aimed a steely look, as if in search of a serpent fork. "About two million dollars in mutual funds." Anisha struggled for breath, one small hand clawing her throat. The lawyer rose to fetch a glass of water from a silver service on the side table.

Reggie's public relations senses recovered as they left the office. He was expansive, shaking hands all around. "Anisha told me how much you've helped one of our students," he said to Maddie, flashing unnaturally white teeth fresh from bleaching. "And as for Malcolm Driscoll, he seems to have experienced a change of heart."

"Almost an epiphany, if I might say. So providential that he was murdered after easing his conscience." Maddie monitored their expressions, then waved her hand casually. "But of course, Florence Andrews has been charged."

Anisha took Reggie's arm, releasing clouds of jasmine perfume. Then she spoke loudly, as if a covey of reporters lurked in the hall. "On that terrible weekend, we were in Detroit at a fundraising event sponsored by General Motors. Whatever our differences with Professor Driscoll, he was a colleague. Surely he has in fortunate hindsight given SWINC a miracle, but miracles are central to our philosophy. Now the swimming pool will proceed, and the exercise rooms as well. Bridge funding for staff will facilitate Rehabilitation Therapy and Sign Language programs. With the current state of affairs, it might have taken years."

Maddie passed a few hushed words with Bridie before heading for the elevator. "I'm unsure if this involves a breach of trust, but do you have any idea what made Malcolm change his mind? He was a fervent campaigner against SWINC. I'm surprised that—"

"Quite right. I wouldn't be able to comment." A question mark divided Bridie's milky brow, and her voice slowed in wonderment. "He seemed a different man on the day he altered his bequests."

"Different? Was he ill?"

"Subdued would be my description. As if he had learned something of great import. An odd blend of sorrow and relief."

Maddie offered Mrs. Bach a ride home. "Fancy that," the old woman said. "Giving his hard-earned nest egg to that Swinky Dink. Malcolm never mentioned anything about his business affairs. And that rude Reggie fellow. Men are such Bavarians. The car's welcome. Took my Maverick to the wrecking yard last week. Not sure what I'll do with the house, though. My seniors' condo is geared to income. Lots of activities. Bingo, euchre, and our annual play. I'm going to be the Grand Duchess in *Anastasia* directly I finish my stint in *Romeo and Juliet* at the university."

Maddie laughed at the success of her casting suggestion to Stephen Glogore. "It's a charming cottage. I'm sure you could get a fair price in the spring. Malcolm may have intended that you sell."

"Oh, I nearly forgot," Mrs. Bach added. "You'll get your invitation in the mail, engraved something posh. The Professor's remembrance dinner will take place Friday night. On his birthday. Thought it was fitting." She mumbled so quietly that Maddie had to strain to hear. "Good riddance to those blasted quail. And the partridge rides along for pâté."

Chapter Twenty Three

Tuesday Maddie spoke with Nancy. Seeing the secretary in conversation with a student, she passed through to Malcolm's office. Twisting a plastic ruler to the snapping point, Nancy had a "They don't pay me enough for this" look. The open door afforded Maddie a glimpse of the girl, an enormous battler built like a backhoe, thighs the size of logs in tights. "I demand to see the chairman. You're just a secretary. I know my rights."

Rights over responsibilities. The "Me" generation. *"In loco parentis,"* the old university ethic, retained only the middle word. Maddie cruised out, bland and official, eyebrows primed for attack. "What's the problem, Nancy?"

The woman sighed, her face flushed with irritation as she pointed to a calendar. "This student wants to drop a course. The deadline was a week ago."

Maddie raised her chin a millimeter, wondering if the lines of gold studs on the girl's ears were near meltdown from cranial steam. Her voice was low but firm. "Is there a medical reason, or some family emergency that prevented you from withdrawing?"

"My point hour's going to be . . ." The pudgy lips toyed with the F sound, eyes squeezing shut in last-minute self-control. "Messed up." Blowing out a frustrated breath, she whirled and banged out of the office.

"Thanks for the rescue. That babe probably beeps when she backs up," Nancy said.

"How did it go at the hospital the other day? Everything in its place?" Maddie asked.

Nancy patted her stomach, pleasantly rounded but far from fat. "A little dusting and cleaning. Frankly I can't wait until the Big M. Figure I'll be ahead ten bucks a month on tampons. Every penny counts with my kid. Roy doesn't get much building work in the winter. So what's the word on Flo?"

"I can't believe I went to see her. Bruce begged me."

"To the jail? Tell all."

When questioned about the petty cash, Nancy gave a shrug. "I'd love to see the little worm caught at something." She choked back a breath, as if remembering the murder charge. "But she paid it back. Malcolm was pretty casual about petty cash. Dipped into it himself when there was a wine sale, and I've taken lunch change. Long as dollars balance by the end of the semester, tra la la. No bloodhounds like at the Accounting Office, thank God."

"So Flo spoke the truth for once. If only she hadn't lied about being at Malcolm's." She poked her tongue into her cheek. "Thinks she's been 'framed.' Wants me to find out how he got poisoned. Some idiocy about a plot against her."

Nancy began stabbing a sharp pencil into a cork ball holder. "She had enough enemies to fill two stadiums. But hold on. This is ridiculous. No one would kill Malcolm to implicate her."

"I agree. So where do I start?"

Their eyes met in perfect understanding. "SWINC. Where else?"

"That was Flo's choice, too, but here's the kicker. I was at the reading of the will. Mrs. Bach got the house and car, the old doll left me money to go to England, but the huge portion of his estate went to SWINC. Can you believe it?"

An astonished laugh burst from the secretary. "No way, Jose. He never changed his mind. Like a dog with a bone."

Maddie sighed. "It's a comic opera. First SWINC had a reason to want him out of the way as an embarrassing gadfly. Flip-flop. Then a motive to send him to heaven as a two-million-dollar friend." She walked over and poured a coffee, sipping in reflection. "I still can't believe Reggie and Anisha had any idea about the bequest. Nobody's that good an actor. A double Academy Award. Anyway, they were in Detroit when Malcolm died. Seen by a hundred people."

"Exactly. The perfect alibi. With that kind of money at stake, they could have hired half of Michigan."

"But it goes to the Center, so I don't see the benefit to them personally."

Nancy gazed out the window. "If I'd known about the money, I would have married the old coot myself. Twenty years ago, more than once he . . ." She pursed her lips and stared toward the door as if hoping for a convenient interruption.

Maddie gave her a curious look. Nancy had been fresh from secretarial school when she joined the department. How those mini-skirts and trim legs had turned heads. "So what now? The police interviewed all of us, and came up with Flo. Yet for all her hatefulness, I believe her. We're at a dead end." After a moment of silence, and a sudden blink, she retrieved a slip of paper from her pocket. "In case someone from the past had a grudge, I checked the files, went back through his history as a chairman, hirings and firings. Zero. Flo mentioned an odd thank-you note. This is all I found. Seems to refer to some kind of art."

Nancy gave it a knowing glance, then went to a tall cabinet to remove a plastic bag from a shelf. "This came a week or so before his . . ." She lowered her eyes. "He opened it, tossed away the packaging, then went to his office and shut the door. He was in there a long time. Never explained. Next I heard he wanted to put it on the wall, but maintenance never got a 'round tuit.' "

Maddie unwrapped a small, plainly framed painting. A bright fall landscape, the brilliant golds, reds, and browns in compelling combinations. Blue water lapped around an island in the background. She was no art history major, but there was something curious about the thick brush strokes, the heavy overlay of paint, like the French impressionists: Seurat's distinctive technique, but dabs instead of dots. Hardly Malcolm's taste, she thought, surveying the intricate Hogarth etchings along the office wall. *Gin Lane* had been his favorite.

Leaving Nancy to her work, Maddie took the picture to her desk. Several ads for new stoves sat to one side, one planned Christmas present for her extra responsibilities. She reached toward a thin red metal box Malcolm used for paper clips. A candy container sent to the troops during the Boer War, which she'd brought him from the Camden Market antique stalls in London. It bore an embossed image of Queen Victoria. South Africa 1900. "I wish you a Happy New Year," her script said. Maddie assembled a few links mindlessly, dangling them in self-hypnosis. What about that photo for his memorial window? Was there a connection? And could Reg and Anisha milk the bequest for their own purposes? Malcolm's radical change of mind had to be the key to his death. When the last clip joined the chain, she picked up the box. It still smelled of chocolate.

Nancy stuck her head around the corner and waved an envelope. "These sessional requests for January and your new scale have to go to Payroll, but Marie needs a test typed pronto. Can you . . ."

A lungful of fresh-frozen air would be welcome. Shrugging into the mammoth down coat that would be her movable house until March, Maddie pulled an angular Norwegian felt hat onto her head and churned briskly through blowing snow to the Administration Building, its bell tower chiming out "The Lusty Month of May." After dropping off the paperwork, she paused in the main corridor. The summer staff might have missed Glenys' creative double-billing, but one man kept an eye on financial pie plates swirling on sticks at Copper. Were there anything suspicious with SWINC's operations, Paul Straten would know. The university would be buzzing over the news.

She climbed to the second floor, passed through swinging doors to Accounting, and knocked at the last cubicle. Paul was inspecting the bottom of a computer mouse. "This damn rodent has been castrated. No wonder it won't move."

"Would you?" Her glance gravitated towards his lap.

Wincing, he removed papers and a squash racquet from a chair and sat her down. A transplanted Charlestonian, Paul had a wisp of a summer-soft South Carolinian dialect, which she savored like a rare wine. About forty-five, curly brown hair touched with gray, other than a stubborn mini-paunch, he kept in fine trim.

When she mentioned Flo's arrest and her suspicions about SWINC, he touched an ink-stained finger to his lips. "I'm afraid they're as clean as anyone, if you know what that means. Even on a small scale, it adds up. Haven't you ever called long distance on a private matter, taken home a ream of paper, or a pack of pens for your own use?"

She bristled and leveled her eyes at him. "Of course not!"

"You may be a certified saint in the corporate world, but make no mistake. The university is a business, as prone to pillaging as IBM. We're trying to run down a part-time lecturer

191

in the Forestry Department who strolled off with a five-thousand-dollar camera lens used for spotting deer. As for Anisha and Reggie, a few expensive lunches, that donated limo that seems to cover the Midwest . . . all justified for the coddling of benevolent patrons. Reggie's raised a potful of private money. But think about it. If they wanted to slop from a loaded trough, they'd pick a more salubrious farm than our floundering university. We're down to our underwear. Watch the students howl at the ten percent tuition hike next fall."

Her fears about the plummeting enrollment received a further blow. "Ouch. But what about the legacy? Could they touch it?"

He rotated the gooseneck lamp on his desk until it cast a circle on her hand. "I heard the details. Turns up the spotlight. They won't be able to hide an escargot, not with Bridie Pedderson administering the trust. She'll make them balance the till to the last penny. If you want a villain, bet on Flo. She always was a cagey one. Played squash with her once and she cheated on every call."

Chapter Twenty Four

On a lunch break, Maddie visited the Webster Fine Arts Building, a handsome structure distinguished by floor-to-ceiling glass in the studios and a Grecian frieze above the portico. Without benefit of double-panes and modern caulking, the building was a thermological disaster area. Heavy sweaters were *de rigeur* in winter.

As she entered the foyer, she noted with irritation that the legendary Babcock collection of classic American art featuring the Group of Eight had been replaced by a multimedia selection of student work. A small tape recorder duct-taped to the wall played a rap song, indecipherable except for "Fiddler, Riddler, and Midler" beside a dark canvas where coarse animal hair of different shades formed a collage. In a sealed case, a greening sculpture of Jennifer Lopez's lips pouted, carved from Spam, alongside a can with the familiar key on a velvet pillow. Scattered on risers were rusted metal forms, like those littering old mine sites or abandoned farms. Giant mesh cobwebs with clinging plastic octopuses and fishing globes hung from the ceilings, brushing her head. Three students were eagerly taking notes, nodding and gesturing in serious appreciation. Modern art? Post-modern? What next, the Apocalypse?

An information board by the elevator listed the sections of the building. Painting, printmaking, pottery, weaving. She roamed the halls, peeking in at a clay-ridden woman sculpting a giant version of a broken thumb, another sketching a bowl of uncooked spaghetti. "Do you know where I can find Theodore Birchem?" she asked.

A few minutes later she entered a spacious room brightened by multiple skylights, but so cold that she could see her breath. Working with a blowtorch at a long trestle table was a bearded man in heavy brown coveralls, ponytail trailing down his back. By his feet, a portable electric heater churned out warmth. Fearing to distract him, she waited. Boxes of colored glass stood nearby strips of metal. The air held a burnt industrial tang, not unpleasant, but purposeful, more satisfying than word-crunching and the plying of dog-eared thesauri.

Finally he switched off the torch and raised his protective glasses, wiping sweat from his eyes. "Are you Theodore Birchem?" she asked, moving closer.

"Ted's fine. Welcome to my lair," he replied in a deep, pleasant voice.

She introduced herself as a colleague of Malcolm, walking in admiration around the large piece before him, a life-sized image of a woman in a flowing blue robe. Opaque white glass, the face had not yet emerged. "How lovely. Up close the effect is so fragile, but they've endured, haven't they, Rouen and Chartres still converting skeptics through sheer beauty."

"Yes," he said. "And we've returned to the original formulas: silver, tin, antimony impurities. Much stronger than pure lead. Some of the Victorian stuff is falling apart."

"The blue is amazing."

"Can't compare with authentic medieval windows. Blue's the one secret they kept. If you know your Bible, it's a Martha motif, sister of Mary. I'm working from a photo, but we can't duplicate the face. It's only a resemblance."

"Could you show me the picture? Reverend Baines told me about it at the funeral."

He removed his gloves, inspected his hands and, when satisfied, disappeared into a small office, returning with a small snapshot similar to Maddie's maiden efforts with a Brownie.

She rotated the picture at angles to the light, trying to eliminate the distracting glare from her glasses. Black and white, taken perhaps at the end of World War II. The girl was a fairy queen of fifteen or sixteen, modeling a white knee-length frock with a self-conscious but proud look, hands folded primly in front. Dark hair in the Andrews Sisters style her mother had worn in her wedding picture was rendered more striking by a widow's peak. On her feet were Mary Janes, shiny flat-heeled black shoes with a strap. Maddie's Catholic girlfriends had said that the nuns warned against too much polishing lest the surface might reflect nether regions. Behind the scene was a large building bearing advertisements too small to read.

She turned to Ted with a question. "I know it sounds odd, but would you mind if I made a copy?"

At his puzzlement, she continued. "Malcolm died under suspicious circumstances. That's putting it mildly. He was poisoned."

"So I heard. Far out," he said, and she placed him as a hippie who had found a home. "Got to watch yourself around here, too. Plenty of evil stuff. Retired a guy last year with neurological damage from paint fumes." He pointed at the ventilation ductwork. "Lots more preventive measures now."

"This picture may relate to a past which would explain some unusual behavior before his death. One of our colleagues has been accused of the murder. Florence Andrews."

He snorted like a friendly bull. "Andrews. Big mouth at HAWG. What a dickhead, gender aside, and pardon my French." He studied her studiously bland expression. "Do you disagree?"

She coughed, not so much from the dust as from discretion. "It would be tempting to have her out of our hair. But I admit that the evidence seems circumstantial." Then she recalled the other reason for her visit. "Ted, now that I'm picking your brain, indulge me once more. A painting arrived at Malcolm's office immediately before his death. We have no idea who sent it. Could you—"

"Like to help, but I'm no canvas man. That'd be Brian Turner. Find him on the second floor, west wing."

Taped to Brian's office was a handwritten message about a conference in Los Angeles that week. Palm trees and balmy breezes, car jackings and drive-by shootings. Thank God for crime-fighting blizzards. Scrawling him a note and tucking it behind his timetable, she bunched up her parka, pulled on woollen mitts, and headed for the car. Snow had been falling heavily, and the wind was swirling drifts around anything perpendicular. She yanked unsuccessfully on the door, then resorted to a no-fail hockey block with her hips. Starting the engine, she chose a weapon from the impromptu arsenal, scraper on one end and brush on the other. The old wooden type snapped by Lincoln's birthday, but this model was made of high impact plastic. Toiling manfully, she raked and swept, glad to be wearing lined jeans.

Maddie took the snapshot to a photo store near campus and spent an hour padding around the Booknook next door, where she picked up a Pre-Raphaelite calendar with *The Chess Players* and *The Light of the World*. God's favorite Son would have been perplexed at Malcolm's locked door mystery. "I must be about my father's business," she said with a grin. "Constabulary's duties to be done."

The rush job cost twenty dollars. To better study the details, she'd ordered a blowup. Stopping for a coffee at Ruby's Pasty Shop, she took a seat facing the street. Feeble November light trickled through the windows as she took out the enlargement and fished reading glasses from her pocket. Now she could make out the advertisements on the brick wall. Ferrous Mountain Shoes. Tige the dog and a grinning Buster Brown. Practical, durable, and in this toss-away world, unfashionable. Ferrous Mountain was a small town in the central ore range, one hundred miles south of Stoddard. She picked up a pound-sized version of the Cornish original, flaky pastry filled with a spicy mixture of beef, potatoes, carrots, and turnips.

"You're trying to lure me into bad habits, veggies or not," Nancy said as Maddie returned, slicing the treat with the accuracy of a diamond cutter and placing each half on a napkin. "Ferrous Mountain. Malcolm's old haunt. Never wanted anyone to know he came from a hick town. 'Eddication' got him out and he stayed out."

"Is his family still there, do you think?" Hungry from the first scent of success, she enjoyed the tender morsels of pasty.

"Really, Maddie. Unless they're nearly ninety, his parents would be pushing up daisies now." Her quick hand snagged the phone and punched buttons for long-distance information.

"Driscoll in Ferrous Mountain. I don't know the address." A minute passed, and she shook her head, hanging up. "No such luck. Did I save you a trip?"

Maddie was warming to her task, intrigued about assembling a history. "What about aunts or married sisters?"

Nancy paused. "Pretty close about his family. For all I know, he might have been an only child."

"Not impossible, but rare in those days." Maddie opened a manila envelope from the photo lab. "A trail at last. Malcolm gave this to Reverend Baines as a model for a stained glass window. Birchem over in Fine Arts is doing the job."

197

Nancy considered it with a nostalgic smile. "Wartime, or not long after, I'd guess. What a beauty. God, think of the hours maintaining those gorgeous rolls of hair. I'd never make it to work." She paused, then tapped her forehead. "Hold on."

She dug into a lower desk drawer and presented a Cornell University yearbook. "His books went to the library, but I saved this."

A graduation picture showed a young man in doctoral robes, confident of his future. So serious. Sixty pounds thinner. With the meticulous hand of a cosmetologist, Nancy traced the patrician nose, the sculpted lips and the widow's peak as Maddie watched hypnotically. "Presto," she said, peering over her bifocals as she sketched the same features on Maddie's photo.

"A sister? The Martha motif of the window." Maddie gave a thumbs-up gesture. "You hit it bang on. I never would have guessed. The old curmudgeon looked nothing like this handsome devil. That widow's peak wasn't so apparent with his white hair." She rushed for her coat as she called over her shoulder, "Hold the fort tomorrow. I'm headed south."

Maddie left the office with a full head of steam. Finally a solid lead. In a few hours she could drive to Ferrous Mountain to scout around and return on the weekend should anything develop. Even if the parents were long dead, in a small town, people had long memories. A neighbor. Tradesperson. How about the site of the picture? Who lived nearby now?

She picked up a Buffalo wings special as a bribe and stopped by her father's. "Could you go over at noon tomorrow and take the dog out? I'll be in Ferrous Mountain all day."

"Sure," he said, wiping his hands free of crumbs and opening the foil box, sending a spicy tomato aroma into the air. In the corner Lucky nibbled on a small pile of shortbread cookies. "What are you doing down in that part of our fair state?"

"Helping Flo," she said, setting the table. "God knows why I'm bothering, but our benighted justice system might convict her. That cheap lawyer Ralph Pool is probably sleeping off his retainer, if she even gave him one. Bet she found his name on a phone booth wall."

Instead of following her joke or defending his colleagues, he turned away and watched a bold jay chase a sparrow from the feeder outside. "Billy called me from Lansing. Staying on with his cousin for some extra tests, but says everything's okay. I hope he's telling the truth. Wouldn't put it past him to lie to make me feel better."

She nodded. "We all have protective shells. An exoskeleton around our fears."

"Exo? Anyhow, I'm going in for those prostrate tests Friday."

Tamping down the fear, she attempted a casual tone scarcely felt. He was a stranger to hospitals, nothing more than a cold and occasional bursitis. Was this the beginning of the end? Suppose he needed an operation and reacted badly to the anesthetic? Her heart started rattling like a caged animal, as she imagined him wheeled into a sterile room of ticking machines, helpless and still. Pathetic visions of nursing homes. Couldn't he boot one last kick at a field goal? "Sooner the better, old pal. Do you want me along for immoral support?"

"Should have got the four-alarm extra-hot." He gnawed at a wing. "You stay put. I'll be out bright-eyed and bushy-tailed in a coupla hours."

Chapter Twenty Five

The next morning Maddie awoke to a foot of fresh snow. To reach his spots in the backyard, Nikon leaped like a gazelle, leaving poing marks every three feet. Balancing a thermal coffee cup on the dash, a soldier's breakfast in a quick get-away, she let the car warm to clear the icy windshield. Ed had opened her drive with his blower, but the town plow had deposited a knee-high ridge. From a selection of armaments lined up on the porch she chose a metal scoop to dig out, wincing at a dull ache in her lower back. "Grow old along with me" indeed. The best was hardly "yet to be" without a remote starter, an in-car heater, or even a garage, not to mention that Korean War veteran of a gas stove. Before leaving, she gobbled a few aspirins for inflammation insurance.

Along the highway, people with grim determination were clearing their driveways, snowblowers spewing fountains into the air. Four-by-fours with private contracts toiled with the fervor of beetles to get clients to work. Passing a semi-trailer, her car shuddered at the downdraft, yet when a sand truck sprayed grit across her windshield, she welcomed the traction against black ice, nemesis of UP drivers.

With the dregs of fall leaves dissolving into forest mulch, the white cover perked up the bleak landscape. The route to Ferrous Mountain rolled through several state forests—Baraga, Iron Range, Sturgeon River—all dedicated to multi-use, a concept which mixed recreation with resources.

So far the plan had been relatively successful, though tree huggers, animal rights activists, and garden-variety malcontents seethed at the logging, hunting, and snowmobile trails. What was their employment plan? Several new lodges had joined the regulars, luring trade from the cities down south and hiring service workers. Besides, no virgin timber remained, just thousands of acres of reforested pine. On the radio, her oldies station was playing "One Tin Soldier." How many aging protesters chilled at the final line, " 'Peace on earth' was all it said"? Maddie had inhaled a lungful of pepper gas at Kent State while demonstrating against the national guard presence on campus. If she earned a sore throat for her pacifism, tossing handy dandelions at the hapless recruits, at least she hadn't been shot down and immortalized on the cover of *Life* magazine. Copper's pampered undergraduates would never comprehend those dangerous, exciting days when issues larger than rising tuition galvanized students.

After an hour, her stomach aching from caffeine and aspirins, she pulled into a truck stop advertising "Mountain Man's Special": two eggs, bacon, sausage, home fries, toast, and dollar pancakes. It would last through lunch, a double bargain. Between luscious bites, she watched truckers punching portable phones. Many had used the free showers, then spent the night in the parking lot, cocooned in luxurious cabs, televisions and CD players for amusement.

Farther along the road, signs warned against picking up hitchhikers from the nearby Escanaba Detention Center. The UP was a natural Siberia for prisoners, imprisoned by a climate as forbidding as stone walls, but occasionally a desperado took jackrabbit parole. At a final turn, she entered the town of Ferrous Mountain, Dickinson County, a tiny enclave of barely eight thousand. Dotting the main street were the usual pharmacy, dry cleaners, restaurants, and a boarded-up

Roxy Theatre where Malcolm might have waited with a dime clutched in his tiny fist. Except for a neon video store, it probably hadn't changed since the last controversial royals, Eddie and Mrs. Simpson, departed into exile on the Riviera.

Pulling into an empty spot, Maddie surveyed the street. Where to start? Though Nancy hadn't found any Driscolls, perhaps they didn't have a phone or were unlisted. People were the best primary resource.

The pharmacy had pleasantly scarred wooden floors with the tang of paste wax and an old-fashioned soda fountain from a dusty decade when Maddie had worn fat, sleek braids. The menu brought a laugh to her throat. "Tin roof? David Harum? Even lime phosphates? And they say you can't go home again."

A sprightly bird-like woman defying retirement was polishing a scalloped dish for banana splits. "Not twenty cents anymore. Meet the last living soda jerkette. Once I go, it's a lost art."

Twirling once on the chrome and red vinyl stool, Maddie ordered a chocolate soda and watched the woman drizzle thick cream into the bottom of a fluted glass, add syrup, seltzer, and a mound of vanilla ice cream. She plied her trade with the precision of an orchestra conductor, topping her creation with whipped cream and a fat red maraschino cherry, and sliding it across the counter. Maddie demolished the tasty concoction with a satisfied sigh and wiped her lips. "Remember suicide Cokes?"

"Sure do. Squirt of every flavor in the line and fizzed up with seltzer as many times as the kid had a burp in his belly. Only made them for pals, though."

The Driscolls rang no bells for the woman, but to Maddie's question about the library, she bobbed her gray head, grabbed a stubby pencil, and sketched a map on the back of a napkin. "Two blocks down Ferrous Mountain Street, new renovations this year. We're right proud of it."

At obligatory compliments about the town, the woman blossomed like a June tulip. "Tell from the name what business ran these parts. The Menominee Iron Range. Kept us steaming during the early depression, least 'til 1935 when the mines closed on account of they dug up all the good stuff. We were getting on to be a ghost town. Only thing saved our sorry bacon was the low grade ore and pelletizing facility at Darkland Mine in 1951. Now we got us a ski hill and the world's second largest fungi." As the door creaked to announce a customer, she cast a glance at the cash register area and called out, "Jennifer Lynn, put down that trashy magazine. You know more about Oprah than you'll ever need to know. Expect to graduate high school on that tripe?"

Entering the library, Maddie approached a bespectacled gentleman at the reference desk who looked like he had founded the place, which perhaps he had. According to the plaque outside, the building was only thirty years old. For all his love of books, Malcolm wouldn't have walked these halls.

He studied her with serious olive green eyes, his gleaming head a duplicate of Dewey's. Maddie said, "A family I'm tracing lived here . . ." She ticked off years mentally. "Certainly before the Second World War. But there are no Driscolls in the phone book."

"Old city directories your best bet. Follow me." He rose slowly, a frail man, bowbent from osteoarthritis or perhaps ankylosing spondylitis. Maddie massaged her neck to ease the tensions of the drive, ignoring a persistent throb in her back.

As they passed a row of computers, he beamed with pride. "On the newfangled Internet here. Problem is . . ." With a frown, he scuttled over to a teenager at a terminal. The screen flashed a colorful close-up of a female crotch. "None of that, Hal. One more time and you're out."

"But Mr. Evans. It's Gustave Courbet. *The Origin of the World.* For my art history project." He waved a battered notebook.

"I'll origin you, laddie. Sign off!" The boy sighed and clicked the mouse.

Evans returned in clear embarrassment. "Never believed in censorship. Might be sitting in a dark corner reading Gray's anatomy book like we did as kids. But some of those pictures'd curl my hair if I had any. Mothers and their toddlers pass by here."

In the yellowing 1934 directory, they found a Timothy Driscoll on Lloyd Street. The listing gave his job as mine foreman. Growing more optimistic, Maddie said, "Whoever lives there now might have known the Driscolls. Even bought the property from them."

He reshelved the books with tender care. "All gone now. Whole block went for a mall when the town got going again."

When she pulled out the photo, he shook his head. "I've only been here the last ten years. Early retired from the line at GM in the Motor City. Like to keep busy, I do."

She cocked her head. "Where's the oldest graveyard?"

He directed her down the road to Maple Ridge Cemetery, closed in 1982. The wind had freshened, and Maddie left the warm car with reluctance, tugging her fleece hat snug around her ears and pulling a scarf over her mouth. Scanning the smooth white vista, she bit her lip. Flat markers would be covered. Footprints wandered in and out of the paths, past bunches of faded plastic flowers and gaudy silver-ribboned wreaths. The natural withering of live flowers seemed a poignant reminder of the life cycle, far more powerful than the obscene persistence of polymers. Following the bootsteps, she made her way with difficulty. Wool pants and long underwear had been a good idea, but even so, the chill was bitter. After thirty minutes, nose running and glasses fogging from her breath, she finally located a Driscoll in a far corner beneath the skeletal arms of a mighty oak. Squinting under the pallid sun, she removed her mitts to rub at the gray marble. Timothy had died in 1965, his wife Jane in 1970. Her maiden name was Ryan. Maddie clapped her icy hands and hurried back to the car, wishing she'd brought a flask of coffee.

Back in town, the phonebook listed a K. Ryan on 1711 Beacon, but the line was busy. Three o'clock. She looked at the threatening sky. More snow? How could she drive back to Stoddard in the dark? Afflictions that defined the territory of age were nipping at the corners of her independence. Calm down, she told herself. You're not young, but you're solvent. Spring for one of those motels you passed, and call Father to collect Nikon.

On Beacon, 1711 elbowed identical neighbors, a trim house with asphalt shingles stamped like red brick, small and practical, four-square against the cruel climate. The tiny porch had been enclosed as a buffer. On the floor sat a desiccated chrysanthemum, a pair of unisex black rubber boots with a zipper up the front, and a thick cocoa mat at the threshold. When Maddie knocked, a bundle of sweaters opened the door, plump Persian cat twirling around the swollen ankles like warm vanilla pudding.

"I'm looking for relatives of the Driscolls," Maddie explained. "By some fortune, I found the Ryan name at the cemetery."

"Get yourself in, girl. Colder than a witch's tit." Gray lisle stockings on her blocky legs above cut-out bedroom slippers, the old woman shuffled into the living room.

Kathleen Ryan was Malcolm's maiden aunt on his mother's side.

She took the news with stoic aplomb, shaking her head slowly. "So Malcolm didn't live out his threescore and ten," she said, pouring strong China tea from a square pot decorated like an English cottage, steam rising from a chimney lid. Reaching from a massive armchair, she drew heavy brocade curtains against the wind. "Was it the drink that hastened him on? Tim liked a drop when he could get it, and the apple doesn't fall far from the tree." Her eyes crinkled more from resignation than judgment.

Maddie sipped quietly, perched uncomfortably on an adamantine horsehair sofa. No wonder the Victorians had looked so crabby in tintypes. "It wasn't liquor. He was poisoned." She explained the bizarre situation and the unsatisfactory answers.

"My word! A good friend you must be to come all this way."

"I've been whirling like a dervish, searching for clues. Perhaps something in his past could help us. It'll be a bore to you, I fear."

"Oh, bore away. I'm eighty-three this month. There's nothing to do in this blessed frozen town except watch old friends buried, and have to wait until spring for that. Tubby keeps me going." She pointed to the cat, encamped like a hairy cannon ball on a tattered rag rug. "Take my advice and retire where you can rock on your porch all year 'round."

"I learned at the library that Malcolm's father worked in the mines," Maddie said, steering the conversation along a more productive path.

"Everyone did, girl, and down on their knees thanking God every night. The Depression left the country in breadlines and yet here they were, the lucky ducks. Weekly paychecks. Company houses. My cousin Arthur's here I bought when they sold them off. Tim's was torn down." Her Wedgwood blue eyes surveyed the tiny room with fondness, from the painted mantel, loaded with souvenir cups and curled photos, to the crocheted antimacassars on the sofa. Then she coughed into a lace handkerchief. "Got wandering again. Let's see, Tim just made foreman when the mines closed. Jesus wept. The whole town took it bad. Like a funeral that didn't quit. No stopping babies, though. They don't read the papers. How he made a go of things after that, I don't know. Decent carpenter. Odd jobs for the town. Jane served potato soup for lunch and macaroni every other night. Only ketchup on top, often as not."

"It must have been hard. My father packed mustard sandwiches to work for years. Still won't touch the stuff."

"Never took the relief, any of our family. The kids used a homemade wagon and scampered down ditches after pop bottles, delivered papers, too. 'Fibber McGee and Molly' after dinner and then off to homework. Malcolm was a stubborn boy when he set his mind, though. Once a pork chop went missing. Dear meat in those times. Jane spanked him, sent him to bed with no supper. He stuck to his guns and marched upstairs. Not a whimper. She found the bone later in the dog house, cried buckets."

"He was like that."

"So he was. Dead set on making a life for himself away from here. When he graduated from high school, some valedictatory, Malcolm got fancy scholarships out East. Then a good post at the university."

"Did he come home very often?"

"That boy seemed to stay in school forever. Anyway, I did practical nursing, over to Ishpeming. Never saw the use of marrying. Went to Boston to take care of my feeble-minded cousin and stayed on. Only came back when I retired at seventy-plus. Wanted to see my friends before they hit the marble orchard. Saw Malcolm at Tim's funeral, then Jane's. He did send his old aunt a nice check every Christmas."

"He acted strangely before he died. Changed his will." She pulled the photo from her totebag. "Do you know this girl?"

The old lady's double chin began to wobble, one thickly-veined hand fluttering to her ample chest like a wounded bluebird. "Lili, his sister. Think Fred took it."

"Malcolm must have loved her very much. At his church he commissioned a stained glass window in her honor." Why hadn't he ever mentioned Lili? And who is Fred, she wondered, swallowing the questions. Old people liked to take their time. Maybe her own impatience would mellow through the years.

With a knobby hand, the old woman brushed at her eyes, voice cracking like shook foil. "Twins they were. Close as sweet peas. I expect Malcolm took that snapshot with him when he left for college."

"Where is Lili now?" Maddie asked, despairing of the answer. Tuberculosis, typhoid, influenza, polio, all the ills the flesh had been heir to before wonder drugs. Stretching with languid innocence, the cat curled toward her, ivory fur fluffed from static electricity, clear blue iceberg eyes. She extended a tentative hand. Cats were unpredictable, perversely landing in the laps of those who disliked them. As one deceptively swift paw grazed her knuckles, she flinched. It gave a sniff and waddled off, amused at the game.

"Remembering is hard. It always makes me sad." Kathleen searched Maddie's expectant face. "But you've come so far. And you're the first outside visitor I've had in years." She took a wheezy breath and leaned back, her swollen feet resting on a tiny embroidered ottoman, her voice assuming a dreamy tone. "Lili, that's with an i. Named after a movie star, Lili Damita. Never forget that *Bridge of San Luis Rey* picture. Half-silent, half-talkie. Only fun we had was going to the old Roxy. Got a whole set of dishes when *Gone with the Wind* opened. Antique dealer passing through gave me top price last year. Depression glass. A windfall for this old girl." She nodded toward the one anomaly, a new, elephant-sized television.

Maddie drummed her fingers out of Kathleen's sight. Should she offer comments, or merely nod, play psychiatrist? Her stomach was beginning to make faint moans despite that monster breakfast. "Where is Lili now?"

"We don't know." Kathleen's damask rose teacup clinked, slopping amber liquid onto the chair arm. She dismissed the accident with a casual gesture.

"So she left town? To marry? Take a job?"

The old woman gave a knowing tsk. "Expecting. You can imagine the shame in those days." She pursed her wrinkled lips. "Lili was a clerk at the five and dime, and I was the county nurse by then. Boarded with them over on Lloyd to help a bit with the groceries. I saw the signs in the morning. Waited for her to speak, but she kept her mouth shut. Then one night she disappeared. Bitter cold. You could hear the trees crack. Not fit for beasts. Valentine's Day, 1957. Took only a cardboard suitcase. Around her neck a gold locket with her parents' pictures. A note by the kettle to say that she'd write when she'd found work."

That explained Malcolm's curious choice of jewelry, or did it? How had he come by the locket? "Did you ever learn who the father was?"

With a sigh, Kathleen lumbered to the mantel, retrieving a

faded snapshot creased with years. A young man in khakis, a fresh buck private, dark hair slicked with brilliantine, eyes sparkling with hope and glory. "That's Fred. Killed in a training accident in California day after he made corporal. Broke his neck on some damn exercise, they called it. His family brought over the telegram New Year's Eve. Only son. The engagement was no secret, though. Made jokes about a cigar band ring. He was coming home first leave to marry our girl."

Maddie rolled along the ebb and flow of questioning, a raft on a slow, lazy river. "Did you tell anyone about the pregnancy?"

The old woman's stooped shoulders stiffened, the prominent nose from the Ryan side hawklike in its pride. "Jane and I didn't see the sense. Expected she'd have the baby and come back. Maybe with it, maybe without. Done all the time. When he heard she'd left, Malcolm wanted to come back from college. But we couldn't have found her, you see. Hadn't the faintest idea where she'd gone. Could have hitched a ride clear to Detroit where all the jobs were. Lili was a resourceful girl." A shiny brass ship's clock on the mantel began to chime.

Some autonomic response made Maddie count. Seven! She stood with an apology on her face. "I'm so sorry. The time got away from me. I must have kept you from your dinner." She drew the curtain aside to look at the snow swirling in fresh drifts, the hazy streetlight barely visible. "Can you recommend a good motel?"

Kathleen hooted and waved her hand. "Never in a million years. If you'll break bread with an old lady, she'll sport you to a room. This brute of a country makes fast friends of us all. That's how we survive."

Maddie called her father collect to ask him to take care of

Nikon. Then after washing up, she was summoned to the small dining room where a clean but threadbare linen cloth lay on the table. Shoved onto the sill above were pill bottles, salves, and other nostrums of the aged. "Breaking bread" brought a tasty surprise, a cold baked ham studded with cloves, honey-sweet watermelon pickles, a whole wheat loaf fresh from the morning, and Kathleen's canned green beans with bacon bits. "Sorry about the lack of fresh vegetables. Thrived like piggies without them when I was a girl. Summer, see those foreign foods at the market. Artychokes, funny flat peas, Mexican chili things."

Maddie spread hot mustard on the crusty end piece, toothsome and spicy. "I've given up on salads. Last week, the tomatoes tasted like pink fibreglass, and the head lettuce had the spark of an Egyptian mummy."

Kathleen laughed and scooped up a gob of butter for her bread. "You remind me of Malcolm and his little poems. What a naughty goose. And that English accent when he got merry on the apple brandy. Hardly anyone interesting to talk to here. If it weren't for Oprah, don't know what I'd do. Liked to tickle me when she hauled in that wagon with thirty pounds of fat. Always got the library to order the books she jawed about."

From a massive glass percolator, Kathleen poured coffee after dinner. "Strong as pitch, but it puts heart in a body," she said, reaching for a wooden match and snicking it into flame with a horny thumb. "Care for a cigarette to settle the stomach? My only vice. Don't know why all the fuss about warnings on the pack. Been calling them 'coffin nails' since Hector was a pup."

Although she had quit years ago, Maddie cupped her hands for the light, whiffing a smell of sulphur. The Marlboro widened her eyes and jolted nicotine into her bloodstream.

Dizzy for a moment, she looked up at a bank calendar on the wall, a tropical beach scene, a wide expanse of white with gentle waves. Islands of bliss, free of blackflies. Mangoes dropping into the mouth. The clink of Kathleen's spoon brought her back to reality. Time was running out, and she had learned only questions. "A painting arrived at Malcolm's office not long before he died. We don't know where it came from. Any art talent in the family?"

Kathleen puffed out a row of concentric smoke rings, grinning like a merry chipmunk. "Malcolm kept his nose in the books. And as for Lili, bless her soul, she was a wizard with a pencil. No money for art supplies, and not much time for hobbies. Her chores were to work in the vegetable garden and mind the animals. A few chickens, Easter lamb. No picky town bylaws in those days." Then a chuckle shook her shoulders. "That time with the lamb, I'll never forget. The ewe had struggled away through the snow. Thick-headed beasts, sheep are. Got good and lost. When we found them, thought the wee babe was a goner. But Lili tucked the sad little creature behind the stove, wrapped in an old sweater. Limp as a dishrag. Not a breath in it. About midnight there was the most awful racket. It was dashing around the kitchen to beat the band. We laughed until tears rolled down our cheeks."

Later Maddie helped with the dishes and then was taken down the hall to a small room. The white curtains were freshly laundered and ironed, the pink chenille bedspread soft as baby skin. Kathleen passed her a flowered garment. "Spare nightie. Soap and towels in the bathroom. Sorry I can't offer other fancies. Oh, and Tubby comes to your bed, you bump him off. Deaf as a post, he is. Blue-eyed white cats often are."

"You're very kind. I'll be quite comfortable." She paused, then asked a nagging question. "Kathleen, that locket of

Lili's. Was there another like it in your family?"

"Nary a one. Pure gold. Twenty-four carat. Passed on from Great-grandmother Lou." The old woman didn't pursue the issue, and Maddie was relieved. It brought back memories of Malcolm helpless and blind on the gurney, an image she'd tried to forget.

After Kathleen trundled away, navigating on posty legs out of sheer will, Maddie headed for the bathroom. A quick splash in the massive lion's claw tub and to bed. Her pants matted with cat hair, she hung her clothes in the empty wardrobe. The room was drafty, windows iced over, fumy oil heat blasting up at intervals, so she kept her socks on under the ample gown and blessed the flannel sheets.

Over a small bureau in a handsome gilt frame was a tinted portrait of a couple, a studio photo with the ubiquitous potted palm. He wore a vested suit, high collar, she a velvet dress with pearl buttons. Lean and raw-boned, widow's peak defining his dark hairline, he placed an awkward hand on her shoulder, the optimism of youth glowing in their faces as they stared into the camera, conscious of the moment, a prosperous time. Before the mine closing, the responsibilities for children yet unborn. A daughter who would vanish into the cold dawn, never to return, leaving them to wonder forever if she were warm or cared for. The thought of Nikon disappearing for an hour would have driven Maddie out of her mind.

The mattress had the resistance of Ferrous Mountain itself: no innersprings, just the stuff of nightmares. What would it do to her back? After pummeling the pillow into submission, from a bookcase she selected *Girl of the Limberlost*, one of her mother's favorites. A feminist tale out of sync with conventions, 1912 Indiana, the Limberlost swamps. A girl with dreams of becoming a botanist. "Lili Driscoll," the inside cover read: "2440 Lloyd St., Ferrous Mountain, Michigan, United States, Earth, the Universe." On the page was the simple pencil drawing of a lamb kneeling in the bracken.

Chapter Twenty Six

Maddie returned from Ferrous Mountain warmed from meeting Kathleen but sensing that her journey had hardly begun. Malcolm had a sister, a twin who had haunted his heart to the final beat. That explained the stained glass window, but not the reversal of his attitude toward SWINC. Lili hadn't been handicapped, after all. And how did the thank-you note and painting relate to the whole? The locket had to be the key. How had Malcolm come by it? If he had found Lili, or discovered her fate, why hadn't he at least told his aunt? Above all, had it perished with him in the fiery furnace?

With a rare nerve, she dialed the Gooderham and Worts Funeral Home. They had handled her mother's accident and burial with dispatch and discretion. Tom Gooderham answered her questions with smooth dispatch, no doubt anticipating future business.

"No, it's not grotesque of you to ask. Many people have those concerns. The client does wear clothing of choice. All the same to the process." He listened while she broached the delicate subject of Malcolm.

"Professor Driscoll? I'm not sure I should . . . But yes, there was a locket. Stipulated in his last will. Molten metal only in the remains. Some prefer it that way. Not pacemakers, though. Lord-a-mercy, is that a mess."

Hanging up, Maddie turned to the painting, now an old

familiar on the wall, and perhaps the last piece of evidence. When would Brian return to help her with the provenance?

Hunched like a frustrated raven at Malcolm's desk, she glowered at the paperwork that plagued a chairman, the moments' monuments of memos. Handling the department and her classes had become an onerous bargain. In one bright spot, Dean Nordman had freed mysterious funds for a web page to attract English majors. A techie whiz from the Computer Services Division had passed her a copy of *Son of Web Pages That Don't Suck*, an outrageously named but thorough book which now sat on her desk, its lessons underlined. For the scanner, she'd chosen pictures of Dickens, Hemingway, Bellow, Updike, Woolf, sound bytes from *Hamlet*, snippets of Romantic favorites, and shots from recent films of Jane Austen's works. Keeping the project a secret, she'd climbed out on a literary limb to test-fly a course in mystery novels, including *Fifth Business*, by Canadian Robertson Davies, and a science fiction and fantasy selection, grounded in basics like Poe and Verne, but including Frank Herbert, Douglas Adams, and Tolkien. Alice Sebold and Jonathan Franzen checked in as Generation X favorites.

Flo had made bail, but she was on an extended, unpaid leave until her case was resolved. Her precious HAWG meetings needed a representative. Perhaps with the thought that extra duty might boost chances for tenure, Gary had agreed to attend, so Maddie had requested minutes of the last sessions. Chairman Bix Wilder, Head of Engineering, had forwarded a distressingly thick folder. Reluctantly, she waded through concerns about venting and storage of dangerous substances in the chemistry labs, proper precautions in the Fine Arts area for fumes and dust. Ripped carpeting was documented, slippery stairs, missing handrails, broken desks and chairs, even vandalism of the bathroom machines selling aspirins, tampons, and prophylactics by a character desperate enough for quarters to jimmy the locks. Busybody stuff, Flo's style. Speed-reading, her finger stopped at one interesting point.

Dumbwaiters. Apparently the library had installed them at the turn of the century. Before elevators, they carried books between floors. Fearful of forbidden food invading the hallowed halls, recently Caroline had grumbled about staff commandeering them to ferry clandestine pizzas. Maintenance had been ordered to board them up. Yawning, Maddie turned the page, when a small voice peeped from a far corner of her brain. Since her preoccupations with the mysteries of Malcolm's death, she hadn't given further thought to Cheryl. It all seemed so cut and dried. A nearsighted lab assistant. The elevator down. A sealed floor. Barring all that, a possible accident or suicide. Yet how big were these dumbwaiters? Didn't slapstick Thirties comedies involve jokesters riding in them? Could that explain how someone could have avoided the stairwell alarms? Hid out in the basement, or waited like a patient spider in the dumbwaiter until the building reopened? As she pondered, remembering the frantic almond streaks of Cheryl's nails, in the margins she drew small boxes with hunched creatures, knees around their heads. Phillips would laugh her out of the police station. She shrugged, tacked on a snarled happy face, and plopped the mess into a large envelope headed for Gary's mailbox.

Sorting through the external correspondence depressed her further—pleas from erstwhile applicants filed away as cannon fodder. Sessionals and part-timers were an economic fact of life, despite her vow to use them compassionately. What did it matter? Soon she'd be out of such pencil-pushing miasma. And if Flo's bargain basement lawyer didn't earn his gin money, an outsider would have to sweep up the debris.

On her voice mail was a message from a student whose

name was unfamiliar. "Um. Dr. Temple," a hesitant male voice said. "I've missed some classes for, uh, personal reasons, and want to make up the work. Call my machine and tell me what I need to do." Personal reasons. Was there any other kind? She consulted her grade book. An invisible man since signing the register the first day. She left a message. "What's the rush? Why not wait until a day or two before classes end to tackle your English assignments? Meanwhile you can concentrate on more serious interests."

She made a quick call to her father, due for tests late that afternoon. How was he getting to the hospital? "No big deal. Billy can drive me. Got back yesterday. You stick to your job, Madeline. I'll be in and out of there like a fart in a mitten."

Though Grace hadn't crossed her path in days, Maddie met her being escorted to the parking lot by a Campus Watch volunteer with a bright yellow jacket. The braids were straggly, her face haggard. Her voice trembled, discreet enough not to let the young man overhear. "I have been getting telephone calls at my apartment in the middle of the night. One ring, two rings. No one ever answers."

"How annoying. Maybe you should get an unlisted number."

Grace drew her coat closer at a gust of wind, looking down the path in apprehension. "I have an unlisted number, and I have changed it twice already. Someone must . . ." She froze as two young men muffled up in parkas approached, chatting and laughing in a musical language.

"I know them, Grace. DeBeers scholarship exchange students from South Africa. Seniors in the Accounting program." She watched the woman waver and reached out an arm in support. Clearly Grace was nearing the breaking point. R and R in Hawaii wouldn't come too soon. "Tonight's Malcolm's dinner. Are you going?"

★ ★ ★ ★ ★

That evening at six, more out of expediency than familiarity, Maddie called out a greeting and let herself into the cottage.

"In the kitchen," trilled a voice amid a clatter of pans. Maddie hung up her coat on the antique hall rack. After smoothing a cream silk blouse over beige linen pants, she wandered through the dining room, where a majolica bowl of delicately spiced potpourri scented the air. The Irish linen tablecloth was set with Spode china for eight. Heavy Georgian silverware and dual candelabra complemented the dishes, two crystal goblets at each place, with a huge centerpiece anchoring the scene. Where had Mrs. Bach found red and white lilies at this baleful time of year? The festive atmosphere lifted her spirits and defused the tension she'd felt recalling her last visit. "Much depends on dinner," the culinary sociologist Margaret Vissar advised.

She popped her head into the kitchen. "May I give you a hand?"

Covering a dark blue cotton dress, Mrs. Bach's apron was starched and white, a flirty mob cap giving her the appearance of a maid in a Congreve play. An outfit from theatricals with Malcolm? On the stove, huge pots bubbled clouds of fragrant steam into the air. "Kind of you to offer," she said, plucking errant pin feathers from tiny forms arranged on a baking dish. "Recognize these poor naked fellows? I think they missed you. Looked downright disappointed to see me pop by." She drew a quick Z with a cleaver. "They might have read my mind."

Maddie remembered the place settings. Surely Flo wouldn't be crass enough to come. "I'm glad you're joining us."

"It's Malcolm, the absent guest."

Swallowing a lump in her throat, she asked, "If I may be so bold, what is on our menu in your grand repast?"

Mrs. Bach took a mock bow and brushed back a tendril of damp hair. "A Restoration feast. That's what he wanted, lawyer said. I got the lay of the land from that Pete's diary we used to read in . . ." Pooching out her bottom lip and turning away, she grabbed a giant wooden spoon, then began stirring a pot of heavy cream soup with wisps of green. "Took me a devil of a time to track down recipes at the library." She offered a grease-stained paper, dishes checked off in pencil.

Maddie read with her mouth watering. Sorrel soup. Roasted quail in red current sauce. Chicken broiled with leeks. Saddle of lamb for the main course. A salad of cucumbers, peas, olives, and artichokes. Boiled haricots. Sautéed asparagus. Apple tart and sweetmeats for dessert, along with fresh peaches and cherries no doubt Fed-Exed from Detroit. A blue-veined wheel of Stilton and cream crackers with the port. She patted her stomach in anticipation. "Well done, thou good and faithful servant. I wonder if I'll survive my gluttony."

Mrs. Bach hummed a little ditty, pleased at the compliments. "As for that Florence woman. She was on Malcolm's invitation list. I don't fancy her nervy enough to show her face. Poison the master and guzzle his wine."

Maddie sighed and sneaked a small slice of Stilton from the hutch. "She says she's innocent."

"They all do. Never a guilty one in jail." The old woman fished in a drawer for a corkscrew, then picked up a pocket encyclopedia. "Don't know beans about wine. Malcolm always chose what he wanted. Take this down to the cellar."

In a neat, dry cold room outfitted with metal racks, under a swinging green glass lamp, Maddie sat at the small table amid the acres of Europe's best vintages. Kid in a candy store, she flipped through the guide, and selected a ruby-rich Chateau Batailley, a cedar-pencil claret from Ducru-Beaucaillou, and for the whites, a crisp Graves by Chicane, not in the senior class with the others, but why compare a frisky Probe with a dowager Mercedes? For dessert, she added two precious bottles of Suduiraut, a legendary Sauterne. The pungent Stilton still deep in her nostrils, she plunged into the dustiest shelves and found a bottle of Quinta do Noval, 1957. At a Christmas party long ago, Malcolm had said that a bottle of port was "put down" when a child was born. She sat in quiet reflection, the familiar date hovering like an insistent spirit. The year Lili might have given birth.

After opening the wine and setting it on a side table, Maddie answered the door, first to a subdued Grace, then to a boisterous Nancy and Marie. The motley crew of men arrived in Gary's pickup, hauling a case of Budweiser. The living room was confining for seven, but Nancy joined Mrs. Bach in the kitchen while Maddie circulated with platters of hors d'oeuvres, featuring oysters on horseback and a peppery partridge pâté garnished with black truffle slices. The mood was guardedly festive, as if they perceived that Flo's mercifully short Spanish Inquisition had cooled under Maddie's limp whip.

George and Rick were vying for connoisseur of the evening, dueling with clichés. "Masculine but gentle," George said, closing his eyes in appreciation as his Adam's apple bobbed.

"I find it supple," Rick countered, wiggling his tongue in a characteristically disgusting gesture. "A tad on the tannic side. Some fatness would help."

With her ample rump propped sidesaddle on the edge of the sofa, Marie sucked back an oyster with a hearty smack of the lips. "Do you think that this closes the books, then? Dear Flo strung up on the gibbet?"

Rick brayed out a raucous laugh, stubbed out his cigarette in the pot of a splendid white violet. "I'd spring the trapdoor on the bitch myself, given the chance."

George's moustache twitched in tart agreement. " 'A night-growing mushrump' like Bussy D'Ambois. So quickly did she sprout and wither. Luckily for us, fellow slaves."

His bolo tie loose around the collar of an embroidered Western shirt, Gary rested silver-studded snakeskin boots on the ottoman, slugging back one beer, crumpling the can, and opening another. "Mushrooms grow in bullshit. Flo's territory. No more ropes, though. Lethal injection, Texas style." When Maddie cleared her throat, he lowered his feet to the carpet like a chastened boy.

As tongues loosened, great debate erupted over which offending terms should be banished from the language. George nominated Flo's "paradigm," at which they nodded in unison. "What about 'eponymous'?" asked Gary.

"I'd favor decapitating 'defenestration,' " Marie added. "Making a fine distinction for killing people by tossing them out of a window is beyond this simple medieval girl."

Irritated with the chatter, preoccupied with thoughts of her father's tests, Maddie combed the record collection. She hadn't played Mozart since that tragic afternoon waiting for the ambulance. Elgar's *Pomp and Circumstance*? Malcolm wouldn't be wearing his moth-eaten doctoral robes, beaming like a benevolent Buddha when the diplomas were awarded. A Bruckner symphony seemed a civil compromise, a balance of harmonic moods.

The men moved into the dining room to arrange bets on the Detroit-Green Bay game, and Marie toddled to the washroom. Settling onto the sofa, Maddie spoke quietly with Nancy. No man was a saint to his valet, nor to his secretary.

"Twins? And the sister disappeared? He was wearing the locket? What a story." She nicked a slice of the pâté and smeared it onto a cracker. "Lili must be dead. Poor Malcolm. Joking through his heartache all these years."

Maddie shrugged, trying to drown her uneasiness in the pleasant treat of fine wines. Ten dollars a bottle was her limit. "Why else wouldn't she have contacted the family? I'm down to my last clue, and the one man who could help with that picture is still out of town. And how in the world did he get that locket?"

Across the room, like an ebony statue, Grace hunched in a deep armchair, leafing in slow motion through a coffee-table book on Scottish castles. Though acknowledging the occasional comment, she had not volunteered a word, tormented with problems only Maddie was privileged to imagine. Faculty get-togethers were not her custom, so obviously she had attended out of loyalty to Malcolm. He had chosen ability over race at a time when she needed a job as far from the big city as possible. Now her safe haven had become another prison.

Half an hour later, flushed with heat from the kitchen, Mrs. Bach passed a platter of English cheeses: Cheshire, double Gloucester, and Lancashire.

"So sorry, good folks. Any minute now. Bear with me."

She left to pats on the back and hearty encouragement as the guests dug in. Well-oiled and the edge to hunger removed, the department was a jovial ogre. Maddie checked her watch. Her father should have the results of his tests. The multi-course dinner might last past his bedtime.

She moved into the hall where she had last dialed 9-1-1, sitting nervously on a ladder-back chair beside a delicate cherrywood table. He answered on the first ring, his voice hearty and jubilant. "All clear, girl. Going to set me up for some doozie of a pill that'll dynamite the pipes. You'll have the old man to kick around until Hell freezes over or Billy quits smoking."

Her blood pressure dropped to normal and a forgotten appetite resurfaced. "This calls for a celebratory feast at Huhtala's one of these nights. Tell Billy to come. They have that private booth in the corner."

"Right-o." He dampened the receiver as he spoke with someone. "Say, Maddie. Our expert gardener found those plants you left on the fridge. Says they're hemlock. Where did you get that stuff? Wasn't that the same . . ."

The phone hung loosely in her hand, words fading in and out like a distant siren. Hemlock! Why hadn't it killed the quail? Aromas of roast meat and vegetables filled the air. In the dining room, a tinkly bell rang.

"Ladies and gentlemen, dinner is served," a voice warbled. Foot shufflings and glass clinks sounded, and a steady current of voices and bodies flowed past her. Chairs scootched across the polished oak floor. Still Maddie sat, paralyzed as Malcolm had been, cold trickling to her stiffening toes like an icy shroud. Then she screamed.

Chapter Twenty Seven

Fleeing the scene faster than escapees from the Black Death, the party vanished to find dinners of their own design. After the police had borne off the suspected quail, Maddie poured two goblets of the Graves and joined Mrs. Bach in the kitchen.

Weeping softly, the crestfallen cook waved a plump hand across the platters and dishes. "Such a dinner there never was. And all gone for nothing."

Maddie considered the savory ruins. "It might have been *The Last Supper*. Plenty of good food left. Drink up and dig in. You worked too hard to go home hungry."

The old woman flung off her apron with a defiant grin and reached for a serving spoon. By the time they sampled the Chateau d'Yquem at one o'clock and cracked the port shortly after, it was time to call a mutual taxi. As Mrs. Bach struggled into her coat, Maddie asked, "I've wondered about your accent. British, of course, but what dialect?"

Mrs. Bach's consonants butted up against her vowels. "I was born and raised in Cheboygan. The Professor and I loved that "All Creatures Great and Small" on PBS. A little game with us. And do you know, whenever I walk through the door here, it seems natural."

Nikon was chasing grouse in his sleep when Maddie turned out the bed lamp and gazed across the snowy lawn, a bright moon illuminating the scene like a floodlight. Out of precaution, she had taken an extra aspirin along with a couple of Tums. Distant in memory were the days of quick recovery from overindulging in food, drink, or exercise. "Gone with the wind," like the poet Dowson, burnt out at thirty-three from a dissipated life, calling for madder music and stronger wine. "Desolate and sick of an old passion" when the gray dawn arrived. What old passions did she have? Bleary-eyed, she fingered Dan's ring, the persistence of memory, or perhaps what imagination served, some ready fiber impulse charging across the brain cells recalling that touch of flame. Fact or fiction? Ed was solid and dependable, but never that spark. All for the better, a certain danger in impulsive decisions soon regretted.

"Toxic to people but not quail?" she asked Phillips the following week in his office.

The detective seemed relaxed and friendly now that the case was closed. He passed her a box of doughnuts, and she took a honey cruller. "You got it. Threw us off at first. I mean we knew he had been poisoned. With the cook out of the running, Andrews seemed the likely candidate, lying about the visit, next in line for his job. Could have distracted the old man and sprinkled the hemlock on the food somehow. Never figured more of those sweethearts were chomping down hemlock out back."

"Guess that's why my pup gets away with browsing on questionable mushrooms in the woods." With dampened enthusiasm, she added, "So Flo's free, or is it too baroque to assume that she poisoned the quail herself?"

"Too broke? They had some minor money troubles, couple of overdrafts, dunning letters from an orthodontist. No, those bushes have been there for years. Common in our area. No problem until the Professor built a new quail pen.

One last live guy the cook kept for a pet for her grandson. Good thing she did. Blood analysis proved our theory." He laughed and took a swig of orange juice. "Andrews owes you big time."

Back at Copper that week, the departmental ship of state shuddered ahead, its captain returned with renewed vigor and no small amount of malice to pound out rhythm for the oars with a what-have-you-done-for-me-lately attitude. Maddie's pity vanished as Flo systematically confirmed an imprimatur, memos pouring from her desk like pernicious lava. A doctor's excuse was required for absences of more than one day. Office hours were doubled. No Fridays or Mondays off, despite the occasional lucky draw of computerized scheduling. Assignments had to be returned no later than the next class.

Maddie heard a familiar snarl as she passed Flo in the hall. "I hope you're collecting your personal effects, especially that garish landscape. It clashes with my Holbein prints and the Van Eyck," she said, without a word of thanks. "And what a stupid idea to send Gary to the HAWG meetings. Do you think I want that dumb cowboy representing us? He has the subtlety of a sack of pinto beans. Probably lives in a trailer with a 'Lawnmowers Repaired' sign." She directed Maddie into her office with an imperious nod, shoving the painting towards her, along with newspaper flyers advertising stoves, two models circled. While Maddie shifted her burden, Flo piled on the Toby jugs and the Victorian chocolate tin. "Nancy told me about your scheme to award a degree to a dead girl. Apparently the thesis wasn't even finished. Are you trying to make a morbid joke?"

"Have a heart for a change. Grace smoothed over the rough spots. And Malcolm put Cheryl's name on the graduation list, so grin and bear it." She narrowed her eyes, then

227

nodded toward a glossy *Crucible* photo of Flo, arms linked with the Dean and President Bowdler. "Good publicity."

Still seething after she rearranged her office, Maddie dropped into the Common Room to collect a coffee and commune with the other whipped dogs. Tempers were boiling. Gossip went as far as a fervent wish that undiscovered evidence would toss Flo back into jail.

"It wouldn't be double jeopardy," George said with a hopeful smile. "She never went to trial."

"It's over, my friend. Deal with the present. Maybe the nail-chewing baggage is right about our future." With a stubby finger, Marie traced runic letters on the Help Wanted section of *The Chronicle of Higher Education*. "Thankfully, my career is drawing to a close. I've read the handwriting on the wall, and there aren't any thorns or eths. The sterile Garden of Adonis versus the fertile Bower of Bliss in *The Faerie Queen*. Without change we're poor metal things with molten hearts. Take my lit course, for example. I've tried, Lord knows, to make material relevant. Plugged the lady knight Britomart as an archetypal feminist: 'I have beene trained up in warlike stowre.' They started snickering about that Gun Heaven place out on the Sault Road."

Rick peered up, rubbing a shredded eraser over a sheet of yellow foolscap. "I may have to go genre with my novel. That's where the money is. What about these titles: *Murder in the Ivory Tower*, *Death Is Academic*, or *Bloody Grades*?" A few discreet sighs answered his question, and he tossed the eraser across the room, scoring three points in the wastebasket.

George shook out a small blue pill and swallowed it dry. "She told me to make more comments on the papers I returned. Can you believe it? One idiot complained, some kid moose hunting in Canada for two weeks. Give him a D, and he wouldn't have read another word. If he could read at all."

The simple truth of that axiom was as bitter as Maddie's coffee. "Isn't that always the case? Don't show up and they want you to teach the material twice," she added. A good chairman knew when to treat accusations seriously and when to protect faculty like a pit bull with a conscience. Years ago, a big-mouthed jock had complained that she'd called him stupid during class. Not a chance. She'd have used more creative and muddy words, "oblique" or "benighted."

After the disastrous dinner, followed by the resurrection of Flo, she had almost forgotten about one last possible door to the truth about Malcolm's past. Like a squirrel tantalized by an unreachable nut, she picked up the phone. Brian Turner was back. Perhaps a filbert had dropped her way.

"So you're the one who left that note. I had it yesterday. God knows where the little sucker went now. Figured if the matter was important, you'd get in touch again. I'm free now. Want to bop over?" he asked, and his slang carried her back to high school. Another soldier in the Gray Power battalion.

Ten minutes later, toting the painting, she entered a cluttered cave of an office, piled eyeball-deep with effluvial decades of university service, a fire hazard HAWG would love to root out. An energetic elf with arms stretching to his knees, Brian wore faded black jeans and a tattered gray sweater with holes in the sleeves. A whiff of what Brits called "pong" drifted her way each time he moved, and the heavy shadow on his face confirmed a dubious hygiene.

"Love that hat," he said. "The Doge of Venice with a pom-pom." Brushing aside a shard of congealed pizza crust on a drafting table, he placed the picture under a bright, adjustable lamp. "Decent technique. Are you interested in the value? Because it's amateur stuff, pleasant pablum though it is."

"The value doesn't matter. Is there anything you can tell me about the painter?"

"No signature, only that sun in the lower corner. Sort of an emblem. The brush strokes are curious. Could be deliberate or . . ." He collapsed a pyramid of papers to unearth a small package. "I'm a sucker for promotions."

Maddie examined the six cards. Artwork by the disabled. A low vision person. A man who painted with a brush in his mouth. A tragic generation of Thalidomide victims now facing middle age, testing limits of diminished mobility. "Are you suggesting one of these people?"

"The styles are similar. It's a guess. No charge." He smoothed back a wave of greasy blond hair, discernibly white at the temples. "But on a different tack, what about the subject?"

"Subject? This nature scene?"

"Exactly. Look carefully. What do you see?"

Grateful for his professional courtesy, still she felt the uncertainty of a callow scholar, catechized for her answers. "Water, trees, an island." She squinted for details, wishing she were annotating a poem instead. "No people. No boats."

"Boreal trees. Granite. What island? Perhaps a landmark."

"It could be anywhere in Michigan, Wisconsin, Minnesota. Who knows?"

"Tell you who might help you. Pat Valentino. She's a photographer in Stoddard. Knows the UP like the back of her truck. Check out Ecovision on Smith Street. Even if nothing gels, you might pick up great Christmas presents. Makes sense to support local artists."

That handicapped idea jibed curiously with Malcolm's change of heart about SWINC, Maddie thought, trudging back across the snowy paths of the Oval. Suddenly, fingers tugged at her sleeve. Someone in a wool face mask, only his earnest brown eyes and mouth showing. A rabbit in a tiny parka rode in the handlebar bag of his mountain bike. "Can I, can I buy you a . . . a . . . cup of coffee, Professor?" Barney whispered. "I need some help on my outline."

Maddie was astonished at the invitation, clearly offered before the request, showing more social savvy than she could have expected. To him it was probably tantamount to a marriage proposal. For the moment she ignored the "can/may" distinction, for practical purposes already on a dusty shelf with Marie's Old English odes.

"It's a deal. Fifteen minutes, and then I have to get back to work."

Seated in the Refectory, she smiled as Barney approached, bearing the porcelain cup like a chalice. She whisked it out of his shaky fingers. Placing a backpack on the floor, he peeled open a carton of chocolate milk and took a few slurps.

The final assignment was a seven-page research essay, rocket science for freshmen. Maddie's no-plagiarism ploy involved letting the students document a major purchase: car, snowmobile, motorcycle, vacation, wedding. Onto the table tumbled a collage of papers he spread out like a Civil War battlefield. Barney was planning a funeral. He had gathered data from respectable sources, including an update of Jessica Mitford's pioneer study, *The American Way of Death Revisited*, *Consumer Reports* magazine, and a pamphlet from Gooderham and Worts: "Where Do You See Yourself in One Hundred Years?" It listed a number, 1-800-ASH2ASH."

"I am having a cremation. The modern way," he explained. "But I cannot decide on burial, putting it in a vault or just to take the urn home."

No use even making a Gordian thrust at untangling the distressing lack of parallelism. "You can't take it with you,

Barney," she remarked, struggling to retain a solemn expression. "Make your choices and document your references. Use that new style with parentheses."

She watched him scribble into a tiny notebook. Then stuttering thanks, he wiped up a coffee ring with a napkin and bussed her cup over to the dish table, carefully depositing the trash into a garbage can. Bless the boy. How was he faring in his other courses?

Back in the department, she smiled absently at Nancy. The secretary's voice had a twinge of panic.

"Grace's gone."

Chapter Twenty Eight

"Gone? You mean she left already for Hawaii?" More benign volcanoes than the one simmering at Copper. Yet the semester had several weeks remaining. How odd. Had she made advance arrangements? Maddie turned from the bulletin board where a Christmas book sale at SWINC was being advertised.

"I don't know." Wrinkling her brow, Nancy inspected a sheet of paper as if it contained the secret to picking winning lottery numbers. "This was slipped under the door when I came at eight. Thought it was a student assignment, so I didn't open it right away. Doesn't even say when she'll be back. God, Captain Bligh'll be in a rage. She'd have torn a strip off the woman face-to-face."

Maddie examined the note, the usually careful script rushed and blotted. "Recent circumstances prevent me from continuing my duties. I hope that my years of service may override this sudden dereliction. Enclosed is a check which will pay a grader to mark the final papers in my courses."

Nancy glanced over her shoulder as if Flo might swoop down on them like a slavering wolf on the fold. "Was she ill, do you suppose? She's been so . . . paler. And strained, like she hasn't been eating or sleeping well."

Maddie fastened her coat and plopped her doge hat back on. "Grace is a professional. She wouldn't have left tasks undone. Something's wrong here. I'll be back in an hour, if anyone asks."

Though Maddie had never been inside Grace's flat, she had given her a ride home once or twice. Years ago, the stately old manor on Brewster Drive had been a private hospital, a "rest home" in more euphemistic terms. She parked along the snowy street behind a row of cars still buried by the plow. Gothic turrets and doorcases, wing-like eaves, and shooting window heads gave the Queen Anne-Romanesque blend the aspect of a bird in flight. Asymmetric, decorated with rounded porches and quirky little balconies, the house retained a certain schizophrenic charm. Maddie walked quickly through the lobby and located the number on the mailboxes, noting the lack of a security entrance, hardly surprising in Stoddard. Polished oak stairs with a plush new runner led to the second floor, where a silver-haired man in dusty overalls was chiseling the edges of Grace's door. He brushed aside wood chips and looked up.

"Tony Christakos, the Super," he said after she introduced herself. "First break-in since I've lived here. Safe neighborhood, but these doors aren't so strong. Cheap retrofittings when they converted."

"I'm looking for Miss Lwasa."

His friendly, gray-shadowed eyes held a guarded worry. "She stopped down at my apartment yesterday. Told me about the damage from Saturday night and said she was leaving town. Nice lady. Paid in advance until the lease is up in August. Maybe she plans to come back." He gestured inside. "I mean, furniture's still here."

"Did she call the police?"

He shrugged. "Don't think so. She said nothing was taken. Messed up, though. Could have been kids fooling around. Parents don't teach no responsibility these days."

Sure, Maddie thought. Snowballs through windows. But this "prank" had pushed Grace over the edge. "May I look inside for a second? She has a book of mine." Responding to her confident smile, he opened the door.

Maddie had little time to admire the decor as she moved into the living room. A general ransacking had taken place. Pillows were tossed around, sofa cushions unseated. Pictures hung at angles and drawers lay open. In the bedroom, shoes and clothes littered the floor. The fractal pattern of order in disorder continued with the added ignominy of panties and bras on top of the uprooted mattress. Maddie's stomach lurched. A rape by any other name. On the dresser underneath an overturned jewelry case, she recognized the signature coral necklace. Funny that it hadn't been taken, nor the heavy silver bangles and gold chains. In the closet, empty hangers askew revealed places where a few outfits had been snatched.

The kitchen was untouched: counters clean and bare, doors closed, no foodstuffs thrown around. The fridge contained salad vegetables, milk, juice, spring water. Wouldn't kids have trashed the place? In the bathroom, the usual collection of aspirin, vitamins, and creams remained, but no shampoo, toothbrush, comb, or brush. A hurried decampment.

In the study, books lay on the floor along with scattered lecture notes and a letter from a local travel agency confirming a reservation on American Airlines. Detroit to San Francisco to Honolulu on December 23rd, returning on January 5th. Growing bolder, she opened an address book in the desk: all African references, except for her own number and an N. Lwasa in New York City, the name crossed out in one ominous stroke. With her father dead, Grace had nowhere to turn. Breathing faster, Maddie felt guilt creep up her spine like a furry, accusative spider. Why hadn't she taken her friend more seriously?

She seized a well-thumbed paperback of *For Whom the Bell Tolls* and waved it at Tony as she left. What bothered her most about the apartment was the lack of wanton destruction. Portable plums like the stereo and television were still in place. Not common thieves then. And professional hitmen would have aimed at Grace herself, or at the very least destroyed the apartment. This looked like a polite poseur had rambled through, bearing a subconscious mindset that breakage wasn't good manners.

She started the car and waited while the flabby heater kicked in. Where had the woman gone? The trip was weeks away. To a motel out of town, then? Except for those near the snowmobile grid, most had closed for the season. And travel in the UP in winter was less than convenient, finding gas at night difficult. Despite the organized efforts at settling her lease and leaving an apology with the department, suppose she'd driven off like a frightened animal, then had a breakdown on some remote road? Grace hated the climate, fought it instead of making peace with its elements. Unlike the local vehicles, the Buick wouldn't have carried an emergency car kit with a sleeping bag, chocolate, and candles. Did she intend to start a new life somewhere under another name? Grace had been on permanent staff at Copper for over ten years, so she must have had a nest egg. Insurance money from her father perhaps. Maddie took a deep breath to dispel the dramatics.

Scarcely had she returned to her office when Flo pounced in, quivering like a raging cougar, angry lines creasing her forehead. "Where the hell is she? I'll tell you one thing, she'll never work at this university again. And those self-effacing phrases about 'service' came from Othello."

Maddie took a deep breath, tempted to mention Iago. "You know, Flo, not long ago you were begging for help. I don't expect any gratitude for my trouble on your beha—"

"What trouble? The answer was underneath your nose. I wouldn't call your efforts brilliant, just lucky."

"If I may continue." Ignoring the red tide rising in her head, Maddie shot her an oblique scowl. "You might at least show compassion for someone with serious problems."

"What problems?" She snorted in contempt.

"Grace was very afraid these last few weeks. I thought a student was harassing her, but it's escalated. Her apartment was vandalized."

Flo tossed her head, tinkling a pair of delicate crystal earrings. "So what? No one's immune to petty thievery."

"It looked more sinister than that. For example, nothing was taken."

"Maybe a seamy secret life. A jealous lover. She's been unstable from the beginning, if you ask me."

"What do you mean?"

"Simply that Malcolm had no business hiring her. She doesn't belong here, to put it bluntly."

"Bluntly ugly. Why aren't I surprised?"

Flo folded her arms and arched an eyebrow at Maddie's jeans. Then she smoothed her pale green silk dress under an ivory mohair sweater. "I don't know if you're merely stubborn about those casual clothes, to use a polite word, or if you don't have any fashion sense. Trying to look like a student at your advanced age. It's pathetic. Why don't you try something useful? Plastic surgeons in Detroit do wonders for gobbler neck." She stamped out, slamming the door and leaving the Toby jugs vibrating on the shelves.

As her blood pressure pounded a Sousa march, Maddie checked the calendar, did some monthly calculations, and ruled out hormones. She opened the window and inhaled the healing cold. Instead of brooding about Grace's disappearance, why not use her spare hour to follow up on Brian's suggestion?

With the painting becoming an accessory, Maddie drove to Smith Street, unsure of what she'd find in the quiet residential area. In front of a small bungalow of native fieldstone hung a black sign resembling a strip of film with iridescent highlights: Ecovision. After climbing the stairs to the porch, she opened the front door, jingling a distant bell.

The living room had been remodeled into a photo gallery: color, sepia, black and white, some representational and others intriguingly abstract. A Georgia O'Keeffe blossom beckoned the viewer into its soft mauve velvet folds. Maddie smiled at the title: *Rose Is a Rose Is a Rose*. Gertrude Stein would appreciate not being misquoted for a change. Moving past a grove of birches mirrored in a still lake, she turned her vision upside down at humanoid tree forms resembling torsos, the skin-like texture of the silvery bark inviting touch. The price tag read two hundred dollars, reasonable with the attractive framing and intricate mat-cutting. Perfect to wean Ed from those muscular horses and lions.

"I'm Pat Valentino. Looking for anything in particular?" a mellow voice asked. Maddie would have handed over a week's salary to exchange her irritating soprano for those resonant tones. A tall woman in navy gabardine slacks and a white rough linen shirt with full sleeves parted a beaded curtain. Her black hair, poodle cut a la early Anne Bancroft, had streaks of silver.

"What amazing work!" Maddie said. "It hypnotizes me, but I can't decipher some of the images." She pointed to a huge diamond nesting on a creamy cobalt background of flowing silk. *"Breakfast at Tiffany's"*?

"I used to do nature postcard pictures, but it got boring. Now I like to challenge people, make them think. That photo was shot in a brook at freeze-up." She mimed a twist with her hand. "Close up. Hundred-and-five-millimeter lens."

Maddie drew closer to a haunting image of wild geese crossing a luminous full moon. "You must have been incredibly patient to capture the shot at the exact moment that the birds flew by."

Pat cleared her throat, a soft smile nudging one corner of her mouth. "It's a composite. A double exposure. And now with digitalization, anyone can stroll across Venus or shake hands with Abe Lincoln."

"Thanks for not stringing me along. Anyway, my neighbor will love it. He's a hard one to please when it comes to art." While Pat prepared the business of the sale, Maddie opened her bag and placed the painting on an empty easel. "I had another purpose coming here. Brian Turner at Copper said that you know Northern Michigan pretty well. Do you recognize this site?"

Pat's heavy, expressive eyebrows rose for a moment, perhaps expecting a challenge. She gave it no more than a brief glance. "Of course. It's a very holy place."

"Holy?"

"To the natives. The Ojibwa. Dreamer's Rock, the island's called. Young boys were taken by canoe and left on the narrow ledge in a quest to learn their animal name."

Maddie cocked her head. "Rousseau would have approved, but not child welfare agencies. Then what happened?"

"Apparently, fasting played a large part. It can induce hallucinations. Chants, drumming, burning sweetgrass. If you've been to the local powwows, you'll remember the aromatic smell."

Maddie felt herself drawn in, the mists of Avalon descending. The painting was assuming a reality of cold, hunger, privation, yet with the exhilaration of transcending the body to find an incorporeality beyond. "Is the site far?"

"Couple of hours. Down to the northern part of Lake Michigan. Fairport peninsula. Pretty raw this time of year if you're thinking of going."

"I might have to." Maddie sighed. "Do you have time to hear about my own quest?"

Pat brewed a pot of coffee spiced with a vanilla bean and pulled up two pressed-back oak chairs. The photographer listened with courtesy and interest. Then she inspected the painting more closely.

"That sun symbol. I'm positive that I've seen it on my summer rambles, but the brain cells aren't clicking." She paused and sent Maddie's eyes an invitation. "Sunday's good for me. Care to take a trip starting about six?"

Maddie returned to Copper with a dose of hope. Lake Michigan had a personality quite distinct from Superior, and a knowledgeable companion would help. En route to her office, she heard the sounds of uncivil broils around the corner and turned with reluctance.

"Are you crazy?" George yelled. "You're signing our death warrant!"

"Lower your voice," Flo hissed, gesturing to Nancy as a student stood gaping in the corridor. "Shut that door and lock it. I don't want this embarrassing argument to become common gossip."

Watching the secretary secure the door as if they were besieged, Maddie stepped forward. "What's the matter?"

George shook a fist at Flo. "Ask her what 'service course' means. It's another word for goodbye English Department. And don't bother to write if you get work. Because you won't."

Flo folded her arms in a smug gesture. "Shortsighted as usual. Don't you realize that enrollment has been dropping? And there haven't been any jobs for teachers since the last baby boomer left college. You all got in under the wire, and so did I, admittedly. But it's quite simple. By ceding degree-granting powers in favor of sensible service courses, we'll save money and guarantee our future."

Ceding. The innocent word belonged to appeasement treaties of the most perfidious kind. Of all Flo's hatchet jobs, this struck at the mission statement of the department itself. Sinking the axe into the heartwood with the pretense to prune. Counting to five, she tried to appeal to reason. "You're the shortsighted one. Boom, bust, echo. The first children of that generation are already entering college. We'll get our students back." Did she really believe that? She thought of mentioning the web page but realized that she hadn't discussed it with Flo. Its failure might confirm the wisdom of her chairman's nefarious plans.

"And what service courses?" asked Marie, a sag to her crumpled body which tugged at Maddie's heart. "We already teach basic grammar to every division."

Flo steepled her fingers, gazing off like Brigham Young in the Promised Land, yet with no inspiration beyond a balance sheet and a ticket up the administrative ladder to a deanship. "Let's face it. The arts are dead. I see three productive streams. Business, health science, and technology. We can specialize as necessary. Nursing might want something different from Engineering. Case notes versus lab reports."

"We're lit people. What do we know about that?" George's voice wavered, his slim body turned sideways like a wary old gunslinger overmatched.

"My point exactly. Look upon it as a chance to expand your myopic horizons. Learn or leave. Teach the new courses

241

or get out. And by the way, I've left sample texts in the Common Room. See that you're familiar with them a.s.a.p."

Acres of sterile lab reports marched across Maddie's mind, moles and stress factors. All that passive voice with complete impunity. Never had Flo been more confident. Nordman must be back on her side. A fatal accident and demographics had brought her evil star into ascendancy at the department's most vulnerable moment.

Chapter Twenty Nine

Hearing a dull roar about six Sunday morning, Maddie flashed on the porch lights and opened the door. A silver GMC 4X4 pickup with an Ecovision decal on the side pulled up in the drive. Nikon charged out, fumbling like a fool around Pat's high-topped Kodiak boots. She let him lick her ear and applied a hearty thump, his waving saber tail a barometer of instant favor. "Great pup! Bring him along. My border collie Angus is in the back."

"I was taking him to my father's, my last-minute babysitter."

"No problem. That's why I got an extended cab. Angus comes on all my shoots."

At Pat's whistle, Nikon leaped into the truck as if born to the manor, mildly received by the polite sniff of a sober black and white herding dog. Next to the camera pack on the generous bench seat, Maddie plopped an insulated jug. "Thermal infusions." She noticed a pack of Winstons on the dash and hoped that the cab wouldn't fill with smoke.

The day was crisp and the sleepy dawn approaching its tardiest. Less than a month until the solstice. Pat eased a Lorena McKennett CD into a slot in the dash and eerie Celtic sounds piped them through the darkness. The shores of Superior appeared for a final time at Marquette as the sun flared onto the windshield.

"Want to stop?" Maddie asked, feeling guilty about com-

243

mandeering the trip for her purposes.

Pat laughed softly. "It's no point-and-shoot. I'd need to set up the tripod. Early morning and late afternoon are the best times, when the land reveals itself by shadows. Even so, that shifting cloudbank's going to cut us off."

Maddie felt chastened, but babbled on in embarrassment. "Have you been to Pictured Rocks National Seashore? I went camping there as a kid. The bugs turned my head into a balloon. Thought I was hardy enough with our blackflies, but those . . ." Her skin still crawled at the memory.

"Cluster flies, Ethiopian flies I call them. Like those pictures of African famines. When I photograph on the beach, they land on my pants by the hundreds."

Heading south on 41 as the hours passed, they entered the tiny towns of Skandia and Trenary, then skirted Hiawatha National Forest until Rapid River. Pat turned east on Route 2 along the Big Bay de Noc, taking a right down the peninsula to Fairport. Snaking in and out of Manistique State Forest boundaries, finally they followed a fork heading into the conifers. Unplowed, it had been broken by other brave pickups and snowmobiles. Maddie wrinkled her brow at the deep ruts and braced herself against the dashboard as the vehicle lurched. "Sure we won't get stuck?"

Pat steadied the wheel, her calm gray eyes assessing each move. "These lug tires are wicked on highways. Too much vibration. They're designed for off-road." She switched to low gear, and they inched forward in a tank complete with stereo sound and velour upholstery.

At the end of the trail, the evergreens separated to reveal a lookout. Pat cut the engine, opened the doors, and directed the dogs to their business. Maddie followed, bundling up her coat and pulling her hat over her ears against the cruel wind across the bluff.

"Exactly like the painting. The artist must have stood here," she said, shielding her eyes against tearing as she pointed with her other hand. "Dreamer's Rock shrouded in mist. I can barely make out the ledge you mentioned. With that pink cloud bank and the dark blue water, it's magical and deadly. The Lady of the Lake reaching up to pass the sword. English poets had no concept of countries outside their benign little island."

Far below, the cold air sucked the last warmth from the steaming water. The gravid lake moved slow thighs, ice tinkling at the edges, crystalline layers piling like broken glass as the flow pushed forward. At what instant would the last molecules exchange states of matter, trade fluid for solid and transform the coastline into a vast white land? Humid air frosted the trees. Maddie admired a gnarly jack pine grappled to the cliff, bunches of tiny needle clusters and small, hard cones decorating its unkempt branches. "So strong and resilient, hanging on for dear life. Farmers used to call them unlucky because the thin soil that nourishes them wouldn't support crops. Forest fires can release the seeds in the cones." Billy had given her a long lecture on trees.

Cigarette between her lips, breath merged with the smoke, Pat fingered the timeline of cones, gray in the interior, dull green midway, and bright emerald at the tip, a natural epigram. "Sometimes it takes a shock to move ahead." She didn't explain, and Maddie didn't ask. They'd known each other scarcely a day, and despite the easy camaraderie, the photographer was yet a stranger.

As Maddie stood transfixed at the edge of the cliff, the heat stored through hours in the cab leached from her bones, leaving her as vulnerable as a sparrow. "Guess we'd better get going, unless you—"

"Too windy for photography," Pat said, tucking her hands

into her parka. "Give me zero and calm over thirty-two degrees and a gale. Pass the coffee, and let's roam around towards the north. Something is nuzzling at the back of my neck, and it's not dog lips."

Another hour brought a troop of snowmobiles, followed by cross-country skiers, angular motions propelling them with surprising speed and grace. In this sparsely populated region, they met little auto traffic. Glad to reach the restroom at a gas station in Manistique, Maddie insisted on filling up the truck, swallowing heavily at the sum in comparison to the teetotaling Probe. Then she treated Pat to lunch at the Anchor Inn. It was hard to see how a town of only three thousand could support much business in the winter. Lake trout was the special, succulent morsels accompanied by piquant cole slaw and mounds of hot, crispy french fries. A bottle of malt vinegar nudged the ketchup, courtesy to Canadian preferences. Bottomless cups of hot coffee cheered them, and they ordered homemade apple pie. Maddie asked the waitress for a brown bag snack for the animals.

"First good meal all week. Guess I'm a typical artist. Too busy working to cook. Kraft Dinner's my staple." Pat regrouped the plates, leaned back to consider her efforts. "Food photography might be a lucrative option."

Maddie forked into the flaky pie crust and moaned with expectation. "I tried my mother's pastry recipe, but somehow it never turns out the same. Lard was gospel. Never a can of shortening in the house."

Released from the truck, the dogs devoured their hamburger patties. Nikon pawed small balls of ice which he crunched happily in lieu of gravel. "One more hour, and that's it," Maddie said, checking her watch. "You've been too generous with your time."

More winding secondary routes led them into a farming

area. Long split-rail fences of durable cedar defined the fields, eight-foot lengths stretched between crosspieces efficiently constructed without the expense of precious nails. Pat rolled down the window for a breath of fresh air while she consulted a map. Closing her eyes, Maddie expected the muted clop of horseshoes or the schuss of sled runners. Only the glimpse of a microwave tower in the distance summoned them to the present. Around the next bend, past a grove of noble chestnut trees, Pat braked suddenly opposite a wooden sign with a huge yellow sun. St. Hildegard's Monastery, it read. They gave each other mental high-fives and gazed up a long driveway. At the top of the hill was a gathering of buildings and the spire of a small church.

"That sun. I should have remembered," Pat said, flicking the steering wheel. "Drove by maybe five years ago. A different landscape in the snow."

"What is this place? A female saint, but a monastery? Monks or nuns? Gregorian chants or guitars?"

Pat smiled in amusement. "Maybe everything. Go on in, request a carol, and see what happens."

Anchoring the complex like the rock that was Peter, the central building of five stories of chiseled gray stone had a slate roof and bars across the windows of the top floor. Pat pulled in next to a white van, where a person of indeterminate sex, dressed in a parka, was unloading cartons. Two smaller brick buildings, offices or residences perhaps, stood on the left, on the other side a white-painted clapboard church, its steeple spearing the blue sky. A metal barn and a manure pile hinted that the monastery owned animals, and a few cornstalks peeked through the snow in a large garden. At the sight of a shoveled play area with swings, slide, and merry-go-round, they exchanged curious glances.

A broad set of worn stone stairs led to the main building.

Maddie paused and contemplated the entrance, cold and foreboding. And those sinister bars far above didn't help, shades of Mrs. Rochester gripping them with bony fingers. "No sign for visiting hours. Could they be cloistered here?" The distant wails of a baby reached their ears. "Not that cloistered," she added.

Pat pointed to a few leathery oak leaves clinging to a tree. "Wind's died. I'll scout around and see if anything's worth shooting. Meet at the truck in an hour, say? Or should I come searching for you in some damp dungeon?"

With a nervous grin, Maddie waved her off and climbed to a huge, blackened double door bearing an iron knocker in the shape of a frame harp. When no one answered her raps, she steeled herself, opened the door timidly, and peered at a cross-stitched motto at the entrance: "All guests who present themselves are to be welcomed as Christ." A young woman in a denim jumpsuit padded forward in sneakers, a nut brown baby on her hip tugging a wooden cross around her neck. "Sorry I couldn't answer sooner. Rather tied up. I'm Sister Therese. How can I help you?"

"I am a bit confused. Is this a monastery?"

After listening to Maddie's inquiries, Sister Therese explained that St. Hildegard's was an orphanage run by Benedictine nuns. Most of the children were refugees from Africa and the Far East, past the adorable baby stage for easy adoptions. " 'Monastery' is a generic term. As for clothing, some of us wear modern dress. Others prefer the traditional habit."

Then she led the way down a long hall of classrooms. At first, Maddie was surprised at the noise, but it seemed to emerge from eagerness more than chaos. Hands shot up at questions, and childish laughter charged the air. For a moment she wished she taught at this exciting primary level.

What happened between here and college to stultify education? Or was the instructor the magic ingredient?

The main office, decorated with a bulletin board of
crayoned efforts, had a desk with a battered Smith Corona
and a deacon's bench against one wall. With a womanly
smile, Sister Therese parked the baby in Maddie's uncertain
arms and knocked at a door before disappearing inside.

Maddie sat awkwardly, retrieving vulnerable parts from
the child's busy hands. With no siblings, she lacked experience babysitting, preferring delivering papers for her first job.
If "dandling" was the appropriate word, how was it done? A
few bounces? Dressed in a light woollen sleeper, the baby
didn't appreciate the strategy, its rosebud mouth blowing spit
bubbles, tiny fingers clenching the drawstring to her hood.
An explosive burp caused her to check her lap with a relieved
sigh. Down coats were expensive to clean. Puppies were more
amenable. And they didn't drool.

On one wall, a gold-leafed ornate frame highlighted a
woman in medieval clothing, gauzy fabric draping her head,
eyes closing dreamily over a naked blond cherub on her lap,
its chubby hand fastened on a bunch of grapes. Children
too perfectly featured, ringleted hair glistening, gathered
round in silk and velvet robes. Cautiously, Maddie placed
her charge on the floor, bracing it between her boots. A
brass plate read: "*The Madonna of Giverny*. Frederick
MacMonnies, American painter from 1863-1937." Pre-Raphaelite influence. No wonder it attracted her.

Sister Therese returned, her friendly face registering concern as she hunted for the baby. Scooping up the bundle, she
motioned Maddie through the door. As if on rollers, a large
woman glided from behind a desk, her long blue homespun
garment reaching to the floor. Twin peaks of white hair rose
like doves in flight on either side of a brow creeping back onto

her skull. A disproportionate distance between the bottom of her nose and upper lip, upon which errant hairs sprouted, lent an apelike appearance. Despite her bulk, she moved gracefully, shaking Maddie's hand with vigor.

"Professor Temple? From Copper University? I'm Sister Blanche, the Prioress. You must be cold from your long journey." She called in a booming voice. "Therese, could you bring some of your hot cider?" Ushering Maddie to an armchair, she located herself heavily and gazed down the broad plain of her bosom. "Our deepest condolences on Professor Driscoll's untimely death. I imagine he told you about us."

In the time it took Maddie to recount her peregrinations, Therese returned with two steaming clay mugs decorated with harps. The tempting aroma of cloves and apples summoned childhood memories, a Halloween punch worthy of the noun, she thought, as she felt her temperature rise several degrees and paused to exhale a satisfying fire.

Sister Blanche coughed discreetly and tugged one drooping earlobe. "It's usually very mild, a well-guarded recipe from the mother house in Germany. But this year Sister Bernadette used old rum casks for the aging process. A serendipitous ticket for bitter months."

Maddie hardly knew how to begin. She was present as Malcolm's emissary, but in a way the Prioress couldn't imagine. "You have a fine school. How long has it been here?"

"This used to be a family farm. The last son sold the acreage around 1900, and on the site the county built an asylum, hence the shameful bars for the . . . violent patients." She frowned with a darkness that could have parted the Red Sea. "Then with modern drugs, psychiatry, and government off-loading, there was no more need for the facility, or so they claimed. The troubled were either cured, and I use the term with attendant irony, remanded to their families, or worst of all, sent to far-off streets with a handful of prescriptions. I cannot comment on the morality of abandoning confused souls to their own inadequate care. In a mixed blessing, we were fortunate to buy it for a fraction of the value."

"You've made a heaven out of hell," Maddie said. "But the painting, how did it—"

"*Dreamer's Rock* was Timmy's last. His work was dedicated to the common good. In self-effacement, he used the sun as his signature, an emblem in one of St. Hildegard's precepts." Her eyes closed, and the great lips moved slowly around the words as if reciting the rosary: " 'I am the day that does not shine by the sun; rather by me the sun is ignited.' "

So many ideas were coming too quickly. Burdened by a heavy coat and the fortifying drink, Maddie felt a rivulet of sweat trickle down her back. Timmy. Timothy. Malcolm's father's name. "The last? Then he . . ."

Chapter Thirty

"Spina bifida children didn't live long when Timmy was born. Thanks to the miracles of surgery and modern therapy, now they often lead quite normal lives." Sister Blanche crossed herself slowly, then reached down with a grunt and turned a knob on a chugging steam radiator. "One ample blessing afforded us is heat."

Placing her bulky coat on a chair, Maddie took out the snapshot. "Is this the child's mother?" Silly, thinking of him as a child. He was a man. Given life only a few years after her.

Sister Blanche nodded, a large, knobby finger pointing at the shoe store advertisement in the enlargement. "Only read the signs, the Bible advises in its simple language. Ferrous Mountain. The Professor told us about Lili's family. If we'd had this, we might have located her parents. Never a word from the girl. So long ago. I only hope that a faith beyond imagining sustained them."

From a nearby cabinet, she retrieved a file. "Not much of a life, one thin sheaf of papers. A helpful priest in Manistique referred the poor girl to us. She knocked on our door a chill day just before Midday Praise, offered to do cleaning for bed and board. Lili Damita she called herself." A flirt of a smile crossed the kindly, grotesque face. "Of course we knew that wasn't true. Our sisters love the films, especially the elders. But we let the fabrication stand. While not a Catholic, she soon discovered a deep commitment to the Benedictine Rule.

It was Lili's wish to become an oblate, a lay person dedicated to a religious life." Her throat cleared as she gazed at a delicate porcelain figure of the Virgin. "But before long we saw that she had more immediate needs."

"Her pregnancy."

"Yes, how I wish it could have been as happy as our Lord's nativity. Lili received the best personal care, but despite that, the birth was difficult. Even now, you must appreciate the shortage of doctors in the Upper Peninsula." She gestured out the window across miles of snowy fields. "We are far from expert help. And she died from hemorrhaging complications shortly after delivery. Although the sisters had stood vigil in the hall to offer transfusions, she had a rare blood type. Timmy she named as she held him in her arms those final hours."

Maddie took a reluctant breath, wondering what more would unfold. "How wonderful that she was cherished here, for however brief a time."

"There is a special providence in the fall of a sparrow. That's Shakespeare, I believe."

"And Timmy?"

Sister Blanche heaved herself over to a battered wooden cabinet, removing an album. She turned the leaves until she smiled broadly. "Here's our little man. His wheelchair wasn't practical on the grounds, so the children pulled him everywhere in a wagon. Still, he wanted to do his part. One favorite chore was milking the goats. As he got older, the Lord whispered the best use for his talents."

Maddie paged through the photos. Timmy had a forty-carat grin, saluting the flag at an Independence Day picnic as the other children gathered around him. Love brightened their faces, arms bolstering his thin frame as they hoisted him onto their shoulders. She marveled at the makeshift ramp for the goat which allowed him to reach from his wheelchair. On subsequent pages, he had grown to manhood, his easel set up in a field of daisies. Backlit by the sun in a halo effect, he shook his brush in mock battle at the photographer. "He looks happy." Were it possible to "adjust" to such a condition, Timmy had surpassed that goal.

"Even so, it was a complicated and narrow world for what people called the 'handicapped' in those benighted days. No easy wheelchair access, assistive devices, opportunity to go outside to high school like the older children. The sisters were glad to tutor him in their specialties, but it wasn't the same." She thought for a moment, checked a silver watch pinned to her breast. "There's someone else you should see. Sister Ursula, his art teacher."

In a colorful room next door, giggling together at oilcloth-covered tables, twenty toddlers were plastering rolls of paper with fingerpainting, smocks covered in paint and faces to match. "Cheer is one of God's greatest gifts, and I don't mean the emotion," said a thin woman in overalls, iron-gray hair gathered in practical braids. "Welcome. We don't often receive the joy of visitors. Forgive me for not shaking hands." She wiggled a rainbow of fingers and wiped them on a rag smelling of turpentine.

"Professor Temple was a good friend of Timmy's uncle. She'd love to see his paintings." Sister Blanche strolled among the desks, patting tiny backs and admiring the work. "I'll hold the fort."

"Timmy's gallery is in the library," Sister Ursula explained in a reverent voice, leading her down the hall. "Some pieces which he gave to the sisters, they keep in their rooms."

As they turned a corner, the sounds of plainsong drifted along the corridor. "Choir practice. Hildegard of Bingen was famed for her antiphons, chanted verse. Spare but eloquent."

She breathed the melody like a warm breeze, and Maddie felt the tension in her shoulders relax. There was something profoundly therapeutic in the gentle roll of *a capella* voices, the purity of Gregorian chants as a refuge from the momentous orchestrations of modern music.

The library served a dual purpose, one side devoted to religious studies, the other containing shelves for children's books. Along the back wall, Timmy's work traced the seasonal beauties of the Upper Peninsula. Walking from one glorious scene to another, Maddie followed the progress of his talents, the fledgling dabbler to the accomplished artist, always signed by the sun. Even in the depictions of late fall, that most dismal time of year, a palpable optimism underscored the burgeoning promise beneath fallow fields, the trees guarding buds for the spring. A simple faith infused the oils. Then something had gone wrong, the last pictures merely roughed in, as if waiting for a better day. She turned to Sister Ursula with a questioning look.

"Timmy's most productive period was during his twenties, when mind and mastery were one," the woman explained. "Later, his reflexes and equilibrium deteriorated." A mentor's pride in her voice yielded to pain. "He wanted to go to college, to travel to museums. It wasn't possible. We didn't even have the vans until a generous donor brought them a few years ago. Only one rusty station wagon and an old school bus for the lot of us. The day he painted *Dreamer's Rock*, I cried. He never left the property again."

Maddie felt a tug at her heart, knowing that Malcolm had heard this wrenching story. No man of stone, that explained his change of conscience about SWINC. Perhaps he had seen Timmy every time he passed a wheelchair. "How did you locate Professor Driscoll?"

"When Timmy died ten years ago, just as the daffodils

bloomed, he was buried next to his mother in our cemetery near the herb garden." As she looked out the window, her eyes closed for the moment. "Lili kept her own counsel until the end. I don't think she knew she was dying. Aside from the clothes in her suitcase, she left only a gold locket. As soon as he was old enough to understand, we gave it to him. He wore the memento night and day."

A locket? The one Kathleen had described? She held her breath, hardly daring to speak. "And?"

"We didn't know that the piece opened, you see. It was quite small and delicate. Even in his best days, Timmy wouldn't have had the dexterity to manipulate it. One of our children was helping to sort his few belongings. Lo and behold, the busy-fingered pup explored the jewelry with her tiny fingernails. We found a picture of the Driscolls with their names on the back."

Maddie felt dizzy at the revelations, weighted with the burden of passing on the information to a brave old woman with a cat at her feet and a taste for Marlboros. Would Kathleen receive the sad news as a balm to ancient wounds, a peaceful closure? "But how did you find them? They died long ago, far from here."

"Very true. Yet Our Lord never closes one door without opening another." She gestured to a desk in the corner where an aged woman in a brown robe bent over a book, her magnifying glass flashing across the page. "This fall, our intrepid librarian saw Professor Driscoll's picture in the *Peninsula Register*. Shameful, that opposition to a wonderful project to help God's special people. Sister Blanche was of a strong mind to write him a letter of admonishment, but seeing the unusual Driscoll name, we wondered if he were related to Timmy. So when she did write, a very different letter it was."

"He must have been devastated." So much, perhaps, that he wore the secret to his grave like a penance.

"Professor Driscoll called immediately, planning to visit as soon as duties allowed. When I described the jewelry, for several minutes he was unable to speak. Of course I sent along the locket and painting. I believe he intended to spend Christmas with his aunt and prepare her for the shock."

"Your thank-you note started me on my quest," Maddie said.

The nun's face shone like a merry prune. "Sister Blanche accepted a generous contribution. Our needs are few, but Christmas was coming, and children love presents. She told him that charity was the best atonement, that he should channel his efforts toward that Center at the university and help those like Timmy. I only trust that he followed her wise advice."

Maddie nodded. And so he had. Where would the money have been better spent, at SWINC or here? Not for her to decide. How many dollars had she banked on the chairman's thankless job? She pulled out her checkbook and wrote quickly, before she could remember the plans for a garage and stove.

Fastening her parka, Maddie hurried out to the truck. The dogs were tied to the back bumper, the camera pack gone. She tramped around back of the church as her boots filled with snow, but the graves were humble white-painted crosses buried under drifts. A poem by Oscar Wilde came to her lips as she stood a friend's duty, her eyes tearing at unbidden connections: "Lily-like, white as snow,/ She hardly knew/ She was a woman, so/ Sweetly she grew." "Requiescat," rest in peace. Malcolm's lost twin was reunited with her brother, and Timmy's legacy lined walls for faithful witnesses. Scanning the area, she saw Pat crouched behind a tripod.

Ahead, blessing his flock, stood a large statue of St. Benedict, and looming in the distance, the microwave tower. As Maddie crunched towards her, Pat looked up. "I'm going to call it *Answer to a Prayer*."

"I've found some answers as well."

Maddie explained in detail as they drove back to Stoddard in the feeble rays of the setting sun. At the halfway point, a busy truck stop dished out hot turkey sandwiches. Fries twice in one day. She grew loggy in the warm cab, woke herself twice with snores. As the town limits appeared, she realized that she had forgotten to collect crucial notes on Oscar Wilde for her Monday lecture. No wonder that poem had sprung into memory.

Obligingly, Pat continued on to the university, parking near Denney. Maddie said, "This is rather creepy. I don't usually come here at night."

Pat opened the window, lit a cigarette, watching its glow with a smile. "Darkness only hides the light. Make your man earn his kibble."

Nikon trotted inside with her, some creature comfort as they walked the quiet halls, black and foreboding except for what filtered through the windows from yellow sodium vapors of the campus poles. Rounding the corner to the offices, Maddie heard a small hissing. In front of Grace's door crouched a figure, its arm moving in circles. "Stop that!" she yelled. A tall image turned, and a can clattered onto the floor.

At the alarm in her voice, the dog charged, a roar erupting from his throat worthy of Cerberus, guardian of Hell. When the man scrambled onto a large plastic recycling bin at the end of a blind corridor, Nikon halted on instinct, pearly whites exposed, the coarse hair on his back raised like a wild boar's hump. "Get this dog off me!" a voice screamed, girlish in panic.

Catching her breath, Maddie sat her protector at attention, softly stroking his chest. "No more Roo-Roo. Barkus is willing at last." She glared at the student's team jacket. "Now that I have your undivided attention, answer a few questions."

"What questions? This is crazy."

"Caught in the act, young man. Did you also damage Miss Lwasa's vehicle?" He squirmed and refused to meet her eyes. "Tell me, or this trained attack dog heads straight for the family jewels. Who would blame me? A poor defenseless woman about to be mugged." She had bit her tongue against adding "old."

His shaking hands strayed towards his crotch as the dog growled softly. "Okay. I keyed her car. Big deal."

"Phone calls?"

"No way, man. She's unlisted."

"What about vandalizing her apartment Saturday before last?"

"Saturday? Shit, I was with the football team in Toledo. Ran for two hundred friggin' yards. If she flunks me, I'll miss basketball season."

"Consider yourself lucky for that small price. When I was your age, a student who couldn't make the grade packed his duffel bag and put on a uniform. You do remember *Vietnam: The Movie*?" Like a grim avenger, she pointed her finger at him. "The department will bill you, Mr. Dartmore. Smarten up . . . and broaden your vocabulary."

Chapter Thirty One

Maddie had sent Kathleen the painting with a long letter. Perhaps she'd assemble a basket of treats and visit the old woman at Christmas. She stood glumly in front of her mailbox, collecting her pay stub, that monthly passport to respectability. Malcolm's magical mystery tour had docked at the last port. Nothing more now than rowing on to retirement on the Ship of Fools. Could she adapt to teaching business English or technical writing? All those dull but practical résumés, memos, descriptions of mechanisms, ponderous troubleshooting manuals. With fewer and fewer people reading for pleasure, was this the dying gasp of literature, despite its inspiration and comfort as writers whispered wisdom across the centuries? An evil imp asked, "Could a poet fix the toilet? Could a dramatist swat a bug in your hard drive?"

Students passed in the hall, wrapped in massive coats and scarves, eyelashes frosted with rime, puffing warmth into frozen hands. Her eyes drifted to Grace's mailbox. Still no word. If only she could let the woman know that Dartmore had shot his last bolt.

In her colleague's space was what looked like a bill, and suddenly Maddie reached out a kleptomaniac's hand and hooked the envelope into her pocket. Suddenly Gary's hearty voice made her jump back, persimmon-faced at her furtive actions.

"Good news," he said, waving a fax.

"We could use some. You've heard about Grace, I suppose."

"Got to be something cockeyed there. She's as straight as an arrow. Anyway, I took your advice about Poe and made the deadline. Got a call that my paper's been accepted for the MLA convention in Chicago. Here's the tentative program. I read right after 'Gogol: Funereal Eroticism and Horny Vampires.' "

"Coleridge had the jump on vampires with 'Cristabel.' Maybe next year for me. So what's your topic?"

He shuffled his boots and rolled dark, boyish eyes as if the Devil'd made him do it. " 'Masque of the Red Death as HIV/AIDS Forerunner: a Comparison of Color Imagery.' Problem is, this dog won't hunt for Flo. Too little too late."

Maddie hoped he were wrong. The *PMLA*, founded in 1883, was the grandfather of English journals. Gary had done well for himself. Leaving him with congratulations, she walked casually to her office, closed the door, then ripped open Grace's envelope. Only one long distance charge, an Ontario 705 area code. She dialed the number. "Lift the Latch Lodge," a cheery voice answered, and she hung up on impulse. Even given the feeble assumption that Grace was there, better to find out more and know what questions to ask. Why jeopardize the situation by acting too fast? Who knew what her friend might have told them?

She revved the Google search engine into action, locating Lift the Latch near St. Joseph Island, fifty miles east of the Canadian Sault, connected to the mainland by a bridge. The lodge, open year-round, sat on a smaller island off the southern tip. Use the private callbox at the landing, and they'd run you across by boat or ice road. A few pictures scrolled down: Technicolor sunsets, grinning tourists dangling gigantic lake trout, snug pine-paneled rooms with striped Hudson Bay blankets. Was Grace really safe in Canada? Could Victor trace her phone records? Instead of letting her paranoia run out and play with the other kids, Maddie took a breath of logic. This wasn't a blockbuster thriller fueled by an international conspiracy. A disgruntled student had damaged the Buick and painted the office door. The apartment was another matter she'd think about later. Following a half-baked extemporaneous script, she dialed again. The female voice answered in the same friendly fashion. Maybe in the bush they were used to line interruptions. "Is a Miss Grace Lwasa there?"

A pause. "I'm sorry. We have no guest by that name."

An exotic black woman traveling alone in Northern Ontario would provide fodder enough to last until spring. Raising the race question would narrow the odds, but tact prevailed. "I'm certain she's staying with you." Her tone became cautious, hoping to ring womanly alarm bells. "Of course she doesn't want her husband to know. There's a . . . restraining order. I have important news from her lawyer." What a screenwriter. And she hadn't watched the soaps since "Search for Tomorrow" went off the air.

There was a pregnant silence on the line, then a throat-clearing. "I'm afraid that you must have the wrong place. Our only lady guest is a Miss Letty Moran. And she isn't taking any calls." Bingo! Maddie rang off politely, replacing the receiver with a whoop. *Moran of the Lady Letty*. Thanks, Frank Norris. Somehow she couldn't picture Grace as a boat captain, but at least she was tucked away. Surely this could be resolved in time for a return in January. Tears of relief gathering at the corners of her eyes, she made a leisurely trip to the bathroom to freshen up. When she came back, Barney stood at her door, his head cocked like an inquisitive sparrow's.

"Uh, Doc-tor? I was here before, but you were not. The lady in the office said—"

Maddie's eyes flashed to her schedule. "What time is it?" She grappled at her wrist, discovering that she had forgotten her watch that morning. And he'd asked Nancy, or worse yet, Flo. How humiliating.

"Do not worry. The students are still there. I told them that a full professor was fifteen minutes." He thrust his Mickey Mouse watch into her face. "Um," he added as she scooped up her notes. "I am finished with my cremation essay, but I would like you to check the biography to see if I have done it exactly right."

"Bibliography." She nearly kissed his smooth pink cheek, but settled for a grin. "Let's get to class. We'll sort it out later. How about five on Friday right here?"

"Okay," he said, taking out a minuscule notebook and carefully entering the appointment after he repeated the date and time twice and made sure she meant p.m. The rabbit in his pack wore a Santa outfit.

That night Maddie cleared her sinuses with a tamale pie, a green chili mixture topped with corn bread. As always in the small kitchen, she worked around the spatial demands of Nikon's pen. Yet he'd been loose on a trial basis for over a week and hadn't set fang to the furniture. Even the toilet paper sat undigested on its roll. Perhaps early parole was in order. And why store the monster when someone on campus might like to buy it? At Christmas, people couldn't resist pet store pups and later regretted the impulse when the realities of sodden rugs and shredded slippers hit home. After dinner, she went to the computer room and typed a "For Sale" sign.

In the bathroom, she squeezed toothpaste onto her brush, then began scrubbing. Suddenly she gagged and spit into the sink, grabbing a glass of water. Nikon's chicken flavor toothpaste. So distracted. End of the semester? Or did this happen to every woman with stuttering hormones? Everywoman. Now there was a concept.

Minutes later, Ed knocked at the door, flourishing a magnum of Veuve Cliquot. "Stocking up ahead of time," he said. "No last-minute runs on New Year's Eve."

Together they sipped decaf in the living room, Nikon begging for pets. "You two belong together," Maddie said. "I haven't given him much regular exercise lately."

"This is a busy time of year for you. And he's a job in itself," he responded with a sympathetic tone.

"It's more than that. I can't seem to concentrate. One problem after another." She paused. "Now there's Grace." She related the recent events.

"Trying to be all things to all people, Maddie." He squeezed her shoulder. "Now that you've found her, you'll be able to get in touch soon. Relieve her mind about that damn boy at least."

"She was so frightened. Scared out of her apartment, her job, her community. And what good did I do?"

"Whatever anyone could under the circumstances. But right now, unless you want a five-hour drive . . ." He stared at her evenly, almost like a father. "Let her take her time."

When she managed a weak smile, he added, "Worries of my own about Clark, my brother in Duluth. He's pretty low. The bypass clogged up again. I've been wondering if I should go out there."

The evening's task was to construct the Victorian Poetry final. Twenty conspicuous quotes to identify and explain in historical context. No prisoners taken. Armed with her anthology, reading glasses polished, she set to work. The first choice was easy. "The Woods of Westermain" stanza about oxen chewing cuds in the primordial swamp drew an accurate picture of academia through the ages.

At eleven o'clock, yawning and sleepy, she went to the kitchen to let Nikon out and discovered that the small television, sound off, had gone to war. CNN correspondents were gesturing as bodies were carried away by figures ducking bullets. As she turned up the volume, the mention of Uganda pricked her ears. In a sudden coup, Victor Abukha had been blown into pieces at a state dinner. His forces were in disarray, fleeing to whatever country would admit them. Certainly now Grace could return. Then she stopped and revisited a question that had plagued her. If not by Victor, how had Grace's phone number been discovered? And what about that demure rifling of the apartment? Occham's sharp razor cut the simplest answer. No international conspiracy, just a devilish little scheme to diet the department for its future service role. Retire Marie, deny Gary tenure, and frighten Grace. Wouldn't Flo love a staff of sessionals, no costly benefit packages and fat salaries? Should Grace swallow her pride, a degrading probation might greet her at best. Flo had the cold facts on her side, abandonment of a post. Could they fight back? Madame Chairman had been so careful at the apartment, no clues and no witnesses. Those love letters from the Dean were embarrassing, but how much leverage would that buy? Maddie felt herself turning into a cheap blackmailer, slipping anonymous notes under the English Department door. How much of a ruse, considering that the letters had been left in a desk she'd occupied, if only briefly? Flo might even cause problems for Nancy, another person with access to the office.

Eleven o'clock. Too late to call the lodge. Tomorrow is another day, Scarlett. In the bathtub, struggling to relax, she simmered her aching shoulders, more tension than arthritis.

Nikon sat companionably, watching the bubbles burst, tiny rainbow animals exploding before quivering brown eyes. He licked soap from her arms and lapped bathwater like a hot toddy. Maddie went to bed still searching for a last quote for the test. What had Grace said about the appointment in Samarra? Fate was one obvious theme. Maybe a night's sleep would recharge her tired batteries.

Chapter Thirty Two

On the office bulletin board, Maddie tacked up the last of twenty ads for Nikon's cage. Nancy was sorting the interoffice mail like a keno dealer, the phone clamped under her chin. "No, you can't. We do not have the money. Plain and simple. Yes, I agree. What a shame you weren't born into a Texas oil family."

She hung up with a weary growl only a mother could give. "Stick with pooches, Maddie. They don't need gold-plated running shoes. And designer jeans. And makeup. Do you know that the average teen spends six hundred dollars a year on warpaint?" She juggled an armful of packages to the mailboxes, stacking them on the floor and rubbing her back. "Say, did you open that big envelope from the library? Ian Macdonald doesn't talk, but he's been giving me owly looks in the Refectory."

"What envelope?" Had she forgotten something again?

"It came weeks ago when you were chairman. Marked URGENT. Didn't you pass it on to Flo?"

With a guilty groan, Maddie headed to her office to deconstruct a lumpish pile on the file cabinet: shipments of sample texts, collections of student papers. Fortunately the semester was ending despite the exponential marking. Too many tasks were escaping her. Finally she pulled the envelope from beneath an untouched set of Matthew Arnold critiques from her seminar. No wonder they'd been so silently expectant lately at the end of class, but she appreciated their not complaining to Flo. Within were two manuscript copies, a note on top.

Typewritten, with Ian's name scrawled below. Given the limitations of his stroke, the effort must have taken eternities. "These photocopies were ordered in September by the student who died in that tragic accident. With the usual delays and routing, they finally claimed my attention. I was taking them to Cataloging, should they contain some research value, when I was trapped in the damn elevator for several hours. It didn't take long to notice that three early chapters were nearly identical. I have flagged the pertinent passages. The second writer is obviously a plagiarist. The mill of God grinds slow but exceedingly fine. Wouldn't you agree?"

Maddie checked the titles. Both dealt with Frank Norris, following a similar path at first, later diverging. One discussed atavism, the other romantic conventions. Cheryl's theme of illness in the American novel sent her looking for any Norris reference in on-line library holdings. A Clarence Springer at the University of Maine had authored the first. Dated two months later, the second was by Lucretia Porlock at the University of Oregon. Paging through the manuscripts, she smiled at Ian's cherry red Post-it notes on key pages. From sea to shining sea, who worried about getting caught years before copying was universal, before computers and e-mail and the Internet? Serious researchers never consulted these moldy oldies. With a wince, Maddie remembered her own barrel-scraping M.A. thesis on the pathetic fallacy in the poetry of Thomas Hardy.

She supposed that she ought to do something. Or rather Flo should. How she'd enjoy ferreting out whether this Porlock woman had gotten a university job where such a lingering venial sin could lead to career meltdown. Academic plagiarism had no statute of limitations. Or perhaps poor LP whose initials topped the pages was self-employed, long gone to fields fairer than the dry husks of literature. After the horrors of the semester, the larger ethics of murder or suicide, for an eyeblink she debated the moral expediency of dropping the sad evidence into the wastebasket. *Ave Atque Vale.* Good night, nurse.

As she was logging onto her computer to check a book order, familiar heel clicks echoed behind her. "One second," she said, typing the password: DorianG. Oh, to have a handy portrait in the attic to absorb the blows of age. Then the screen came up. No mail.

With Estee Lauder assaulting her lungs, Maddie hoped that the next wave of political correctness would ban perfumes. Flo hovered hawklike at her shoulder and stubbed a rigid finger at the wall calendar. "I'm warning everyone not to end classes one minute earlier than five o'clock on December 18th, the day grades are mailed. The specious 'working at home' ploy does not fare well with me. Faculty must report to campus daily until the official break. People have been seen at airports when they are not technically on vacation."

Maddie blew out a contemptuous huff and shoved the envelope forward. "M.A. theses sent over from the library. Cheryl Crawford ordered them, the student getting that posthumous degree."

Flo's nostrils flared as if presented with a rotten sardine. "Yes, very rash of Grace to authorize the payment in perilous financial times. I would have countermanded it, had I known."

"You'll be delighted she did. The thesis with the later date is plagiarized. A couple of chapters. And who would have discovered the similarity? Those little black covers gathering dust, ink fading on that erasable paper we used."

"Really?" A pencil-thin eyebrow lifted as she snatched up the papers. She tipped back jewel-winged glasses to inspect the title pages with an assessing leer. After a few moments of flipping pages, a tsk sucked through her sharp teeth. "Twenty years ago. Getting away with murder all this time."

"You might have read about that movie *Amistad*. Seems Spielberg cribbed from an earlier novel. Then that author confessed to having lifted passages from a Thirties history book. *Roots* all over again."

"I'll see that the universities involved are made aware of this outrageous theft. This woman's career will be over. And it's quite a wake-up call for our students as well. The Internet has become a veritable garbage dump for essays. Nancy will memo the faculty about departmental policy on plagiarism. Instant dismissal. No second chances here." She paused. "Speaking of which, you haven't heard from dear Ms. Lwasa, have you?"

Not for a heated double garage with automatic doors would Maddie relate recent developments about her friend. "She may be back in January, or even sooner. I'm keeping my fingers cr—"

"Your precious goddess can keep her statuesque legs crossed on the unemployment line for all I care. How are we supposed to plan around an invisible woman? I've been scheduling faculty for classes. Nancy may have to work late tomorrow. Since you're still coordinator, you'll do the final loading Monday. And by the way, on those numbers you gave me, it was twenty-seven for Grace's poetry class, not twenty-four. Haven't you ever seen a continental seven in all of your worldly travels? Not that it matters. We'll have to cancel now, and students will pay the price." With a pivot on one stiletto heel, she slammed the door.

Taking deep breaths, humiliated by her latest error,

Maddie stared out the window at the falling snow. Flo was ruthless but right. If Grace didn't return soon, she might never teach again. She dialed the lodge a third time, writing a note to pay for the long distance charges. Flo would relish discovering another petty offense. "Please tell Miss Moran that there has been a military coup in Uganda and that she should return home. I'm her colleague, Maddie Temple," she said, hanging up with a prayer.

Late that afternoon, she caught a message on her voice-mail. "It's Ed. Clark passed on, I'm afraid. Got to rally round Maureen. Can you keep an eye on the house, collect the paper, feed Peep? I'll be back in plenty of time for our date. That new BP med seems to be working, if you get my meaning, old girl." The radio predicted an incoming storm, so he was leaving immediately.

Chapter Thirty Three

For one brief, shining moment, forecasters earned their pay. The blizzard arrived in gale-force, scattering the campus chimes of "In the Good Old Summertime" to the corners of the Oval. Maddie dismissed the seminar students early, since many had begun staring out the window with growing alarm, checking their watches and whispering. It was poor pedagogy to demand concentration on Kipling's "The White Man's Burden," even with the blatant racist overtones which always stimulated debate.

Around the parking lot, people crouched against the swirling blast, plunging forward with tubular hoods like down-filled Pez dispensers or shielding their faces to hack and sweep at their windshields. The exhausts of cars disappeared in the gusts. As Maddie wheeled onto the main highway, spinning thick treads in the heavy snow, the wind was a ravenous banshee. Visibility had dropped to less than twenty feet, the center line obliterated.

The plow hadn't arrived at Prospector Road, only the ruts of another car breaking deep grooves, a railroad track to follow. The Probe gripped like a puma, but its clearance was barely six inches. Along one blustery stretch, even snow fences didn't prevent whiteouts. She forged along in near blindness, then braked suddenly as red taillights blazed a warning. Fearful of being rear-ended, she switched on emergency flashers. Out of the chaos, a woman appeared and tapped on her window. It was Clarice Hodgson, a neighbor who assisted Nikon's vet. She cupped a shivering kitten in her gloves. "I had to stop. Can you see ahead?"

"No. I nearly hit you." High beams flooded Maddie's rear window. She elbowed out of her warm seat and yelled to a man looking out of his truck cab.

"We're quite helpless here. Can you go ahead and lead us past this mess?"

The convoy snailed another mile until a stand of heavy pine screened the wind, and signposts and directional markers appeared. Soon the truck accelerated with a toot. Maddie honked back, watching Clarice aim deftly into her property, where her husband had turned into Frosty by clearing a path with the blower.

The last steep hill was always a heart-stopper. Like a slow motion videotape, her car inched to a near-standstill on the slippery ice beneath the snow. She'd have to back down and try again using second gear, a dangerous maneuver which might skew her over the embankment. "Come on, Sweetheart. Another ten feet and take the weekend off," she pleaded, white-knuckling the wheel. Nanoseconds short of inertia, the tires bit on grit and provided enough traction to reach the crest. Downhill and home. Breathing a prayer of thanks, Maddie eased to a stop in the drifts of her driveway and cast a sad glance at Ed's house. No cheery window lights greeted her. After dinner she'd go over and feed Peep. No use shoveling until morning. Calling for a quick plow would be a better idea.

Nikon seemed perturbed about missing his walk. After staring at her in *j'accuse* mode, he scrounged up a broken tennis ball and worried it until a curious 'pock pock' caught her attention. Apparently his sharp teeth had bisected the toy, connected only by a shred of ragged felt. "It can't be a bra," she said archly. "Looks more like your first jock strap. You'll have to grow into it. Or maybe not. The jury's still out." Still pouting, he disappeared down the hall.

Eager to divest herself of bulky clothing, she pared down to forest green silk long underwear. Thawing a chicken breast in the microwave, she started chopping a wizened zucchini for souvlaki. Watching the snow accumulate on the deck and knowing that she was well-provisioned made her feel warm and comfortable, an optimist's response to a storm. Christmas was around the corner. This weekend she'd string a row of bulbs on the eaves, forgoing a tempting tree for a curious young dog. The presents were heaped in the closet: lime aftershave for Billy, an in-car heater for her father, Ed's ice diamond photograph, and a party pack of pig ears for Nikon. On the compact disc player in the living room, the King's College choir sang an uplifting "Jerusalem," and she was humming along in festive mood, about to pour a glass of Gallo tankcar Chablis, when a knock sounded at the door. For illogical seconds she hoped Ed had returned.

"What brings you out in this weather?" Maddie asked, stepping back from the blast. She might appear an elder elf in that outfit, but she wore what she pleased in her own home.

Setting down her exercise bag, Flo brushed snow from the sleeves of a full-length lynx coat and wiped her boots, a delicate suede pair more suited to balmy Manhattan. "My Cherokee Nellybelle goes through anything, unlike your impractical sports car. I wanted to discuss that graduation presentation to learn more background about Cheryl Crawford. After catching up with paperwork, finally I was able to give the thesis a quick scan. The girl worked hard. And for all her shortcomings, Grace did a decent job splicing it together."

Nikon galloped into the room, tail knocking against the

cabinets. Stepping behind a chair, Flo blinked, then reached out a timid hand for a perfunctory pat. "This is the dog I've heard about. He is a big fellow, isn't he?"

Resisting compliments was hard, even coming from an ass, but Maddie didn't like the way Nikon snuffled at the fur coat as if examining another species, no matter how distantly alive. She yanked his collar to make him sit. "Nearly six months and sixty pounds already, this unruly adolescent."

"Exactly like children. I wish I could have left Jason at the Animal Shelter the day he turned fourteen." Flo chirped at the rare joke, then grew thoughtful. "After my neighbor lost all her jewelry in a robbery, I considered getting a watchdog. It might be a companion for Bruce, coax him out for exercise. But purebreds are expensive. And those vet bills."

"Worth every penny." Maddie felt disposed to show off her man. "Lie down, Nikon. Flash those toofies." His loose lips waffled to let her roaming fingers expose huge, crushing molars. "No vandal wants to deal with a barking dog, even a Heinz 57. Avoid one break-in and you've made up the difference."

Profit and loss clicked in Flo's cash-register eyes. "Now that you put it that way, I understand the merits." She placed the exercise bag on the top of the crate and took out a plastic makeup kit. "May I use your little girls' room to powder my nose?"

"Right down the hall." In a blizzard? What a Miss Priss act. Dean Nordman might be titillated at the charade, but it was one thing to affect a delicacy, quite another to possess it. Those pathetic love letters might be the only weapon in maintaining the department's integrity. Messy, though. Marital cheating wasn't a crime, simply not worth the risk, as Clough advised: "Do not adultery commit./ Advantage rarely comes of it."

When the dog followed, Flo froze, her eyes apprehensive. Maddie said, "It's territoriality. Nikon isn't used to . . . strangers moving about the house. He's a pussycat. Guaranteed."

Several minutes passed while she prepared the customized souvlaki sauce, mixing baba ganoush, sour cream, and salsa. Dropping by at dinnertime. So awkward. Should she ask Flo to stay? Hard to stretch one piece of meat. Just then, her guest returned briskly down the hall, brushing back a lock of hair and checking her watch. Nikon had probably relaxed his diligence and dozed off in a corner. All for the best. Regular socialization would teach him not to be such a nuisance.

"This won't take long." Flo removed her coat and groped in a side pocket of the capacious bag for a pad and pen. "So tell me about Cheryl. I'll need a few cogent remarks when the diploma is awarded. Nancy said that the family will be present. Such a sad Christmas for them."

Maddie felt disarmed at the uncharacteristic empathy. Could the lynx change its spots? Grudgingly mindful of hospitality, she brewed a pot of aromatic Earl Grey and spun a tidy story scripted by vintage Disney, tactfully downplaying the dysfunctional sister. Settled at the kitchen table, her chairman jotted notes in careful fashion, pausing to sip tea and nod in occasional acknowledgment.

Finally Flo stood, tucking in a dotted Swiss blouse and flicking a black dog hair from her camel wool skirt. "That sounds perfect. You've been very helpful." She returned the pad and pen to the bag in exchange for car keys. "So you didn't sell the kennel yet. I saw the ad. It takes up so much space. Are they necessary?"

"The pen simplifies house training. Especially at night, unless you want to sleep with a pup for two months like I did." Amused at Flo's raised eyebrow, she recited the tenets

276

of the bible while she finished her tea. "Of course, Bruce may be home during the day to supervise."

Flo touched the top and sides and peered into the pen. "Very strong. What a comfy little mattress. Does it lock, too?"

What a naive question, as if the dog were a wild beast. Good thing the woman had no pets. Maybe she was considering using it on her teenagers. Wouldn't she love an electronic collar or two? Maddie operated the vertical catch. "It fastens. But why bother adding a lock, unless you were traveling and concerned about theft?"

"I see." A fluttering motion dropped the keys into the cage. "Oops. Be a dear and get them, will you? I did too many sit-ups yesterday at a wicked forty-five degrees. Shouldn't push myself, but you know me." Her lips drew back in what passed for a smile, a waxy cerise smear on her teeth, even after an eternity in the bathroom.

Perturbed about damaging her back, Maddie humped in, stretching to the far corner for the keychain, a bronze disc with a circlet of pearls and the initials LP. That's curious, she thought. Not FA. Maybe a keepsake, or an item the cheapskate had claimed from the Lost and Found. Still, the letters rang a bell. A metallic click sounded, and she turned with difficulty, her knees creaking, only to find herself trapped. "Stop kidding, Flo. Open the cage."

"It's Florence, and I've never been so serious." She leaned forward, holding a compact, shiny object. It snapped around the bars and dangled like Svengali's watch.

"What are you doing?" Maddie looked again at the keychain, swallowing heavily. Suddenly the metamorphosis was complete. Turgid waves surrendered into a surface of clear ice with a realization that froze her blood. "Lucretia."

"Even frumpier than Florence. What were my parents

thinking? That's why I took my middle name after marriage. Along with the very important reason that I wanted to absent myself from a silly mistake. Time was running out. I had to finish that useless thesis and move on to the Ph.D. The University of Michigan had offered me a fellowship." She paused and gazed at the ceiling, her voice for once moved by genuine emotion. "Mother was ill. It was the end, you see, but not as serene as we all would prefer. Long and ugly. Months after her death, I still couldn't concentrate. At the MLA conference I thought I might find a temporary lectureship to give me breathing room, clear my head. I met others in my field at the cattle call, some with completed theses. Poor Clarence. He never suspected, flattered with my offer to proofread his work. A gift from God. Along with the invention of Xerox."

Maddie kept her voice calm. She was in her kitchen with supper assembled on the counter. "Not much of a gamble. Oregon and Maine are a long way from Michigan. Anyway, I thought your area was the Renaissance."

"Everyone I knew was choosing the American novel. Competition would have been fierce when I finished the doctorate. I simply changed majors and spent an extra year catching up on courses."

Cramping at the confinement, Maddie dangled the keys. "I still have these. So what's your plan? Cut and run?"

Flo's smirk sent a sucker punch to her stomach. "*Semper paratus*. The last time I lost my keys, Bruce attached a magnetized case to the wheel well. A thoughtful man. And by the way, running's not a plan. Running's what you do when plans fail." She peered out the icy window. "And your only neighbor is away."

"What's the point in leaving me here? I'm not going to starve to death. And I have your keys as proof." She paused and firmed up her voice, confident in the logic. "On Monday they'll be looking for me, if not before. In weather like this, my father always calls by seven to make sure I got home safely."

"But you won't be in a cage, not for long." Flo gazed at the stove. "I saw those ads you clipped. Gas is an economical choice. Too bad you haven't been as efficient lately in your own job. So forgetful. Nearly missing that class. Your error in reading those figures. Driving all over the state in an obsessive compulsion to trace Malcolm's family. I nearly laughed out loud when Nancy told me. Time of life, is it?"

One small word sliced through the jumble of Maddie's transgressions. "Gas?"

"Then when you're nice and comatose . . ." Flo checked her slim gold watch with an appraising eye. "In another hour, to be on the safe side, I'll discover the tragic scene."

So there was a timetable. Maddie had to keep her talking, work with insecurities. Raising the specter of the letters might only antagonize her. "Remember Malcolm? You nearly went to trial as an innocent victim."

"And so I was. Hot dogs and grilled cheese are off the menu. But this time I've planned against every expediency. Nancy is working late with faculty loading, terribly grateful when I offered to pay double overtime. I assured her I'd deliver her home safely, said that I needed to pop over to fix Bruce supper. Poor man's in bed with a head cold, or at least he'll say so if he knows what's good for him. When I return to the office, I'll call you with an important question. Your line will be busy . . ."

Maddie's head was spinning with a baroque plot outdoing the turgidities of Hardy's *Dynasts*. "It's not busy. What are you talking about?"

"Another precaution. While you were preparing a meal you'll never eat, I logged onto the campus mail system from your computer. What a telling password you used the other afternoon: DorianG. More pitiful than amusing. When we can't reach you, I'll hit 'sho users' and discover you on-line. Very interactive. Quite an improvement over the old take-the-receiver-off-the-hook ploy, which can be checked with phone records." Her pointy teeth nipped at a cuticle as she paused to gather her thoughts. "Then we'll drop by to find you passed out over your computer."

She was so pleased, Maddie thought, eyes glittering, self-congratulatory. Complicity in Grace's disappearance she'd suspected. But not a motive to murder. Now it was making tragic sense. Cheryl. That dumbwaiter.

"Nikon!" she yelled. Where was he? Clearly Flo feared him. He could be a distraction until Nancy called Bruce to see where Flo . . . But the rest was silence.

"If you're wondering, puppy's in slumberland with a delicious Italian meatball. Deli meal I picked up for my sick husband. Feed a cold, etc. Not to worry, though. A half-tablet of Bruce's Xanax won't hurt him. After all, the animal's a valuable asset, and so friendly. He followed me to the bathroom, and that's where I left him. The door's closed and the window open. Don't worry. He'll be my little prince. I love him already." She gave an ugly wink. "You must admit he likes me."

Maddie felt hot tears flood her eyes, a curious, natural balm, but resisted begging for her life. Instead she shook the bars in useless rage. "You bitch!"

"Coarse words don't become your late profession. Try not to fuss about and cause yourself needless pain." She stepped back and framed Maddie with her hands. "It's ironic, but I'm reminded of a scene where Tamburlaine puts his enemy in a cage."

Maddie bit her lip, tasting blood as it trickled across her

tongue. "I read *Tamburlaine,* and you're no Scythian warlord, Flo. *'Tis Pity She's a Whore* has the role for you."

"Shut up! What does an old bat know about love?" Flo gave the cage a wicked kick with her boot. Slipping on a pair of whisper-thin leather gloves, she washed both teacups, put one away, emptied the pot, and restocked it. Then she closed the doors to the kitchen. "We'll get all snugged up. No need filling the house. Gas bills can be murder." A spasm shook her padded shoulders, "Bwhhahahahahahah" like typed laughter on the Internet newsgroups. "Later, I'll return to 'lug the guts' as Hamlet said. What do you weigh? One fifty?"

"One thirty." Maddie felt hot shame at rising to the bait.

"Fudging during the last minutes of your life. I'm appalled. Anyway, I bench-press double the limits for my size, so it shouldn't take but a moment. Balance, leverage, the readiness is all." Flo stared off for a moment as if short-circuited, one eye twitching. "Let's see. Nancy stays in the car until I need her as a witness. I'll collect those keys quickly in case she . . ."

Maddie sneaked a peek at her watch while Flo put on her coat. Seven ten. If her father were getting a busy signal, he'd be mad as hell. Mad enough to take the Dynasty out in a storm? "And what about Cheryl? I deserve to know that at least."

Flo sighed elaborately. "If you insist. She was in my Shakespeare class last year, and I'd seen her studying in the literature stacks every afternoon. When Grace said that those Norris theses were ordered, I had to act fast. Some acknowledgment about her scholarship, calling attention to a bird outside, an open window." Suddenly her voice grew caustic. "I dumped the laptop into Lake Superior. There wouldn't have been any complications. Then you found the disk.

Scribbled about dumbwaiters on the HAWG minutes. Biding your time. For all I knew she had them already."

Her careless pronouns indicated growing mental confusion. Maddie searched for a ploy to drag out the moments. "Cheryl never even read the theses. And certainly Grace didn't. They didn't come until after—"

Flo pounded the table, spittle forming on her nether lip. "And you did, Ms. Butter-Wouldn't-Melt-in-Your-Mouth. Always standing in my way. Taking my job when I was helpless. Isn't it ironic? She died for nothing, and her death led to yours. A chain of paper clips. No, dominoes is a more precise analogy."

"Grace may figure this out when she returns." Maddie was grasping at straws, bits of Nikon's foam mattress in her trembling hands like fluffy dice.

"Not unless she buys a ton of glue and likes Dumpster-diving. I shredded the manuscripts yesterday after thanking Ian for his diligence. At any rate, don't dream that our timid colleague will crawl back after the scene at the apartment. Overhearing a phone conversation about her sordid past gave me enough ammunition to scare her off. Now that's enough delay. Your tactics are so transparent." She turned to examine the stove. "An old fossil, isn't it? Oh, present company excepted." Then with a merry "oops" she blew out the pilot, switched the gas on high, filled the kettle, and placed it over the burner.

"You'll never grow old, Maddie." She patted her firm jaw and bared her teeth like a jubilant crocodile. "Or older, rather. And to leave you with a last beautiful thought, didn't your Keats say, "Ever may she . . . long may she . . . oh, who cares? Soon you'll be in a Grecian urn, not talking about one."

Flo closed the door firmly, leaving Maddie to the quiet syllables of the gas. Her grandfather had killed himself, a victim of manic-depression in the days when the only treatment was a straightjacket between ice baths. Stuck his head in the oven and left his wife with six young children. No wonder her father checked his own stove in a nightly ritual, balancing back and forth in a compulsive dance. She'd laughed once as a toddler and caught a spanking from her mother. With her first paycheck at Copper, she had bought her parents a new electric range and taken this one. Her death would destroy him, especially disguised in this way.

An acrid taste nipped the back of her throat. In desperation, she threw herself against the cage, moving it mere inches and wrenching a shoulder. Quality construction. That's what she'd paid for. Moaning softly, she rubbed her arm. What a dramatic concept, Flo running around in a blizzard, but perhaps she was counting on absurdity. And even the most suspicious mind would conclude that she had nothing to gain from Maddie's death.

As her head swam against a rising nausea, she reached out to the larger whole, her father's reliance upon her, the human fabric that knit a fragile triangle with Billy and Lucky. In his loving eyes, whatever she had ever done had been the "right thing," always forgiving, not judgmental like her mother who speared the lone B amid the A's. And Ed, the understanding man. Not much time for you lately, she thought with rue. The champagne might serve as a funeral toast.

Nikon under Flo's control was the "most unkindest cut of all." While she could hope that her father would adopt his "grandson," a full-grown GSD would prove a handful for an elderly man accustomed to a lethargic dachshund. Paralyzed by grief, her father might be easily led by her helpful chairman. What kind of food would Nikon get at the frugal Andrews house? No more pig ears or mashed carrots. Bargain basement specials based on corn. Invalid hobbles with Bruce instead of forest romps, or worse yet, confinement in the house as a living burglar alarm.

Her eyes watered from the fumes. Why struggle against the cage or scream? Even without the roar of the storm, Clarice's place was half a mile away. She peered myopically at the lock. Her reading glasses sat on the kitchen table. And besides that technicality, she didn't know the combination. Then an inkling of hope rose like that thing with feathers Emily Dickinson invented. The lock seemed to be a cheap variety she'd used in high school. Always three numbers: right, left, right. More than once after the summer break had washed the numbers from her teeming teenage brain, sensitive young fingers had deciphered the subtle clicks and pulled the casing like a grenade. She crouched into a sitting position, reached around the steel bars for the lock, turned it in her hands like a surgeon, explored every curve and groove to read a silent heart. Dan's ring tinked against the metal, so she fumbled it onto the mattress.

Without energy to concentrate, her hands dropped listlessly. Breaths were shallow, self-preserving drafts, the besieged organism sensing that air was necessary but resisting the poison. She felt drowsy, fatigued as if climbing Everest. How tempting to curl up in the fetal position on Nikon's soft mattress in hopes that someone would ride to the rescue. Ed, her father, or even a remorseful Flo. She choked back a sob. Not with a long-feared secret turning to papier-mâché in a landfill.

Maddie forced herself to the lock, pressed her ear close. Turned it once, twice. Nothing. The serpentine hiss of the gas whispered honeyed Tennysonian endearments into her ears. Come into the garden, Maude. Her eyes wept like raw wounds. Everything was blurring. Then between coughs, she thought she detected the faintest click, a cylinder meeting its mate. With all the spent force within, holding her breath as her chest burst, she turned it again, back, forth, click, click, pull. Still it resisted. She vomited the tea into a corner of the pen, recalling with humiliation that Nikon had never soiled his bed. Blood pounded out the rhythm of death. She twirled it to clear the mechanism, then gave one last try.

The Gods smiled, or chuckled. The lock came free, and she pawed at the clasp of the cage, forced it up, and lurched forward onto her knees. No power now to cross the kitchen to shut off the gas, to fling open the door for a clean drink of cold liquid air. That a man's reach should exceed his grasp. Browning's line had new meaning. She crawled by inches, head barely off the floor, retching in dry heaves until her diaphragm ached, her legs trembly appendages of a marionette. Dizzy and weak, she slumped against the counter and knew she would not rise again. As the room darkened into a swirling vortex, she imagined a noise outside. A car door? Flo was back to finish the job. She wouldn't even have to open the stupid lock, just lug the . . . Maddie's face sought the coolness of the linoleum.

Chapter Thirty Four

From somewhere over the rainbow came a banging, an icy wind, then a tinkly song. It sounded like "Easter Parade."

When her eyes opened, Maddie was lying on the living room sofa, a worried face hovering overhead, breathing Juicy Fruit gum. More delicious than the finest perfume. The house was freezing, turned inside out. "Doc-tor. Are you all right? I called 9-1-1 to get an ambulance. But I had to log off your computer first. And I opened the windows and turned off the stove. Your face was so red."

The choppy syntax spoke endearing poetry. "Barney? How did you get here?"

"I have my mountain bike. Our meeting. Five o'clock p.m. I knew you would not have forgotten. Something was wrong. The secretary was still working in the office. She said that you lived on this road."

"You came through all that snow?"

Face mottled with frostbite, he swiped a chapped hand across his runny nose. "It was not easy. Many cars went off the road. I passed a Jeep Cherokee in the ditch after that big hill. Some people had stopped to help."

As quickly as it had risen, the wind had dropped to a whisper, like a quieted child. With the windows open, she could hear the welcome scrapings of the plow. Maddie wondered if she should cancel the ambulance, earn a sharp rebuke from the dispatcher. What would they do except give her oxygen, and she was breathing more than her share. Struggling to her feet, willing wobbly knees to connect, she closed the windows and turned up the heat. The beginnings of a massive headache fogged her brain. Something was missing. Nikon!

Barney at her side, she shuffled down the hall, bracing against the walls like a drunk Peter Pan. In the bathroom, head on a slipper, Nikon snoozed, opening one bleary eye at her prodding.

"This is a wonderful dog," Barney said, kneeling to stroke the silken coat, product of fatty acid supplements and brewer's yeast. Then he sneezed. "My parents would not allow me to have one because of my allergies. I have a Pentium 4 computer instead."

Marginally coherent, Maddie went to the kitchen phone. First she dialed the ambulance and the police, then the English Department.

Nancy's voice rose into the stratosphere. "I'm marooned here and out of spring water. What's happening? Flo went to check on Bruce, never came back. That strange boy from your class arrived around five thirty. Insisted that I call you. But your number was busy."

Maddie took another blissful breath, stretching her legs onto the bench seat in the alcove, and gritted her teeth. "Pour yourself what's left of the coffee. Find Malcolm's hidden bottle, if he left one. You'll need a jumpstart . . . and a taxi."

Jeff Phillips arrived with siren blasting. He took their statements, scratching his head at the cage. A phone call confirmed that Flo's car had gone off the road, nearly covered by the plow. Unconscious, she had been taken to the hospital. He ordered her room placed under guard.

"She came to pretty quickly, wanted to leave, but they were waiting for the concussion scans. With the boy's testimony, the keys, the lock, she'll be charged with attempted murder."

Maddie shook her head quietly as she thought of the unwitting victim that had begun this mad march. "A bare fraction of what she deserves. What about Cheryl Crawford?"

"We'll dust that dumbwaiter, but Ms. Andrews sounds like a crafty one. Depends on her lawyer."

Maddie patted his arm with an evil grin. "In that case, she'll be fasting until the next millennium."

Later that night the phone rang. It was Grace. "The lines have been out for days. I cannot tell you how sick I am of baked beans. And there is a large animal in Canada, a moose. They consume it in ragouts, chops, and even in sausages. Your message arrived not a bit too soon."

Before she closed her eyes that night, Maddie recalled the cliché that in academia the viciousness increased conversely to the size of the stakes. All those years, Flo's fate had waited like a rejected lover. "Alien they seemed to be:/ No mortal eye could see/ The intimate welding of their later history."

"The Convergence of the Twain." Thomas Hardy and the *Titanic*. Maddie had the last quote for her test.

Epilogue

Once again Maddie took the helm of the department, but the search committee had established a short list, so her reluctant chairmanship wouldn't extend beyond June.

"The Seventh Cavalry has galloped to our rescue." Nancy piled a load of letters on the desk. "E-registrations are off the map. Thanks to that neat web page, enrollment for next year's doubled. Strike up the band."

Scooping up a set of exams, Maddie made her way to the Victorian lit final in a classroom she had requested. Sofas and armchairs were awkward for extended writing. Blooming on the desk was a huge bouquet of bright red roses. The students applauded as she opened the card: "Roses, roses, riotously."

"Who told you that Dowson is on question two?" she asked, sniffing one of the blossoms and smiling. Passing out the blue books, she explained that they would have three hours to write the test, text allowed but not notes. The thin pages of the mammoth poetry anthology fluttered through sweaty hands. She drummed her fingers, irked at having forgotten to bring reading material.

Picking up a blue book, she started a letter to Dan. His ring was part of her past, relegated to a drawer now, but their time together still brought smiles. Outside the frosted window, a raven swooped by, a faithful winter bird, inured to the cold. More snow was falling, one hundred inches so far, right on track. At least Iceland had thermal springs. An hour passed as she began Christmas notes to old friends. Then her eagle eye caught something bright and colorful at the back of the room.

She walked on cat feet. "Mr. Boothby," she said, deliberately formal. "This time is offered so that you may locate relevant passages from the text. Are you so cavalier about your mark that you are squandering a precious advantage?"

He grinned and presented his booklet. "Sorry, Miss. I am finished."

With a wink, she appropriated the magazine instead. "Never hurts to do another proofread. Especially your dangling modifiers, as I recall."

Back at the desk, she opened the latest *Playboy*, cruised through an article on the gun lobby, another on censorship of the Internet. Flipping past the glossy centerfold which had captivated Mr. B, she turned to the Jokes page. "A wily old harlot from Akron . . ." Her peals of laughter raised every head.